A Pirate's One and Only

Amy Valentini

A Seekers of the Past Novel

A Pirate's One and Only

Contemporary/Historical Romance

A Pirate's One and Only

Amy Valentini/Romancing Editorially

Amy Valentini

Dedication

To my faithful readers who eagerly await each book—

Thank you.

You are the reason I keep writing.

Amy Valentini

Family Tree

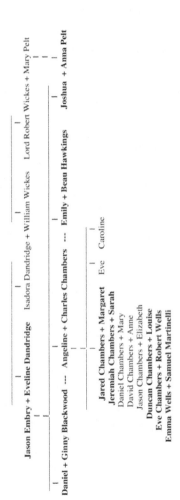

Emma's Family Tree (10 Generations)

Jason Embry + Eveline Dandridge   Isadora Dandridge + William Wickes   Lord Robert Wickes + Mary Pelt

Daniel + Ginny Blackwood --- Angeline + Charles Chambers --- Emily + Beau Hawkings   Joshua + Anna Pelt

Eve   Caroline

Jared Chambers + Margaret
Jeremiah Chambers + Sarah
Daniel Chambers + Mary
David Chambers + Anne
Jason Chambers + Elizabeth
Duncan Chambers + Louise
Eve Chambers + Robert Wells
Emma Wells + Samuel Martinelli

Amy Valentini

Present

Two weeks had passed since Emma Wells and her husband, Sam Martinelli traveled back through their reading to experience Emily and Beau's adventures on the high seas and watched them fall in love. Sam finally agreed to take Emma to New Orleans to do more research and she fell instantly in love with the city. She had never been before so was enjoying Sam playing tour guide and showing her all the best places off the beaten track. After two days of playing tourist, she knew they had to get down to work.

Having located a treasure trove of information in the city archives, she was delighted with some of the answers to questions that allowed her to fill in the blanks somewhat regarding their doppelgangers. But she knew they still didn't have all the answers.

One of the first things they found out was La Coeur de la Terre had existed but burned to the ground around eighteen hundred and twenty-six. The cause of the fire was not known but had destroyed the entire main house and nearly all of the outer buildings. It was most likely caused by a misplaced lantern or kitchen fire but forensics at that time in history was not proficient enough to give any definitive answer.

A new home was built some years later but by the time it was finished, the War Between the States had begun.

They could only presume the owners were descendants of the Hawkings but that was yet another question needing an answer and one Emma was determined to find.

"I'll leave you to your reading while I look up my family records," he whispered to her as she sat at a table in the quiet room, possibly a bit louder than appreciated judging by the sound of someone clearing his throat.

Emma grinned. She knew Sam wasn't a fan of libraries and archives but it pleased her immensely he was willing to accompany her. She thought maybe he was beginning to appreciate the search for treasure among the many documents from the past as much as she did. He was actually getting quite good at finding things most would miss.

"I'll be right here and later, I promise, I'll make it up to you for having to hang out here," she said kissing his mouth.

"I'll hold you to that, my sweet girl," he said with a chuckle before kissing her again.

While he was off seeking his family information, she had found some documents pertaining to the Hawkings family which was providing some interesting information. Even as it was hinted at in Emily's journal that the line of succession to the title of Earl of Parkhurst had skipped a generation, she had wondered why. Was it because Thomas had left England to make his way in Louisiana or simply because he had married a woman his father disapproved of because she was French? Among the many documents connected to La Coeur de la Terre was a letter from a solicitor in England addressed to Thomas Hawkings. It stated that since Thomas had chosen to abandon his family, his family's wishes, and societal post that he would not ever be entitled to the title which was to be bestowed on him by right of birth. His father had indeed disowned him.

Thomas Hawkings had chosen love over family honor and she appreciated that very much. She understood the prejudice which existed in that time in history toward anyone different and wished everyone could have been as open-minded as Thomas Hawkings. Despite being cut out of his father's life, he had obviously found a happy life with his beloved wife and family in Louisiana. They had integrated themselves into a society much different than England, a place where Louisa must have felt more at home surrounded by people who spoke her language as well as English. It also explained Beau's propensity for using French endearments which she found quite amusing since Sam was prone to using pet names in much the same way. She had always attributed it to his being born and raised in the south. Perhaps it stemmed more from his years growing up in Louisiana.

Sam had insisted there was something familiar about the family name Beauregard and his possibly having a however many greats grandmother named Gabrielle. She had suggested to him that he call his uncle but he had ignored her so she decided not to bring it up again, at least for now.

"Look at this," Sam said in a low voice nearby.

When he pulled his chair closer to hers and it made a scraping sound, someone across the room cleared his throat. She shrugged her shoulders at the man. It was a hazard in libraries and archives which were very much the same thing. Sam spread out a large book in front of her with handwritten entries.

"It shows here that Emily and Beau had four daughters," he said pointing to a section about midway down the long page. "I thought you said they only had twin daughters."

"That's what it showed in the list of births in the bible," she said with a shrug. "I suppose the other two girls' births and names could've been omitted. Let me see."

She pulled the book closer and read the list under the name Hawkings. There *were* four daughters.

"Interesting. Even more interesting is the two other siblings are older than the twins." She rubbed her chin as she tried to reason why their names and births weren't registered in the family bible.

"Felicity and Caroline," she read the names aloud in a low voice. "Okay, this is weird. Sam, Felicity was far too old to have been Emily and Beau's. She was born years before they ever met."

"What? How is that?" Sam leaned in to look closer at the ages next to the handwritten names in the city census.

"I'm wondering if they were adopted children," she remarked as she mentally did the math to figure when the two girls were born. "Hmm…it wasn't uncommon for there was a high rate of mortality among both birthing mothers and infants during this time. Perhaps they were birthed by a family friend or perhaps they found Gabrielle and these two girls were hers. I suppose anything is possible. More questions needing answers, I suppose."

She leaned back and stretched her back. She still wasn't feeling well and had a niggling suspicion of why but had she told Sam she was pregnant, he probably wouldn't have allowed her to come on this trip. She knew she was going to have to tell him sooner rather than later.

"What we really need is more information about Gabrielle," she said, turning in her chair to look at Sam.

He was staring off into space.

"What?" she asked.

"Huh? Yeah, Gabrielle…yeah, we need to find out more." Sam seemed preoccupied with something.

"What are you thinking?"

"These names all seem so familiar. I'd like to know more about Beau's family tree," he said then pushed back his chair with another scrape so the man across the room scowled at them again.

"Sorry," Sam said as he stood.

She watched him head off into the stacks again and smiled. He really was beginning to enjoy a paper trail as much as a physical dig.

She did too if she had to admit it. It was addicting to find one piece of information and then another until the blanks get filled in and the story of the past starts to come into view.

Emma only wished she could convince him to contact his uncle. The man lived right here in New Orleans and she was sure he could probably shed a lot of light on the family history and perhaps could help them locate the origin of the gold. But her husband was a stubborn man, almost as stubborn as she was. After all, he hadn't given up on the two of them getting a second chance together even after five years. Of course, she hadn't made it easy for him, but he hadn't given up either. Thank goodness for his stubbornness for she was so pleased he had forced her to admit she still loved him, even after she'd convinced herself she didn't.

Smiling, she began looking over the other names in the census logs. She doubted there was anything further but possibly Gabrielle's name was further down the list under a married name. Fascinated by the names before her, she hadn't realized how long Sam was gone until he appeared alongside her and placed a book in front of her. The overhead lights in the archives had been turned on and the man who seemed so annoyed by them was no longer at his seat across the room. She glanced at the clock on the wall. It was after five in the evening. No wonder her belly felt like it was trying to gnaw through her backbone.

"What's this?" she asked looking at the leather-bound book.

"You're going to love this, Emma girl," Sam said opening the cover and turning a single blank page.

When she saw the handwritten name on the title page, she gasped.

Emily Hawkings.

"Oh my gosh, is this another journal?" she asked flipping the next pages.

"Yep," Sam said taking a seat.

She looked at him and grinned. Was it possible the magic could work with this one too? She turned the pages to where the writing began.

"Sam, this isn't about Emily and Beau," she said scanning the page in front of her.

She looked up at Sam and he was grinning like he'd found some incredible treasure.

"I know. It's Gabrielle's story," he said with a sparkle in his eyes. "Can we check any of this stuff out? I'm hungry, but I think we need to read this."

"I'm starving. Let me go check with the desk," she said, closing the book and standing. "Do you think...could the answer be in here?"

"One way to find out, darlin', we need to read it," he said with a nod.

Emma grinned with a feeling of elation and took the book to the desk to ask about checking it out.

~*~

Two hours later, after a delicious and filling meal at a quaint New Orleans restaurant off the beaten path, Emma and Sam returned to their hotel room, kicked off their shoes, and curled up on the bed together. She held the journal on her lap, her fingers tracing the embossed leather worn from the time gone by since it was first owned. She was nervous because she feared it would just be a journal and they wouldn't experience the same rush of watching history unfold as they had enjoyed with Emily's previous journal.

When she hesitated, Sam opened the book and looked at her.

"We won't know until you start reading, honey," he said putting his arm around her and pulling her against his chest.

He pressed a kiss against her hair and she looked up at him.

"What if it doesn't happen this time?" she asked not wanting to hear it might not.

"Then it doesn't...but we read it anyway," he told her before pressing a hard deep kiss against her lips.

"You keep doing that and we won't read anything tonight," she said with a laugh.

"Oh yeah...well then—" He leaned in to kiss her again but she turned her head so his kiss landed on her cheek. "Hey!"

"As much as I would love to play honeymoon with you, Martinelli, I think we need to find out what's in here. Don't you?" she said with a smile and tapping the book.

"Yeah...we do. Okay, but I get some of your time later, right?"

"I promise. You've got all of my time for the rest of your life."

"I like that. Okay...let's do this," he said nodding his head to indicate the book in her lap.

She sighed on a nervous exhalation and opened the journal. She turned the pages. She turned past the title page where it read Emily's name and the year the journal was begun— eighteen hundred and seven. There was no end date so Emma had no idea what period of time might be represented within the pages, but it was definitely after Beau and Emily had married and returned to Louisiana. She turned to the first page of full handwritten prose and began to read.

"The following is an account of my beloved sister-in-law, Gabrielle's life after the fire which took her home and family as she told it to me." She looked at Sam. "And then she signed it— Emily Embry Hawkings."

"Okay." Sam waggled his dark brows.

Her excitement made her voice shake as she began to read. "It was New Orleans and the year was 1798..."

The sensation began and she heard Sam chuckle. She glanced over at him and he grinned. "I feel it," he said.

She smiled. "Me too."

As Emma read the words in the journal written by Emily Embry Hawkings, the scents and sounds of activity along the docks surrounded her. The magic was there again, just as it had been with Emily's original journal. This time it was pulling her and Sam back through time, back to New Orleans at the end of the eighteenth century—to the past.

Chapter One

New Orleans, 1798

As if the room was not already too warm causing perspiration to drip from her forehead into her eyes, a new ship had recently docked and the crew had piled into the tavern demanding rum. Whenever the common room became over-crowded with unruly sailors, Gabrielle Hawkings broke out in a cold sweat, tucked her chin deeper than normal, and tried to deliver rum and food as quickly as possible. Crowds made her very uncomfortable on a good day but the heat of the room, the smell of sweaty bodies, and the noise level sent her spiraling back to the day when her family's townhome caught fire, burned to the ground, and changed her life forever.

It had been over four years since the second fire in less than ten years ravaged the city of New Orleans. This one, however, devastated her life. The fire took her parents and her best friend. It left her scarred and alone at not even fifteen years of age. She had no one and nothing now for she had no idea where her older brother was. Being a sea captain working in import and export, Beau was probably somewhere in the world. She was not even sure he knew about her burn injuries or their parents' deaths. After months of healing and nearly dying, she found she had no choice but to try to survive on the streets of the city. With no other family to care for her and no word from the family plantation, La Coeur de la Terre, she wished many times she had died in the fire.

It had not been easy at first. She had to sleep wherever she could and had resorted to stealing bits of food to survive. Then one day, she happened across an old neighbor who recognized her. Having lost his home in the same fire, he had taken up residence on the other side of town near the docks. James Fieldmore was an older man with graying hair who was also alone without family but he took her in, making sure she had a roof over her head and food in her belly. She knew he felt sorry for her but she was grateful for his caring assistance.

"Tis a shame such a pretty young girl was ruined by the fire," she had overheard him say to the cook one day. "I doubt she shall ever have any real prospects for a good match now."

She remembered looking into a mirror and tears filling her eyes as the reflection confirmed his statement. Her parents had always told her she could choose whomever she wanted as a marriage partner, but now she had no hope of ever accomplishing such a thing.

The old man had even attempted to find her a husband a few years after taking her in but none of the young men he introduced her to had given her a second look after seeing the ugly scars on her neck. It was fortunate they could not see the thick scars which ran down the right side of her body or the ones on her arm under the long sleeves she had taken to wearing. If they had, they would have run away in horror.

Knowing her future was limited, Gabrielle had spent her days as a companion to old Mr. Fieldmore. She rarely ventured out because she could not tolerate the stares and whispers whenever anyone noticed her. She took to keeping her head low and her scars covered.

A year ago, old Mr. Fieldmore died. He went to bed one night and simply did not awaken. The bank man came and locked all of the doors. Gabrielle was only allowed to take a few of her things but was told there was no money to inherit even if she could prove his promise to ensure her care. Once more, she was on the streets of New Orleans with no means of support. With only a few coins to her name, she could not afford to send word again to La Coeur de la Terre or travel there, which she had often considered. If her brother or any of the servants had thought her still alive, someone surely would have come in search of her. She knew she was on her own. However, luck had blessed her this time for a tavern near the docks was hiring. At first, the owner was wary of her appearance, but he had agreed to hire her as long as she did not cause any of the patrons to complain.

Her scars might be objectionable to most but they had one beneficial side effect—the men let her be once they saw them. The other girls who worked as servers had to contend with being manhandled by the rowdy men who frequented the Sea Crow Tavern but once the men saw her scars, they pulled away leaving her safe from their advances. However, sometimes a patron or more would notice her and start making snide and cutting remarks about her scars. The words cut deep even as she was thankful they left her alone.

Today was no different. A few of the sailors called her over to give their orders, slamming down small bags of coins. One of them grabbed hold of her arm and pulled her into his lap. Before she could refuse his attention, one of his pals noticed the scars on her right arm.

"Bloody hell, Jacko, I suggest you throw her back. She might be catchin'," the man hissed in a disgusting tone and pointing to her scars.

"Arrgh! Be off, girl."

The man they had called Jacko shoved her off of him so forcibly he caused her to stumble into another man at the next table.

"What the hell—"

The man came to his feet with a growl. He was a big man, brutish in face with a white slash of a scar tracing down the left side of his face from next to his eye, past his grimly set mouth, across his jaw, along his neck, and who knows how much further since it disappeared under a filthy, sweat-stained blouse. He had a sprinkling of silver throughout his dark hair in the front and in his unruly beard. She noted how no hair grew where the scar ran through his beard. She had been fortunate not to have had any burns on her head. Her beautiful blonde hair had been spared by the fire.

Immediately tucking her head, she gathered her things and climbed to her feet.

"My apologies, sir, I shall get you a rum," she spoke in a low voice, not much more than a whisper in the loud raucous room. "...on the house."

Without waiting, she scurried from the common room to the back room where the rum stock was stored. Tears burned her eyes as she remembered the cruel words spoken by the sailor implying somehow her skin condition was contagious.

The sound of someone entering the room behind her made her freeze. Patrons were not allowed in the storage space. She turned and saw the brutish man she had fallen against standing there. Her sorrow turned to bone-chilling fear seeing him there. She backed away, glancing about for a way around him.

The man raised his hands as if to show he meant no harm or perhaps to keep her cornered. She thought about screaming but then she remembered the owner's threat if she ever caused a problem among the patrons, she was out on the street.

The man took a tentative step forward and she gasped looking around for an escape. He stopped.

"Tis all right, Miss," he said in a gruff course voice making her wonder just how deep the scar on his neck ran.

"I just wanted to apologize for hollerin' at you," the man said, his mouth spreading in what she imagined was his smile since only one side lifted while the other side hung unyielding. "Many are cruel to those of us who have suffered such pain."

22

He lifted his hand and ran his finger down his scar. Her heart softened suddenly, and she relaxed.

"I am sorry for your pain, sir," she whispered.

"These young asses have no manners. Then again, I suppose you wish not to deal with their advances so tis probably for the better, eh?" he remarked with a chuckle. "Do not worry 'bout me, girl. I have a remarkable wife at home and two daughters. I wanted simply to know if you are all right. You got someone to look after you..."

His voice trailed off as his eyebrows lifted in question. She suspected he wished to know her name.

"Gabrielle. My name is Gabrielle," she answered his unspoken question in a quiet voice.

"A beautiful name for a beautiful girl," he said with a big lopsided grin. "They call me Cuddy as my real name is McGillicuddy—Sheamus McGillicuddy."

"Well, Mister McGillicuddy, tis a pleasure to meet you," she responded with a smile.

It was strange to feel her face light up with the first real smile since Mr. Fieldmore's death. It was good and when Sheamus McGillicuddy busted out in a loud boisterous laugh, she smiled even more. She liked this man.

"Missy, my father's name was Mister McGillicuddy and he was not a very nice man. I am just Cuddy," he said putting his hand out.

She accepted his hand and nodded. "All right then, Cuddy it is."

"I worry 'bout you working in a place like this. Might I make a suggestion?" He scrubbed his hand over his salt and pepper beard. "My girls need someone to teach them to be good ladies and something tells me you had some learning. Am I right?" he asked with a questioning tilt of his head.

"When I was...before my family...yes, Cuddy," she answered, not sure how to phrase where she came from or how she came to be at the Sea Crow. "I believe I could teach your daughters well enough to step into society without embarrassment. I am a bit rusty but I would be honored to teach them."

"Missy, your manners are already far beyond what even my wife can teach them," Cuddy said with a chuckle. "But do not tell my wife I said that."

She laughed. "Certainly not, sir...so are your wife and daughters here in New Orleans?"

"Nay. We live on the island of Jamaica. My Siobhan provides us a very good home for me and my girls. Tis a comfortable house but we can make room for one more. Siobhan has been talking for some time how she would like to see her girls have a chance at good marriages, possibly even bringing them here to New Orleans when the time is right. She says if they have some learning it might do it for them." He grinned with such pride she was surprised he did not puff out his chest and rock back on his heels.

"Jamaica! I am not sure about leaving the city but it does sound far better than working here." She glanced around her. It did sound like a much better opportunity. "Can you afford wages as well as room and board?"

"Aye, I am the captain of my own ship, and I make a good living," Cuddy remarked then frowned. "If you are interested, that is. Tis all right, if you say no. You do not know me from Adam. I do understand your hesitation."

"Well, tis something I must think about," she said, glancing to the open door and seeing her employer waving her back to the common room. "Right now, I must get drinks to those men out there. And I owe you one on the house."

"Do not worry your pretty little head over me," Cuddy responded, taking some of the mugs from her hands and setting them on a tray.

She could feel his eyes on her as she filled each of the mugs from the tap on a barrel. When she picked up one of the mugs, filled it, and handed it to him, he grinned at her.

"Thank you for being so kind to me, Captain Cuddy. I appreciate your offer and I shall give it much consideration. How long are you in port?"

"Only two more days, Missy. You shall need to consider quickly if you wish to travel with me. If you decide to come, however, I shall make you a deal. If you do not like our home or do not feel right with my wife and girls," Cuddy said with a chuckle as he accepted the drink. "Although, I think you shall love them as much as me...I promise to bring you back to New Orleans on the next sail."

She liked this man. She should be wary because as he said, she did not know him from Adam but for some unknown reason, she had a feeling of comfort with him.

"Tis a fair deal, Captain. Thank you," she said with a genuine smile for him.

"Good. You can find me at the ship called the Scarlet Lady."

"The Scarlet Lady? What a beautiful name for a ship."

"Aye. Tis a beautiful ship named for a beautiful lady...my love, Siobhan. She has the most amazing flaming red hair," Cuddy said with another big prideful grin and a raised toast with this mug.

Gabrielle enjoyed how proud Captain McGillicuddy was of his ship, his family, and how even with a damaged smile his big grin still communicated his joy. The thought of leaving this tavern and being with a family again was a great incentive.

"I shall give it great consideration, Cuddy. Thank you. Should I decide to take you up on your offer, I shall seek you out at the Scarlet Lady," she said, patting him on the arm before picking up her tray and heading back out into the common room.

When she reached the table surrounded by rowdy sailors, the one who had been so rude to her before started to speak, undoubtedly eager to demean her appearance yet again but then stopped, his words frozen on his tongue. He turned away and did not look at her again. She set the mugs down in front of the men to take from the tray. When she turned away to return for more, she found Cuddy standing behind her with his hands on his hips.

He grinned down at her and she smiled then mouthed, "Thank you."

It felt nice having someone looking out for her and she liked Captain McGillicuddy even more for it. So in that moment, she knew she would take him up on his offer. Tomorrow, before starting work, Gabrielle would seek him out at the docks to arrange to travel with him to the island of Jamaica. Her day was suddenly much brighter even as she dealt with all these rude and rowdy men.

~*~

Almost seven years had passed since the fateful day when her guardian angel, Captain McGillicuddy rescued her from a life of serving drinks in the Sea Crow. Life with the McGillicuddys was good. The island was beautiful, the people friendly, and soon the McGillicuddys treated her as if she had always been a part of the family.

Siobhan McGillicuddy was a gentle loving mother who treated her well and allowed her the same attention and love as she gave her two daughters, Sara and Fiona. The girls had been only nine and seven when Gabrielle came to their home to be both a companion and surrogate older sister. She had not been able to teach them much in terms of studies but was able to assist them with their lessons as well as teach them to play the lovely carved virginal which Cuddy surprised them with after one of his journeys.

This day began a bit rainy but by noon, the sky was clear and the sun bright so she decided it was a good day to shop for a gift to present to Siobhan in honor of her birthday. She knew Cuddy and the girls would have gifts for her and so she wanted to share in the celebration. She had saved some of her wages the past few months to purchase something special and hoped the lovely shawl she had seen in one of the finer shops in the town of Kingston was still available.

Wrapping a scarf around her neck, and a shawl around her shoulders to cover her scars, she set out toward the town. It was about a mile walk from the McGillicuddy's lovely home nestled among the palm trees, pines, and flowering plants indigenous to the island. The air always smelled sweet and clean here. She enjoyed the walk, passing small farms and vendors who set up to sell fruit and flowers along the busy road. Having come to know most of them, she never worried about walking the island as she would have in New Orleans. However, once in the port town of Kingston, she knew she had to be on guard for as in New Orleans, ships from around the region docked there and rowdy sailors frequented the taverns seeking to imbibe far too much rum.

As she approached the area of the town where it became the busiest, she maneuvered past men unloading goods from the ships. Cringing, she tried to ignore the whistles, hoots, and remarks she would much rather not hear. Gathering her shawl tighter around her, she tucked her chin and headed toward the shops she wished to peruse for a gift. Once she found what she wanted, she hoped to stop at her favorite vendor—the bookseller.

The shop, which was her destination, was just ahead and relief began to relax her shoulders when a strong hand suddenly grabbed her arm.

"Daisy? My sweet, Daisy," a slurred gruff voice exclaimed from behind her before the hand spun her around and pulled her against a large, smelly, and very sweaty body.

The stink of rum filled the air around her face as he tried to kiss her.

Pulling as hard as she could manage, she turned her head away from the stench and cried out that she was not Daisy. The man was not listening but cooing his thrill over having his Daisy again.

"Please, I am not Daisy! Release me at once," Gabrielle cried out, fear gripping her for she knew not how to escape him. "Please let me go!"

The man continued in his attempt to capture her mouth, missing each time but slobbering on her cheeks and neck, pulling her scarf from around her neck. Bile rose in her throat and spots began to form in front of her eyes.

"Basta! Stop now! Leave her alone," she heard a loud commanding voice sound off from nearby.

Suddenly, she was free of the disgusting stench, the crushing hold, and the slobbering mouth. Her legs failed to hold her however, so she slid to the ground.

"Get this drunken animal out of here before I order him strung up for attacking a woman," the voice ordered in a deep, accented voice. "Is he one of ours, Liam?"

"Nay, Cap'n," another man answered.

"Then give him to the constable," the commanding angry voice ordered.

Strong arms came around her and lifted her from the ground.

"Out of the way," the deep voice commanded yet again.

The sound vibrated against her side and pulled her back from the fog which had begun to envelop her.

"You there, have you any agua—water?"

"Aye," an answer came from someone before those arms settled her onto a firm lap.

Still resting in those strong arms, a new scent of leather, sea breeze, and something familiar which reminded her brain of her brother surrounded her instead of the sickening stench from before. Her eyelids fluttered trying to open but she feared facing that awful man again.

"Here, querida, take a sip," the deep voice said, now sounding gentle and soothing.

Her eyelids fluttered again and this time stayed open a bit. Above her was a face wearing dark brows knitted together in concern over dark eyes and surrounded by dark hair.

"Just a sip, little one, just a sip," the handsome face told her.

She did as she was told and a refreshing bit of water slipped past her lips. She swallowed because her throat was so dry. When more flowed over her lips, she drank some more but too fast for she began to cough.

"Si, yes, too much that time...I told you to sip it."

The face grew a smile, a brilliant cheerful smile surrounded by facial hair but not so much as to hide full beautiful lips. The man holding her sat her up straighter, an arm supporting her back and the coughing subsided. He held the cup to her lips and this time with one of her hands guiding it, she drank more.

"Better?" the man asked.

She nodded and focused her gaze on him. He was the most handsome man she had ever seen and he was smiling down at her.

"Hello," he said stroking her hair back from the side of her face.

She gave him a smile in return but when she felt his fingers touch the side of her face where her scars lived on her neck, she stiffened. Her hand reached up to push his hand away and she realized then her scarf was not there.

"Please, release me," Gabrielle muttered, closing her eyes and tucking her chin.

~*~

Tomás Alvarez deplored the manhandling of any woman so when he saw the drunken oaf clutching the young woman and slobbering all over her while she screamed for him to release her, he knew he had to halt the assault. Had he not been standing in the middle of the town and not wishing to draw attention to his presence, he would have snapped the man's neck and left him lying in his own filth. Any man who assaults a woman was lower than low in his mind.

Now he was looking down into bright sky blue eyes in an angelic beautiful face surrounded by silky blonde hair the color of spun gold. A pert little nose, cherub mouth, and smooth skin rounded out the beauty of this little woman. Smoothing a strand of wayward hair from the side of her cheek, he noticed scarring on her neck. *Who did this to her?*

Before he could react in any fashion, she stiffened in his arms, her hand came up to push his hand away, and she demanded to be released. Not one to deny her, he assisted her to an upright position but when she pushed off his lap to stand, she wobbled as if her legs would not support her.

"Please, little one, let me," he implored her as he scooted to the side and helped her take a seat alongside him.

"I am sorry. My scarf—"

He noticed how she tucked her chin and pulled her hair in close around her face. Suddenly, he understood. Her scars embarrassed her. This saddened him for she was a beautiful woman and her scars were nothing. He wanted to soothe her ego and tell her to hold her head high, to be proud but he knew how such a thing could plague one's thoughts.

Glancing around, he saw a piece of brightly colored cloth lying on the ground nearby. He stood, moved to it, retrieving it then he shook it out and brought it to her.

"Tis yours?"

She glanced up at him, nodded then took the cloth, and looked away. Wrapping the scarf around her neck, he knew she wore it to cover her scars. It was then he noticed she wore long sleeves even though the temperatures were far too high to warrant them. Had she more scars?

"Thank you. You have been most kind..." She peeked out at him from under smoky dark lashes, the color of which fascinated him since her hair was like captured sunshine.

"Capitán Tomás Alvarez, at your service," he said with a slight bow of his head then glanced around to make sure no one overheard him giving his name. "And who do I have the pleasure of addressing, mi linda?"

"Me—no, my name is not Linda," she said, her delicate brows which matched the color of her lashes knitting together in confusion.

He laughed making her frown harder.

"No, no, mi linda means my pretty one," he said smiling at her and receiving a chuckle and grin in return.

"Oh! My mistake...my name is Gabrielle," she said once again averting her eyes and tucking her chin.

This time Tomás was not going to allow her to hide so he tucked two fingers under her chin and gently lifted until her eyes met his.

"My honor to meet you, Gabrielle and yes, you are very pretty...beautiful," he said in a low voice as his gaze dropped to her lips and he wondered if they tasted as sweet as they looked.

Once more she reacted by pulling away. His hand dropped and his heart ached for her pain and desire to hide even as his mind pushed back fury at whomever or whatever caused it.

"Thank you, Captain. I appreciate your assistance," she said looking around as if looking for something or someone.

"If you are looking for the beast who attacked you, he has been dealt with and is in the hands of the authorities," he told her. "May I see you home safe, Gabrielle?"

As if he had just proposed something wholly inappropriate, she jumped to her feet with her hands fluttering around her scarf then tugging at her shawl to cover her further.

"That is quite all right, sir, I am here for shopping and wish not to return home yet. I shall be fine. Thank you again." She turned to leave but he caught her hand, stilling her.

"Might I accompany you, in case you feel ill at ease on your feet again?" he asked still holding her hand and surprised she was allowing it.

Gabrielle slowly removed her hand, her fingers trailing along the tips of his and he swore the sensation traveled straight down his spine and ignited a fire in his loins which had him wishing he could sweep her off her feet, return to his ship and sail away before anyone stopped him. He did not know what it was about this innocent-looking young woman but she enchanted him the moment she opened her eyes.

"I suppose it would be all right," she remarked looking around them. "As long as we are in full view of others, that is."

He was about to comment on her not trusting him when she gave him a smile which told him she just might and was teasing him. Then it was gone and she tucked her chin once more. He wished he could explain she had no need to do so for he found nothing unattractive about her.

Standing, he gave her a quick bow and waved her to start. He joined her walking just one pace behind her and to the side to allow her to lead while he followed. His action must have surprised her for she kept peeking at him over her shoulder as if to see if he was still there. He grinned watching her. She was a delight.

When they reached a small shop with hats in the window, Gabrielle stopped and looked at the items then glanced at him.

"You shall probably not enjoy this shop," she said.

"If you enjoy it, I shall," he told her with a grin then opened the door and waved her inside.

The quiet chatter of women inside told him he was probably going to be quite a surprise to them. Tomás chuckled and stepped inside to the sound of a collective gasp.

~*~

Gabrielle did not know what to make of this handsome and charming man. There was a kind gentleness to him but somehow, she knew there was an underlying dangerous side as well. Perhaps it was his swagger, his commanding demeanor, or simply the small gold hoop earring he wore in his left ear. He made her nervous but not in a scared way. No, it was something she had never experienced before. It was something rather thrilling, which made her insides quiver when he touched her. Something which had her wishing her scars gone more than ever before and made her palms dampen as if in anticipation of something exciting.

She watched him enter the small shop filled with ladies' items of clothing and accessories and grin when the women inside gasped as they turned to look at him. She had no doubt they had not noticed her.

"Greetings, sir, may I assist you," one of the women exclaimed as she hurried over to him.

She was an older woman, probably the owner of the shop. Gabrielle nearly laughed aloud at the way she was fluttering her hands in front of her breasts and blushing like a schoolgirl.

"Not me, madam, but my lovely friend here," Tomás remarked as he turned slightly, placing his hand on her elbow and drawing her forward. "I believe she requires your assistance in making a purchase."

The woman's gaze shifted to Gabrielle and as she did, her smile waned.

"Ah yes, welcome, madam," she said, her gaze narrowing on where her scars peeked out from under her scarf near her jawline.

Under her scrutiny, she immediately wished to retreat and began to step backward but Tomás did not allow her. His grip tightened slightly on her elbow and he pulled her closer.

"Madam, you shall show my friend anything she wishes," he said in that particular voice which held so much command Gabrielle thought even the King of England would do as he ordered.

"Of course, sir. Is there anything in particular you wish to see, my dear?"

She knew the woman was only turning her attention on her because of Tomás but she did not care. There was something about him, which gave her increasing confidence.

"Yes, please, there was a scarf in the window last week which I wish to purchase as a gift," she told the woman turning to peruse the display. "It had colors of green and gold."

"Ah yes, I have some, in the back here. If you will follow me," the woman said indicating a table toward the back against the wall.

Gabrielle stepped up to follow her expecting Tomás to stay near the door but he surprised her by placing his hand near the middle of her back and walking along with her, pushing past tightly set displays including one of undergarments. She heard the other women giggle behind her when one of them remarked how she would not mind modeling anything at all for him. She smiled thinking how they must think she belongs with him. It was a powerful feeling having other women being jealous of her for a change.

Not wishing to dawdle or take up any more of the captain's time than necessary, she quickly made her purchase, and foregoing a perusal for her own pleasure concluded her business, and headed for the door. Tomás caught up to her, holding the door and allowing her to precede him in exiting the shop while bidding the women good day.

"So where to next, Gabrielle," he asked once they were outside on the street again.

"I have taken up quite enough of your time, Captain Alvarez—"

"Please, say not my name quite so loud," he interrupted her in a low voice while glancing around them over her head. Since he stood over a head taller than she, it was not difficult for him to do.

"Why ever not?"

"Well...perhaps I shall just say the authorities here might not be pleased I am in port," Tomás said with a sly grin and a naughty wink.

She gasped in response. Perhaps he *was* just as dangerous as she had thought...perhaps even one of the notorious pirates she had heard whispered sometimes frequent the port of Kingston.

"Ah, now I have worried you, Gabrielle. Please, trust me, I would never allow any harm to come to you because of me," he said in a low voice near her cheek which sent a shiver over her.

Not a shiver of fear, however...no, it was something else she did not recognize. The sensation intrigued her. He intrigued her.

"I must finish up my shopping and return home now," she said turning to head in the direction of the McGillicuddy's home, but his hand on her arm halted her.

Turning to look at him, she looked up into dark eyes shaded by thick dark lashes beneath dark brows furled together.

"Do I frighten you, Gabrielle, for tis not my intention?"

Tucking her chin, she shook her head.

"No, Captain, I simply must return for I have duties and responsibilities," she told him, not wanting to admit he made her nervous.

She knew not why he was so attentive but she was enjoying it very much. Most men ran from the sight of her scars yet he had called his pretty one. What did he want from her?

"Then I shall see you to your home," Tomás announced standing tall and extending his arm for her to take as if they were about to walk a promenade.

A sudden nervous laugh erupted from her before she could stop it causing him to frown and drop his arm.

"You do not wish my company anymore, Gabrielle?" he asked looking dejected.

Before she had a chance to answer, a ragtag looking young man ran up to Captain Alvarez and whispered in his ear. Tomás looked around with sudden and obvious nervousness having descended on him. He looked down at her and gave her a quick smile.

"I fear I must take your leave, my beautiful Gabrielle," he said taking her hand and lifting it toward his lips as he bent. "We shall meet again, my sweet. Tis a promise and I always keep my word."

Tomás Alvarez pressed a kiss to the palm of her hand, which sent fire and ice over her skin while causing her insides to quiver with nervous energy so strong she gasped.

"Adios—for now," he said and then he was gone.

Gabrielle stood there, her hand out as if he still held it, his lips caressing it even as he disappeared into the milling crowd. Had she only imagined him? Was the entirety of the afternoon simply a manifestation of the heat and attack by the drunken man? She *had* felt faint earlier. Perhaps she had only imagined the attentions of such a handsome and charming stranger.

Shaking her head, she glanced around but no one watched her. She was after all so unattractive and unimportant despite her handsome captain's sweet words. Perhaps he had been mocking her as so many others do. Tucking her scarf up around her chin, Gabrielle set her gaze on the ground and started walking. She wished only to return home. She would visit the bookseller on her next visit but she would not return to the market alone ever again. No, not again for strange and dangerous things happened when she did.

Chapter Two

Gabrielle mentioned nothing about her visit into town to her employers, her charges, or anyone else at the house so the next day when she overheard Cuddy speaking to a man who had knocked on the door, her heart clamored in her chest and her palms grew damp with fear. The man was asking if anyone from the household had been in town the day before and seen the villainous pirate, Tomás Alvarez or any of his wretched crew.

So her handsome captain *was* a pirate. She cared not for he had been a perfect gentleman with her whereas others with much more reputable social standings acted as rude despicable curs when they saw her scars.

Flattening her body against the wall, she strained to hear more about her captain but the man must have turned away for his words sounded muffled. She was about to step closer to the door when it suddenly opened drawing a deep inhalation of air from her and a surprised expression from Cuddy.

"Gabrielle? Is something amiss?" he asked with concern.

"No sir, no, you just surprised me when you opened the door. I did not know you were home," she lied to her guardian angel, the first time ever in the time she had known him and the way it had rolled off her tongue surprised her.

"Were you by any chance in town yesterday, Gabrielle," Cuddy asked with a glance to the man standing alongside him dressed in a uniform.

"Me...no, Cuddy, no...you know I do not like to go around people," she lied yet again, and again it had rolled off her tongue as if she had been doing it every day of her life.

What was wrong with her? Why was she lying about going into town?

"I did not think so, but had to ask since the lieutenant here seems to think some pirate named Alvarez is stalking the town," Cuddy said with a mischievous wink of his eye and a lopsided grin.

"This is not a laughing matter, Captain McGillicuddy. Alvarez is a dangerous and wanted man. We have no need for his likes in Kingston and since you have a family— daughters, I believe—I would think you would take this more seriously, sir."

The lieutenant obviously did not appreciate Cuddy's sense of humor.

"Aye, yes, Lieutenant, my apologies...tis very serious," Cuddy said clearing his throat. "I shall ask my crew if they have any news of his presence. They would probably know better than me or Miss Gabrielle."

"Yes," the man said suspiciously knitting his brows as his gaze raked over her. When his hand lifted toward her scarf, Cuddy grabbed the man's wrist.

"I worry less about some pirate than some other men on this island, sir," he growled before releasing his arm. "We do not touch women without permission in this house."

The lieutenant stepped backward, rubbing his wrist.

"Of course, my apologies, Miss Gabrielle...Captain—" The man nodded his apology, turned, and stormed out the front door.

Cuddy followed him to the door and slammed it with a loud exhaled hiss. Turning, his face immediately softened and he walked to her, wrapping his arms around her in a comforting fatherly embrace.

"I apologize for that man's rude behavior, my sweet. He had no right to try to touch you. No man does without your permission," he told her patting her on the back as if she had been injured.

"Tis all right, Cuddy. I am used to it. People are curious," she said pulling back and looking up into the kind man's face.

Cuddy had seemed to take it as his duty to be her protector since that day they first met in the Sea Crow. New Orleans seemed a time long past now. Her life was here on the island of Jamaica now even as she often wondered whether her brother ever knew about her and her parents. She supposed he must have learned of the fire once he returned to New Orleans if he returned at all. But would he know she was still alive? There really was no one to tell him otherwise. Perhaps she would send another letter to La Coeur de la Terre, their plantation home outside New Orleans. Surely, if Beau returned, he would return there. Although, she had sent word there a few times after the fire and once she was released from the hospital without any response.

"He still had no right even if he had suggested—"

Cuddy's words brought her attention back to the moment.

"Suggested what?" she asked, fearful someone might have recognized her in the company of Tomás Alvarez.

"The lieutenant implied you might have been with this pirate, Alvarez, in town yesterday. Gabrielle, you can tell me the truth," Cuddy said looking her in the eye.

Even though she had already, she could not lie again to this man who had taken her in, given her a job, a home, a family, and had taken such good care of her. Taking a breath and releasing it slowly, she lifted her eyes to meet his.

"I *was* in town yesterday. I wished to buy Siobhan a birthday gift. A drunken sailor accosted me and a man intervened." She dipped her gaze in shame. "Captain Alvarez."

Stepping from his arms, she wrung her hands but avoided meeting his gaze. She did not wish to see the look of disappointment on his face because she had already lied to him and now he knew it.

"But I did not know he was a pirate, Cuddy. He was very much the gentleman and acted as my protector as I shopped."

Cuddy grabbed her arm and spun her to face him.

"He did not harm you?" he asked with concern.

"No," she answered in a quiet voice then met his gaze. "He was kind and charming and made me laugh. Cuddy, he did not shame me for my scars even though I know he saw them. If he is a pirate, it is only his profession. He is not a bad man."

"Well, that might be true, my sweet but here on Jamaica, he is a wanted man." He pulled her close again then lifted her chin to look into her eyes. "This shall be our secret but I prefer you not visit Kingston alone anymore, please."

She nodded. That was a conclusion she had already come to on her own.

"If you see this man again, you will tell me. Understood?" Cuddy asked, sounding very much like a father and making her smile.

"Yes, sir. I understand," she said before pushing up on her toes and planting a kiss on the gruff man's scarred face. She loved this man. "Is he really so dangerous? Why is he wanted by the authorities?"

"Never ye mind your pretty little head about such things. Tis simply best to steer clear of such men," Cuddy said.

Gabrielle was a bit put off by his statement for his attitude was so condescending she was surprised he had not patted her on the head before sending her off to her room.

~*~

Tomás knew he was tempting fate by returning to Kingston but he had not been able to get the beautiful Gabrielle out of his head. Forced to leave her so abruptly, he had not even been able to give her a proper farewell or ask where she lived, if she was spoken for, or even obtain her last name. He knew not where to find her yet yearned to know that and much more about her.

Having managed to avoid the constable and his men as well as the British navy vessels, which followed him for two days after he and his men set sail, he had finished a delivery of rum obtained in a less than honest manner to the towns on the northern side of the island. The taxes on rum had increased so much, as well as the cost of transport of the rum from Kingston to the other towns on the island, that his services as well as the services of other less than reputable ship owners had become quite necessary and profitable. It was far more profitable to steal the rum from the docks in Kingston and sell it to the towns elsewhere at a lower price than buy it legitimately, and then raise the price to make a profit.

Of course, he was wanted for more than stealing rum or other goods. There was the ridiculous charge of murder hanging over his head for which the British would like to put a noose around his neck. He was no more guilty of murder than sweet Gabrielle was guilty of anything other than making this harsh world more beautiful. But the wife of the man he supposedly killed had sworn he had done it. She was only angry he had not given in to her advances so when her husband assumed she had, he came at him with a pistol. Tomás had defended himself and simply knocked the man to the floor. He was halfway down the street from the inn where it all happened when he heard the pistol shot. He suspected the wife had decided she wanted nothing more to do with her husband but someone had to take the blame and answer to the hangman, and she probably had no plan to do so. A warrant was sworn out for his arrest that very night and he had not had a peaceful moment since—especially in Kingston.

"Cap'n, tis dangerous coming back here so soon...we barely made it out of here in one piece the last time," Liam, his second in command, said from alongside him as they watched the men secure the ship.

They had set anchor outside the reef along the peninsula where the town of Port Royal had become a haven to those who now thrived by doing business with the British. Tomás was not one of those free enterprising men of the sea who now worked for the British plundering Spanish and French ships for ill-gotten gains to serve the King of England. No, his hatred for the British began when they had not taken any pity on his mother and two sisters after sinking the ship they were traveling on from Spain. Due to arrive in Mexico, they were joining him and his father. His father had already set up a fine hacienda in Mérida after he was given land and a high ranking position under the viceroy. Tomás had only been ten years old but his loss was great and his hatred for the British permanently defined.

By the time he was a grown man of twenty, his father had passed from illness and unending grief for the loss they had suffered. Tomás

47

wanted nothing to do with titles and obligations to governments who used innocents as pawns so he set out to see the world. He signed on to a ship leaving for the many islands of the Caribbean. He soon discovered most men had no use for the innocent ones of this world either. He swore he would never sacrifice an innocent for his own gain, and he never has.

Life had not been easy but he was smart and skilled. He had been taught well the use of swords and pistols so the men he sailed with found him useful. He had not lost a fight yet but only fought when necessary.

There were very few in his life he trusted implicitly but Liam Campbell was one. He had known Liam since his first days on the high seas and they quickly became fast friends. They shared a tragic fate which had left the crew of their ship dead and he and Liam in the hands of the British. Liam had suffered injuries, which left him barely conscious. Therefore, the Englishman wielding the lash to get answers chose Tomás instead to practice his handiwork. Only no one realized until Liam was awake enough to speak and told them but Tomás did not understand enough English to answer. By that time, the man had reduced the skin on his back to shreds before Liam was able to answer the questions which finally freed him from the post.

The Brits left them on a nearby island and went on their way not getting anything more they needed from them. They had taken the cargo and left them to die without remorse for the deaths of their crew and the sinking of a ship. To this day, he searched for the big man with the scar marking his face who had whipped him nearly to death. He wanted revenge.

When his monies grew large enough to purchase a ship of his own, he turned to Liam to partner with him. Liam had refused the offer to be his partner for he said he was not a captain but just a simple sailor. However, he was more than willing to assist him in building a fine crew and keep them in line. They struck the deal and even though Liam claimed no partnership, Tomás had always made sure his profits were the same as his own.

"Have you ever seen an ángel, Liam?" he asked his friend.

"An angel? Tomás, I think you have been in the sun too long," Liam said with a laugh. "There be no such thing as angels. Trust me...I got some strange superstitions but angels...never seen one."

Laughing, Tomás slapped a hand on his friend's shoulder and squeezed.

"I think I met one on that day and I plan to find her," he said.

"The girl you pulled the drunkard off?"

"Yes, my friend...she is an angel. A beautiful sweet angel...and I wish to find her," he said smiling.

"You are going to risk going back into the midst of the authorities to find a girl you met briefly...one with scars—"

"Careful, my friend, you know better than anyone such things should not matter," Tomás hissed in a low voice.

"I know...I know, but she is a—"

49

"A what?"

Liam sighed. "A woman—and a woman, even one as pretty as her should not be marked like that."

"True. Tis not her fault, I am sure. Tis one of the things I wish to know about her," he remarked while looking out over the coast and as always, delighting in the way the sun sparkled on the water and the soft surf rolled up on the sand.

He thought of her blue eyes, how they had reminded him of the serene waters around the island and the way her hair captured the sunlight. Scars be damned. She was more beautiful than the purest skinned woman.

"She might be a Brit. You thought of that?"

Tomás turned to look at his friend. He had not considered that detail. She did live with the Brits on the island of Jamaica. However, she had not sounded like a Brit. Her accent was different. He could not place it. Something more he needed to learn about her. With every new question, she intrigued him more.

"I shall worry about that if it is so," he remarked. "Besides, I can ask around about a certain man with a scar while I seek her. Are you accompanying me or have you no desire to tempt fate once more?"

He gave Liam a big grin and laughed when he got his answer.

"Damned right, I am coming with you. Wouldn't miss watching you run scared from the Brits again so soon."

Tomás laughed and pulled the man who was slightly shorter, leaner, and slightly older by five years with a crazy head full of reddish-blond hair and a scruffy beard into a big hug then pushed him away with a snort.

"I always manage to outrun *you*," he said poking his friend in his belly, which seemed to get a bit bigger each day.

Liam placed his hands on his belly and laughed heartily. "Very true, Cap'n. Very true."

As he prepared to head into Kingston in search of Gabrielle, Tomás hoped he would find her. Nearly two weeks had passed since their encounter. A lot might have changed in that time. She might have left Jamaica. She might have married or worse, found out about him and wished nothing more to do with him. With all of the questions he had considered as well as Liam's regarding her possibly being British, he had not asked himself the most important— what was he going to do when he found her? He had not asked it because for the first time ever since setting out on his own, he had not a plan. Tomás had no idea what he was going to do when he found Gabrielle.

~*~

The last two weeks had passed without further event since her more than eventful visit into town and the subsequent visit by the British officer. Gabrielle went about her usual days assisting Siobhan with meals and in the garden, instructing the girls in music and reading, as well as social graces. However, no matter how normal her days seemed, her mind continually wandered to thoughts of the handsome dark-haired pirate named Tomás with sultry dark eyes. She remembered how they crinkled at the corners when he smiled and made her feel beautiful and cherished under his watchful gaze. She could not help but wonder what happened to him. Had he escaped the island uncaptured or was he languishing in the constable's holding cell awaiting judgment? She was still curious about what his crime was which made him so sought after by the authorities. She wished Cuddy would confide in her.

Today began as most days do. She woke, dressed, and then woke the girls. The morning meal was always one filled with chatter and excitement over whatever her two young charges had planned for the day. Today, Sara and Fiona were especially excited. They had been invited to a friend's coming out ball in two weeks and today was their appointment with the best dressmaker in town. Since there had been word of some trouble with runaway slaves who had taken up residence in the mountain territories. This area had once been home to the Maroons deported from the island only a few years earlier so Cuddy was insisting one of his men accompany them into Kingston. Although she had a strong suspicion it was also to protect her and his daughters from encountering any more scurrilous scoundrels like Captain Alvarez. As much as Gabrielle half-wished she would, she doubted very much she would ever see him again.

Once the girls had been fed and suitably attired for the ride into town, Gabrielle joined them outside in front of the McGillicuddys' modest home. Although not as grand as other plantation houses on the island, it still presented itself well to anyone of lesser means. The McGillicuddys did not live grand but they did live very well. Back in New Orleans, she had no doubt they would have easily been welcomed into the best of society. That was if the somewhat stuck up society types would accept Cuddy's gruff appearance and Siobhan's down to earth manner. Then again, perhaps they might not have been any more welcome than she was with her disfigurements.

A brief rain burst that morning had left the air fresh and clean. The scent of banana flowers floated on the wind, which daily rustled the treetops. It was a beautiful day, a good one for her and the McGillicuddy girls to travel into town for their dress fittings.

Gabrielle only hoped the day would pass uneventfully for she had no wish for her young charges ever to experience what she had under the assault of the drunken man on her last visit. Both were beginning to come of age and were most impressionable. She wished their innocence to last as long as possible.

As the carriage rumbled along the dirt road filled with far too many ruts, she thought about the exciting, charming and oh so, very handsome man with long almost midnight black hair, brooding brows, dark enchanting eyes trimmed in lush dark lashes, a smile which could light the darkest night, and a gold earring in one ear. Her pulse quickened at the mere remembrance of the touch of his fingers stroking the side of her face. The man incited feelings in her she had never experienced in all of her short previously uneventful spinster's life.

Shouting ahead on the road had their driver pulling up the horses and slowing their progression in the carriage. Her two young charges began squirming in their seats to see what was happening.

"Girls, please...you are making this carriage sway like a boat. Sit still and stop rocking it, please. I am sure we shall be on our way in a moment or two," she told Sara and Fiona then grabbed each girl by a hand and squeezed. "Whatever the problem, I am sure tis none of our business."

She called over the man Cuddy had sent to accompany them.

"Martin, can you see what it is happening?" she asked the young man as he reined his horse in alongside the carriage.

"Aye, two men have been apprehended. I believe I heard someone say tis that pirate, Alvarez," he told her, his horse shifting and maneuvering.

No, it could not be. Please no.

"I see. Well, I hope we are on our way soon," she said trying her best not to display any concern or worry for Tomás Alvarez even as her pulse quickened, her palms grew damp, and her heart tried to pound its way out of her chest.

"Girls, stay right here. Martin, keep an eye on them and do not allow them out of this carriage for any reason." She stood then opened the door on the open carriage and began to step out onto the road.

"Miss, you should not leave the safety of the carriage either," Martin exclaimed.

"If Captain Alvarez has indeed been apprehended, I wish to verify it for myself and make sure the authorities know tis him," she explained. "Before you start asking questions, yes...I have met the notorious man and so I can verify if the man they have in custody is truly him."

"Still not safe, Miss Gabrielle. Cap'n Cuddy will have my hide if somethin' happens to you," Martin complained and looked highly anxious about what she was asking him to do.

"I shall be just fine, Martin. You said the men had been apprehended," she said with a shrug of her shoulders, careful not to dislodge her scarf or shawl.

Stepping carefully alongside the carriage so as not to slip into the culvert lining the side of the road, she started toward the commotion. She passed another carriage and two men on horses. In her usual manner, she kept her chin tucked so her scarf covered her scars so when one of the men on horseback began following her, she did not notice right away.

"Querida," a low deep male voice said from nearly alongside her, startling her.

Stepping to the side with a surprised gasp, Gabrielle shaded her eyes to look up at the man on the horse. Another gasp escaped her lips but then she quieted when he put his finger to his beautiful lips. The men ahead of her had not captured Tomás Alvarez because he was here, beside her, on a horse and smiling down at her.

"Where are you going?" Tomás asked her.

Knowing now he was a pirate and a wanted man, he looked all the more the part in Black and brown brocade coat over an embroidered waistcoat, a linen blouse open at the neck, and suede trousers tucked into high black boots with silver buckles. Sunlight glinted off his gold earring and he wore a large full brimmed black hat with a beautiful red plume tucked into the band. He had either cut his luxurious long black hair or tucked it up under the hat. She hoped it was the latter for she envied him his ebony locks.

"What are you doing? The authorities are looking for you. They believe they have you apprehended just there." She pointed to the commotion ahead.

Tomás laughed.

"But as you can see, my sweet Gabrielle, they have not captured me," he said with a grin.

He remembered her name. Her heart skipped a beat at the sound of her name on his lips. *What is it about this man?*

"Not yet, you mean. If you stay here, they shall," she scolded stepping closer to the large black horse who was fidgeting.

She put her hand out to stroke the animal and it immediately settled down. Animals did not care about her scars and she had always had a love for their ability to see good in a person despite an outward appearance.

"You are a fearless one, little one. Why were you going there?" He indicated with a tilt of his head the direction of the soldiers still trying to gain control of the men they believed to be pirates.

She tucked her chin more to hide the blush of heat rising on her cheeks than her scars.

"I feared they had captured you," she admitted.

"So you were worried about me?"

Glancing up, she saw a big smile on his handsome face and could not stop her own from spreading her lips. She nodded.

"I do not wish you to end up in the hangman's noose. I do not know your crime but I suspect you are not guilty of it."

"Oh, I am guilty of many crimes, but not the one for which they seek me. Of this one, I am innocent," he told her.

Suddenly, shots rang out and the yelling increased. His horse reacted by stepping erratically, frightening Gabrielle. Stumbling, she fell to the ground nearly getting stepped on by the large animal. Tomás pulled up the steed, jumped down from the saddle, and pulled her into his arms.

"Are you all right, Gabrielle? Please say you are not hurt?"

She looked up at him and nodded. "I am fine."

"Cap'n, it might be a real good idea to get out of here," the man who was traveling with Tomás said in a low voice from atop his horse. "Now."

Several soldiers were running in their direction. Gabrielle understood the faster the men came upon Tomás and his friend, the more likely they were to be discovered.

"You must go or you shall be caught," she said to him even as she wished him to keep her in his arms.

Tomás pulled her to her feet and kept her close. The soldiers drew closer. They were chasing one of the men they were attempting to arrest but he had broken away. As the soldiers neared, she watched Tomás glance around the area. She feared it was too late for there was nowhere for him and his friend to go. Suddenly, he looked down at her and grinned. She frowned because the soldiers were nearly upon them and surely, they would recognize him. She started to warn him but his lips silenced her.

He was kissing her.

Everything fell away as she surrendered to his lips, his arms, his masculine scent, the strength of his body against hers, and the delight of her very first kiss. She no longer heard the shouting or even cared about what was happening around them. All she wished to focus on was the scintillating sensations running through her body as his arms wrapped around her, his lips explored hers, and when his tongue slipped along the seam of her mouth, she relaxed with a moan, and opened to him.

His kiss was exquisite, exciting and terrifying at the same time, and she wanted it to go on forever. However, it did not and when he broke it, she groaned in disappointment. Tomás did not move away, however, but instead allowed his mouth to hover above hers. His breath was warm on her cheek when he spoke in such a soft voice it caused shivers to race over her skin.

"I enjoyed it as well, beautiful Gabrielle and as much as I wish to continue, I must away," he said in a voice not much louder than a whisper. "For now."

Tomás lifted his hand, smoothed hair away from her cheek, and then pressed a kiss to the tip of her nose. She closed her eyes and prayed desperately he would kiss her again. Suddenly, the warmth of his body was gone. She nearly cried out wanting him to return, to hold her again, to take her somewhere and make her his but she knew this was all far too dangerous for both him and his friend, as well as her.

If Cuddy ever finds out...

"My heavens...I must return to my charges," she exclaimed and started to move away back toward the McGillicuddys' carriage.

"No, please, I cannot lose you again. Tell me, please, where I can find you again," Tomás pleaded, his hand clasping her arm just above the elbow. "I came back in search of you."

His admission stunned her. He came back, putting himself in danger of capture and hanging to find *her*.

"At least, tell me your surname so I might seek you out later," he said in a low voice, the sound making her heart leap.

"Hawkings," she said on a whisper just as Martin called out to her.

"Miss Gabrielle, please, you must return to the carriage. Cap'n Cuddy will have my head," he yelled as he maneuvered his horse through the crowd of people, which had gathered to watch the activities of the soldiers.

"I must go," she told Tomás.

He nodded and released her arm but grabbed her hand and lifted it to his lips. Pressing a kiss into her palm, he winked at her.

"I shall see you again, Gabrielle. You have my word," he said then climbed onto his horse and rode along the culvert with his friend behind him before disappearing into the jungle growth.

"Miss Gabrielle, who was that man you were talking to you? Did he harm you?" Martin was insistent on playing her protector, which made her smile.

"I am fine, Martin. Come...we must get the girls to their appointment," she said as she grabbed his horse's reins turning the horse and its rider around then began walking toward the carriage.

I shall see you again. You have my word.

Those words echoed in her head making her insides quiver and happy contentment settle over her. Gabrielle hoped she would see him again—soon.

~*~

"What were you thinking back there, Tomás? You could have gotten both of us a date with the hangman's noose," Liam grumbled as he reined in his mare alongside the other horse.

Tomás had been more than careful since setting out in search of Gabrielle but he understood Liam's concerns. He had taken them almost directly into the center of a hornet's nest where, had they been found out and arrested, he might well have put Gabrielle in danger as well.

"She is the one, Liam," he said knowing his heart was now threatening to be lost forever to a woman he hardly knew.

Life had a way of playing cruel jokes on men but never had he felt so vulnerable—or lost. He could not explain it but Gabrielle Hawkings held his heart in the palm of her delicate hand and he would move heaven and earth or chance being arrested and hanged simply to be near her again.

"The one?"

"Yes...the one I wish to share my life with," he said, and when Liam gave him a look of incredulous disbelief and shook his head, he frowned at his friend. "Have you never been in love, Liam?"

"In love? Tomás, you barely know the girl. How can you believe yourself in love with her? Ridiculous, man," Liam exclaimed.

"Tis how I feel, my friend. Tis true," he explained. "Had anyone told me love at first sight was a reality, I would have laughed in their face then shot them."

"Tis infatuation is all. You have not had a woman in what—two months?"

"More than three actually, but who is counting now? Gabrielle, no, she is different. She is not a woman you bed and abandon. She is an angel."

Liam laughed but Tomás did not appreciate his friend's humor.

"You do not understand," he growled.

"I understand, Tomás. I get you are infatuated with this girl, but is she worth gettin' your neck stretched to see her again?" Liam asked.

Tomás frowned and wondered the same thing. *Si, she is worth the risk.*

"So where do we find her again, Capitán?" Liam asked probably thinking he had lost the battle.

A very good question for Tomás had her name but still did not know where she lived.

"Tis my next problem, Liam, I had to leave her so quickly I did not learn much more than her name. Her man was worried about someone named Cuddy," he complained knowing his lack of information was his fault and no one else's.

"Cuddy?"

"Yes...I believe he referred to him as a captain," he answered.

"Cap'n Cuddy?" Liam began to laugh making Tomás scowl.

"And this is funny...how?"

"Not funny so much, Cap'n, but very informative." Liam clasped Tomás's shoulder and squeezed. "Tis your lucky day, Tomás...for if she is under the protection of a sea captain, he must be known in town."

"So you know this man?"

"No...but someone most certainly will, if he docks in Kingston and lives on the island. However, we might not wish to cross paths with him if he sails for the British. Unless he placates the authorities much as we do to hide what we really do," he said making Tomás grin and nod.

"So if we find this man, Cuddy, we find *her*?"

"I suppose so. If it is what you want to do?"

"Yes...tis what I want to do. But in the meantime, I suppose we must find somewhere to lie low for I suspect the constable is in search of my head on a stick," Tomás said with a laugh then gained a nod from his friend when he suggested where. "Perhaps our old friend will be willing to shelter us."

The two of them turned their horses and headed deeper into the jungle growth.

Chapter Three

Sitting in the dressmaker's shop, Gabrielle waited for Sara and Fiona to finish with the seamstress making their dresses for the coming out party but could not keep her thoughts from traveling back to the moment on the road when Tomás pulled her into his arms and kissed her. Never had she experienced such a thrill. She could not resist wondering if all men kissed the way he did or were the sensations he inspired racing over her body, across her skin, through her blood, and into her heart unique to him. It had been the most breathtaking moment of her life. He had kissed her and she had enjoyed it. She had enjoyed it so much she wished he had not stopped.

Fiona appeared in front of her with two swatches of cloth, one in each hand.

"Gabrielle, which do you prefer?" she asked.

"Both are very pretty, dearest. Which do you like more?"

"I like them both. I cannot choose," the girl said with a woe be gone frown.

"Which one makes you feel the most happy in the thought of wearing it?" she asked the girl.

She watched Fiona look first at one swatch then the other and back to the first. When the girl suddenly smiled and held up the first one,

Gabrielle knew she had her answer. Fiona turned and hurried back into the other room to give the seamstress her answer to which cloth to use to make her dress. She nearly laughed aloud for knowing her young charge, she would probably change her mind again before she got there and on the night of the party, she would cry over not having picked the other swatch.

Shaking her head and wishing she had such decisions to make. It had been far too long since she had to choose between more than one cloth for a dress or specialty combs for her hair or as in both girls' futures, the choice of a husband from multiple suitors. She never had a coming out for she had not reached such an age yet and now at nearly five and twenty, she feared she would never have any suitors. Of course, since men tended to turn away when they saw her scars, she knew she was destined to be a spinster.

Only Tomás had not turned away. Did he not see them or did he choose not to see them? Why had he kissed her? Was it merely to hide from the soldiers as they passed or had he wanted to? Shaking her head, she decided it had all been a ploy to evade the soldiers for no man, especially one as handsome as he was would wish anything from her except possibly a night in her bed—with the lights out and only if she kept herself covered.

A tear formed at the corner of her eye at the thought the kiss which had made her heart race, her palms dampen, and her legs feel weak was nothing more to him than a tool to escape the authorities. A clock on a shelf chimed the hour. She swiped away the tear and checked the time. They must finish up and begin their journey home if they were to arrive in time for supper. Standing, she gathered her things and walked to the curtain separating her from her charges.

"Girls, are you about finished? We must be getting home or your father shall have a search party sent out for us," she said through the cloth wall.

Sara popped her head out through the curtain and smiled.

"Yes, Gabrielle, we are almost finished. Fiona is still deciding on her fabric," she complained.

"As I suspected. Tell her I think the one with gold in it tis the right one for it accentuates her hair," she told her young charge.

Sara nodded and disappeared again. A few minutes passed before the curtain was drawn back and both girls emerged.

"So Fiona...which of them did you decide on?" she asked the girl.

"The one you suggested. It was the one I loved best but I just liked them both so much," Fiona remarked. "Tis the right choice, is it not? Perhaps I should look at them both again—"

"No. No, Miss Fiona, your friend is right. The gold in it...it flatters your beautiful hair," the seamstress interjected, obviously exhausted by the girl's indecisiveness.

Gabrielle nodded and waved the girls along.

"Come, girls, tis getting late and we have a bit of travel yet to reach home," she remarked. "When do you wish them to return?"

"End of the week should do for a fitting then I shall bring the gowns to them for the final fitting before their party," the woman explained.

"Will it be enough time? Oh Gabrielle, what if they are not finished in time for the ball. Tis less than a fortnight and we have so much to do to prepare." Sara wrung her hands in worry.

Gabrielle knew how excited her young charge was to be attending this party for it would be her first foray into society and she would surely be having her own coming out before long.

"Do not worry, tis plenty of time," she reassured both girls and received a nod from the seamstress who then promised the dresses would be ready in plenty of time, and that they would be beautiful.

Finally, Gabrielle was able to usher the two girls from the shop and signal Martin they were ready to head home. After seeing they were comfortably settled in the carriage, she told the driver to proceed. As the carriage made its way along the busy street, she could not resist checking the crowds for a certain dark-eyed man. Since the man was so tall and his hat bore such a beautiful red plume, she thought he would be easy to spot if he were there.

Just as she thought she might have spotted him, the girls began bickering over whose dress was going to be more beautiful. Their argument drew her attention back to them and when she looked back to the spot where she thought she saw Tomás, it was too late. She sighed in disappointment.

"Do not be sad, Gabrielle. Mother said she is going to allow you to wear one of her older dresses. She is going to have the seamstress fit it to you," Fiona said patting Gabrielle's hand where it lay on the seat beside her.

"Fiona! Tis supposed to be a surprise. You have ruined everything," Sara chastised her younger sister making tears form in the girl's eyes.

"Do not fret, Fiona. Your mother already told me of the dress and had me pick one. No surprise has been ruined," Gabrielle told the young girl making her smile.

In response, Fiona turned to her sister and stuck out her tongue making Sara gasp.

"Girls, please behave. I want you both to rest before supper or your developing moods shall upset all at the meal—especially your father."

Both girls folded their arms across their chests and stared out their respective sides of the carriage. Gabrielle smiled. The threat of upsetting their father's meal was enough to quiet them for they knew he might retaliate by denying them attendance at the upcoming party. Peace at last—at least for a while.

Having already left the bustling activity of the town, the ride was quieter with the scents and sounds of the lush jungle surrounding them. She closed her eyes to enjoy the peace. Dappled late afternoon sunlight filtered through the treetops glittering across the backs of her eyelids, the sensation relaxing her almost to the point of sleep. She enjoyed the restful feel and nearly dozed off.

"Hold!"

The command and immediate halt of the carriage brought her out of her meditation.

Ahead of them was a group of soldiers, they were blocking their entry to the drive which circled in front of the McGillicuddys' home.

Martin rode forward and inquired as to why they had stopped them. One of the soldiers walked alongside the carriage and stopped at the door. He looked at the two younger females, raking his eyes over Sara and making Gabrielle very nervous.

"May I ask why you have stopped us, sir?" Gabrielle asked drawing his attention away from her charges.

"You. You are Miss Hawkings, are you not? Please step out of the carriage, madam," the man said opening the door.

"I do not understand," she replied, not making a move to do as he told her.

Glancing toward the house, she saw the front door open. Cuddy stepped out onto the porch. Martin moved his horse forward and one of the soldiers lifted a gun and pointed it at him, halting any further movement.

"Step out," the man ordered her.

She looked to Cuddy who had started toward them but when a soldier called for him to stop, he did. She feared she had no other choice but to obey.

"Gabrielle," Sara exclaimed grabbing her arm in an attempt to keep her in the carriage.

"Tis all right, Sara. I must do as he asks and discover what this is about. Stay in the carriage with your sister," she told the girl who looked as frightened as her younger sister.

Gabrielle stepped from the carriage but as soon as she did, the soldier grabbed her arm alarming the girls who cried out. Martin demanded the man stop and two more soldiers drew guns on him. She had no idea what this was about but knew she must do as the soldier required or Martin and the girls might be harmed.

"Please explain, sir, what—"

"You are under arrest. A witness charges you have been seen you in the company of a man wanted for murder. You will come with me," the man ordered her as he dragged her forward.

"Under arrest? I have no idea of what you speak, sir."

She turned as the man dragged her along and called out to Martin. "Get the girls to the house."

She heard Cuddy yell out demanding to know what was happening. She hoped he would know what to do.

Please, help me.

The officer dragged her along until they stopped in front of two women. She remembered seeing both of them in the shop the day she bought Siobhan's scarf. One of the women nodded.

"Tis her...she was the one with that pirate, Alvarez," she said with a sneer.

The second woman hesitated but when the first nudged her ribs, she nodded as well.

"Aye, tis her. He accompanied her while she shopped."

"Thank you both. You shall be notified when to report for the trial," the officer who had her by the arm said then nodded at another soldier and the man pulled the two women aside. "What say you?"

Gabrielle knew better than to say a single word in her defense for it was her word against two others. She only hoped Cuddy would be able to convince them of her innocence in being only in the wrong place at the wrong time.

"Take her back to town and give her to the constable," the officer ordered two of the men who stepped forward.

One of them tied her hands even as tears slipped from her eyes and down her cheeks. She shook her head and looked to the women who had accused her.

"I did nothing wrong. You must be mistaken," she pleaded and for a moment, she thought she saw a flash of compassion cross the face of one of the women.

The one who had hesitated in her accusation started to speak but the other woman glared at her making her shift her gaze to the ground.

"Ye need me for anythin' else, Lieutenant?" the first woman asked.

"No...no, go away but don't leave the island. You shall be needed at her trial."

The woman nodded, gave Gabrielle another glance then grabbed the other woman's arm and the two hurried down the road leading to town.

"Lieutenant? You *are* a lieutenant. You have authority," Gabrielle addressed the officer, but he was ignoring her. "Please, hear me out, sir."

"What right do you have to arrest her?" Cuddy yelled from where soldiers were holding him at bay with guns pointed at him.

"I have my orders. She has cavorted with a known criminal. She will be interrogated and stand trial," the Lieutenant called out then he walked away from her and the two soldiers assigned to take her to the constable turned her toward town.

One grabbed her arm while the other held a gun on her. Gabrielle stumbled as her eyes blurred and suddenly lightheadedness clouded her brain.

This cannot be happening.

~*~

"Liam—over here," Tomás called out as he jumped from his horse and led it into the brush.

When Liam reached him, he dismounted and pulled his horse behind the brush. Leaning down to where Tomás was peering through the brush at the activity in front of them, Liam groaned when he saw what was happening. After telling their friend, Celie, about Gabrielle and her protector, Cuddy, she had told him exactly where to find them, only it seemed they had arrived too late and now Gabrielle was in the custody of the British.

"She looks mighty upset, Cap'n. It will not bode well for us if they catch us here," he asked swiping a dingy looking kerchief across his forehead and around the back of his neck under his queue of reddish hair before settling his hat on his head.

"Aye. It appears that witch from the shop is accusing her of cavorting with me. The authorities might be using her to ensnare me and then both she and I shall face the noose." Tomás could not allow such a thing to happen.

"We must do something. Perhaps we can cut them off and prevent them from ever reaching the jailhouse."

"Too many armed soldiers with her, Tomás," Liam told him.

"Yes, and there are only two of us...but if they are not expecting—"

His attention was suddenly drawn to the big man the soldiers had detained near the house.

"What is it?"

"That man...the one yelling to know what is happening—"

"He must be the captain she works for," Liam said.

"Why does he not do something?"

"I guess—" Liam's words were cut off when Tomás grabbed his arm in a tight grip.

"Bloody hell—" His heart stopped for a moment when he saw the scar running through the man's beard. "Is it him?"

Tomás looked to his companion who was now staring at the large older man arguing with the soldiers.

"Hard to tell from here but he kind of looks like—bloody hell...do you suppose it is him?"

"I do not know, but I plan to find out," Tomás said with a growl and started to stand but Liam grabbed his arm.

"Cap'n, now is not the time for it."

Tomás hesitated, his eyes going to Gabrielle. Liam was right. Now was not the time. He knew where the man was and if it was the man he sought, he would take his revenge in due time. For now, his concern was with Gabrielle and her freedom.

"Aye...we must assist Gabrielle. If it is him, he shall meet his fate later."

When he saw one of the soldiers tie her hands, he growled. He wanted to attack them now but knew it would be a great mistake. When he saw the man begin leading her away with only one soldier accompanying them, he knew they had a chance.

"Looks like the numbers are more in our favor now, my friend. We can cut them off further down the road near the bend where the others might not see," Tomás said with a grin.

"Aye...I hope you are right, for if not, they shall be stretching our necks by morning," Liam said with a frown.

Together he and Liam rode through the cover of jungle growth until they reached a bend in the road, which was not in sight of any of the farms located nearby. Tomás pulled up his steed and leaped from the saddle taking cover from the road. Liam joined him there. Checking their pistols and pulling their blades from their sheaths, they readied themselves for the two soldiers to pass by with Gabrielle.

A few anxious minutes passed, but then their prey was there. Tomás saw one of the soldiers had a gun on her while the other had hold of a lead attached to her wrists and a hand on her arm. Since the soldier was charged with restraining her, he had no weapon at the ready so he only needed to take out the one with the pistol trained on her back. He had to be careful for if he surprised the soldier too much, he might fire by accident and shoot his angel in the back.

He motioned for Liam to take the one restraining her while he dealt with the other one with the pistol. As the men began to pass with Gabrielle, he made his move with Liam on his heels. Grabbing the man with the pistol from behind, his one hand restrained the pistol while the other slid his blade against the man's throat. Tomás was not a murderer despite the charge against him of which he was not guilty so he simply used the blade to prevent the man from doing anything other than freezing in his grasp. The man would not resist forever so as soon as he relieved him of his pistol, he hit him alongside the head with it then dragged his body off to the side of the road. Meanwhile, Liam had grabbed the other soldier, wrapping a rope around his neck and pulling it tight but only until the man passed out. Once that was done, his body was also dragged from the road.

Gabrielle looked around her in dismay but did not say a word. Tomás wondered if she was in shock for she said nothing even when he turned her to face him so he might untie her restraints. It was only when he touched his fingers beneath her chin and lifted her face that her eyelids fluttered open and he realized she was terrified—and crying. He pulled her into his arms and cooed comforting words to her in his native tongue. When he realized what he was doing, he pulled back and apologized in English.

"My sweet, I am so sorry this has happened to you," he told her all the while wishing he could have protected her from all of this.

When she looked up at him, she blinked her blue eyes and tears slid down her cheeks. The pain and fear in her eyes made his heart ache.

"Cap'n, we had best get out of here unless you plan for the three of us to spend the night in the gaol," Liam remarked in a low voice as he glanced in each direction of the way the road traveled.

Gabrielle looked at Liam and started to pull away from Tomás.

"Who is he?" she asked, her voice barely a whisper and her eyes large with fear.

"No worry, he is with me. Liam is an old friend and he wishes you no harm," he explained to her since it was obvious she did not remember Liam from before.

"Liam Campbell, at your service, m'lady," Liam said in greeting with an abbreviated bow.

"I wish to go home," she said without looking at either of them.

"Tis no longer safe for you there, Gabrielle. They will simply return and arrest you again, only then the charges will be worse," Tomás explained.

She turned her gaze on him and the anger he saw there surprised him.

"This is all *your* fault then," she hissed at him, yanking at the hold he had on her arms.

"Please, I did not intend any of this. I am sorry the authorities looked to you to try to trap me," he said.

She stopped her movements and stared at him.

"Trap you?"

"Yes. I am sure your arrest is a ploy to apprehend *me*," Tomás said relaxing his hold on her arms.

"You really are a wanted man then?"

"Yes. I have done things of which I am not proud but the charge they want me for is false. I swear it, but I do not wish you dragged down with me," he told her taking her hand in his, but she pulled it away.

"Then I will explain I am not with you in any manner, and I do not know you. They will leave me be," Gabrielle said, glancing around. "What you have done will only make things worse for both of us. Leave now or I will scream."

"No. No, please, the damage is done. I fear they will not believe you. Tis me they want...not you," he said glancing over his shoulder in the direction from where they had come.

He knew the soldiers would be heading this way and they needed to get moving.

"Would you rather go to jail and possibly hang for something you did not do? I certainly do not. I committed no murder, yet I shall hang for a crime I did not commit and you shall hang alongside me," he said grabbing her arm. "Just for knowing me. Gabrielle, is this what you prefer?"

She stood looking at him, her eyes wide with fear. She was trembling. He wished more than anything he could change things and tell her all was well, but it was not and never shall be for her again. He was sorry he had caused this unfair situation for her but now it was up to him to keep her safe and away from those who would do her harm.

"Come with us, Gabrielle, I promise to do whatever I must to keep you safe. I shall lay down my life for you if need be. I swear to Dios, I shall," he told her.

"Why did those women tell the authorities such a thing?" she mumbled looking around her and he suspected she was not speaking to him directly.

"Whatever the reason, it has been done and if you go back home, they will come for you again," Tomás said in a harsher tone than he wished but she must understand the danger awaiting her with the authorities.

"I-I do not know what to do," Gabrielle said pulling away from him and wringing her hands while looking around as if in search of something or someone.

"Come with me, my dear, please," Tomás pleaded in a low voice. "We shall go to where we can be safe, far from here. We must sail away from Jamaica, but you shall no longer be in danger of the hangman's noose."

Her eyes grew wide with the mention of the hangman's noose. She looked at the two men in front of her and he supposed she was weighing her options. She closed her eyes and he imagined she was probably wishing she was elsewhere.

"My friends...my family?" Her eyes filled with tears.

He understood what she was leaving behind, and he despised being the one who took her from all she knew. Although, she would despise him even more if the man she thought of as friend and family was the man he sought, and he exacted his revenge on him.

"I am sorry, Gabrielle," he said. "My only concern right now is your safety."

She looked up at him. Tears slipped down her pale cheeks and he thought she would refuse, but then she nodded.

"Good," he exclaimed, grabbing her hand to lead her into the brush with Liam on their heels.

Soon they reached a small clearing where they had left their horses tied. Again she hesitated, pulling against his hand as they approached the large black horse.

"Do not fear him, he is gentle as a lamb," Tomás said with a smile and stroking his hand along the large beast's massive neck. "You met him earlier. He is a good horse."

He watched her as she stepped up then looked the great horse in the eye. The horse whinnied softly and nudged her side with his nose. She smiled and stroked her hand gently along the bit of white on the beast—a small star-shaped burst on his long head.

"I-I remember him but," she murmured then leaned her forehead against the horse's head. "I don't know—"

"Are you willing to ride with me?"

Gabrielle looked up at him, staring at him as if weighing her options then nodded. Moving closer, she looked at the distance to the saddle but when he knelt lower and cupped his hands, she lifted her skirt and placed her foot in his palms while grasping the side of the saddle. When she stepped into his hands, he pushed her up and assisted her as she threw her leg over the animal and into the saddle. Her skirt lifted high on her legs but he quickly pulled the cloth to cover her as she did on the other side. Once she settled, he grasped the reins and the saddle and joined her atop the horse. He wrapped his arms around her as she clung to the saddle.

"I shall always take care of you, Gabrielle," he told her alongside her ear, and she looked at him over her shoulder.

"We shall see," she whispered then looked ahead.

Tomás wondered what she meant but then grinned. He would bring her around. She might not trust him now, she might even despise him right now, but he would win her over for she had already bewitched him.

~*~

Gabrielle had no idea what was going to happen or where they were going but she knew her only other choice was to go to jail, be tried for a crime she could not defend against, and possibly be hanged. Tears filled her eyes as she rode on the great beast of a horse with her back pressed against the hard chest of a man she had once been enamored of, but now wished she'd never met. Now, with his arms wrapped around her as she had daydreamed about earlier, she only wished to start the day over.

He had created this situation and now she was caught up in whatever nefarious deeds he had committed. The authorities were seeking Tomás for *murder*. What if it was true? What if he had murdered someone? A murder he claimed he was innocent of but wanted for nonetheless, and now she was wanted for conspiring with him. As if her life was not difficult enough already, now she was a wanted criminal.

She had been foolish to think him a gentleman, even a hero of sorts. She wished now she had never met him. He had destroyed her life and was taking her away from the only people who cared about her and for that, she would never forgive him. Perhaps she had made a mistake agreeing to go with him. Perhaps Cuddy might be able to protect her from the charge and save her. Then again, why would he? She was not his real daughter. She was not family, and he had his daughters and their futures to think of, and an association with her might ruin their chances in society. She shook her head knowing there was no other choice but the one she had made.

"Where are we going?" she asked not looking at him.

"We must leave Jamaica, Gabrielle," Tomás answered, his voice deep near her ear, the sound sending shivers over her skin which she pushed away.

"And then?"

"I shall take you somewhere safe. Do not worry?" he told her as they moved through the jungle.

"I wish to go to New Orleans."

"New Orleans? Is there a reason you wish to go there?" he asked, suddenly slowing his horse as they approached a clearing.

"Tis my home," she replied thinking of the life she once had.

"Shh..." The soft whisper came alongside her ear as he signaled Liam to halt.

Tomás leaned past her looking out from the brush. She realized he was seeking to ensure it was safe for them to enter the clearing. Ahead of them was a sandy beach and nothing else but open blue water beyond the breakers.

Her insides shook, her palms grew damp, and sweat broke out on her brow wondering what he had planned. Had he brought her here to murder her and dump her body in the sea? She knew nothing of this man, other than he was a pirate and wanted for murder.

"I wish to go back," Gabrielle whispered but then gasped when the sudden sound of shouts filtered through the brush toward them.

"I believe it is too late for that."

Chapter Four

Tomás jumped down from the saddle and turned to look up at her. He put his hands out to assist her, but Gabrielle held tight to the saddle horn and shook her head.

"Please, Gabrielle, tis not safe for you to stay in Kingston now," he said to her in a low voice. "We must make our escape now or we will be apprehended. We must go now or all three of us shall meet the hangman."

"But my father was English, and my mother, French. They must give me a fair trial," she said even as she knew she would not fare any better than anyone else.

"They shall not care what country you hail from, my dear. If they do not hang you, they most certainly shall put you in prison or worse, sell you into slavery. Would you prefer this to taking a chance with me?" He held his hands out to her again.

She looked out across the sand then back to him. If she could convince him to return her to New Orleans, she would never have to face any of this again. She would rather return to her employment at the Sea Crow than go to jail or worse. Her shaking grew worse and suddenly, the air seemed very heavy around her so much so she could hardly breathe.

"Gabrielle, I know you are frightened, and I understand. I returned to this place even though I knew I was putting myself and my friend in danger, but I did so for you. I shall protect you with my life. I wish you no harm, but I knew I had already put you in danger and I could not think of you paying the price for my misdeed. Please..."

Tomás reached his hands higher for her to take them.

She might never know what it was about his plea which persuaded her, but she believed him. Placing her hands on his arms, she allowed him to grasp her waist and assist her from the back of the horse. Settling in his arms, she looked into his dark eyes and saw something there, something which told her Tomás was a good man. She hoped her instincts were true.

"Cap'n, we best go now before we are discovered," Liam said from alongside them.

"Yes, we must go."

Tomás took hold of her hand and moving as fast as possible, they hurried across the sand toward the water. Her skirt tangled in her legs almost knocking her to the ground a few times as she attempted to keep up with the men. She still wasn't sure where they were going or how they would leave the cove by way of the water—except to swim.

When they reached the rocks at the edge of the cove, the surf was splashing against them but then she realized the water hit higher on the rocks after a few waves crashed against them. The tide was rising.

"Come, please, tis safe."

When Tomás began moving forward leading her, she wondered again if she had made a mistake. The man planned to lead them into the surf. Not knowing how to swim, she trembled as the water rushed up around her legs, soaking her skirt and weighing it down. What if she were dragged out into the water? Would he save her then? She glanced back to see Liam following them. What she saw past him at the jungle's edge made her heart nearly stop. Two soldiers had emerged from the jungle.

"Tomás."

"Do not worry, we only need get past these rocks," he said as he maneuvered them through the water.

"Soldiers," she said and pointed behind them.

Tomás and Liam looked in the direction she indicated and they both cursed.

"Come, Gabrielle, we must hurry," he said clasping her hand tighter and moving faster.

With the sand pulling out from under her feet, she stumbled and fell face-first into the water. She sputtered and splashed trying to get upright. Tomás grabbed her and lifted him into her arms. Her shawl was lost to the waves.

"We must hurry."

A few moments later, they were all clear of the rocks and standing at the opening of what appeared to be a cave. Tomás set her on her feet and held her until she was steady in the moving water. It was shallow but rising as the tide came in faster. She glanced behind them and the surf was now pounding at the rocks they had traversed. She saw no sign of the soldiers.

"They will not follow, Miss," Liam told her as he caught her arm when she began to stumble on the rocky floor of the cave.

"Where do we go now? The tide will surely fill this cave," she remarked covering her arm with her other hand suddenly self-conscious of having lost her shawl and knowing her scars were on full display.

Tomás yanked his damp coat off and placed it around her shoulders. She slipped her arms into the sleeves with a whisper of a thank you. When he stroked her cheek gently pushing wet hair away from her face, she looked up, and he nodded. He understood and his showing her such compassion warmed her heart. Perhaps fate had led her to this man for a reason.

"The cave shall fill soon enough and though we have time, we must move before the soldiers figure out how to access it," he said then assisted her in maneuvering the rocky floor of the cave as they climbed higher but deeper into the dim light.

The temperature of the air was dropping around them and she was grateful for his lending her his jacket for more than covering her scars. It was also growing darker as well as the air danker. She began to tremble not from the chill but from fear they would be trapped in here to drown. When Tomás squeezed her hand tighter, she blew out a nervous breath.

"We are almost clear, Gabrielle, do not worry," he whispered, the sound seeming loud even over the sound of crashing waves.

She nodded but remained fearful all the same as they moved further into the darkness.

Suddenly, it grew lighter and as they moved forward, a breeze of fresher air touched her skin. Then without warning, they were in full sunlight and on an open beach. She gasped in relief. They were clear of the cave.

"We are safe now, Gabrielle," Tomás told her as they moved through the sand.

Her wet skirt became caked with sand and she struggled to walk. Would she slow them enough for the soldiers to catch them?

"But they can come through the cave just as we did," she remarked, worried she would hear the shouts of soldiers behind them at any moment.

"If they do, they shall most likely get lost and if they attempt to retreat...well," Tomás said with a shake of his head. "If you do not know the correct path, you only move deeper into the cave. Not a wise thing when the tide is rising."

"Aye, not a good thing," Liam exclaimed with a chuckle.

"Oh, my...you mean they will drown?"

Liam shrugged in response and a flash of guilt washed over her making her tremble.

"Where are we going now?" she asked relaxing a bit now knowing it was doubtful the soldiers would be following, but all the while hoping they would be safe.

"To my ship," Tomás said, pointing to a dinghy which had been hidden among some rocks. "You will be safe."

Safe. Gabrielle had been safe living with the McGillicuddys. She had a safe, simple life until this man appeared in her life. Ever since the day in the market, her life seemed to be spinning out of control. What was to become of her now?

~*~

Tomás hurried her along the sand even as he could feel her resistance against his pull. When he glanced at her, he saw her looking back toward the cave from which they had emerged. He knew she was not sure of him and wished he could calm her fears but now was not the time. Once he had her aboard the La Bella Dama, he will have time to ease her worries and gain her trust.

When they reached the dinghy, he dropped her hand so he might assist Liam in taking it to the edge of the water. Once there, he turned to see she had not moved an inch. She was looking back toward the cave and he wished he could change it all for her. He wished he could take her home and court her properly but the world was a cruel place, and sometimes it dealt far too many a raw deal. He closed the distance between them and turned her to face him.

"Please, Gabrielle, I promise to keep you safe but for me to do so, you must come with me," he told her and pulled her into his arms.

At first, he felt her start to pull away but then she trembled and buried her face against his chest. It was then he heard her sob. His heart broke into a million pieces hearing her anguish. He stroked her hair and rocked her gently.

"You will see your friends again. I promise. I do not know how, but I will make sure you do," he told her.

She pushed back and looked up at him. Her eyes and cheeks wet with tears and her lips quivering as she fought back more. "You promise?"

"I promise...I promise on the lives of my beloved friends and family," he told her and meant it. "But we must go—now."

She nodded and wiped away her tears with the backs of her hands. She put her hand in his and followed him to the dinghy. When they reached the small boat, he helped her into it then he directed Liam to push at the front while he pushed near the back. Soon they had the dinghy in the surf. Liam jumped into the front and grabbed an oar while Tomás climbed in behind Gabrielle and began maneuvering the small boat in the rising surf.

The wind was whipping up more than usual and it was then he noticed storm clouds on the horizon. They needed to get back to the ship fast before the storm struck the island. It wasn't safe to be out on a stormy sea in only a dinghy. He looked at Gabrielle and saw she was gripping the small wooden plank on which she sat. Her hair was no longer wet but wind dried and whipping around her head in a tangle. She didn't even let go of her seat long enough to remove the hair from her eyes.

"Gabrielle?"

She turned her head to look at him and shook the hair from her face. She was pale and her eyes watery.

"Are you all right?"

She shook her head. "I do not know how to swim."

He immediately understood her fear.

"Do not worry. I am a strong swimmer and will not let anything happen to you. We will be there soon," he told her and lifting his chin to direct her to look ahead of them.

Having rounded a curve in the beach, they were now in sight of his ship. Gabrielle looked in its direction then looked back at him.

"That is *your* ship?"

He nodded and grinned proudly at her. It was a fine ship and her being impressed with it pleased him.

"Oh no...Tomás...soldiers," she exclaimed and for the first time since boarding the dinghy let go of her seat to point behind him.

He looked over his shoulder and saw two soldiers, wet and stumbling as they emerged from the cave.

"Liam, we're going to have company soon. We need to hurry," he called out to his friend.

Liam glanced back, cursed, and started rowing faster. Tomás picked up his efforts as well. If the soldiers followed the curve of the beach, they might be able to keep them in their sights but unless they had a boat, they would not be able to follow. He hoped.

Suddenly, shots rang out from the beach. Gabrielle squealed and covered her head.

"Lie down, Gabrielle," he told her as he rowed harder.

She did as she was told and dropped to the floor of the dinghy. He watched as she wrapped her arms over her head and did not need to hear to know she was crying. He felt horrible for all he was putting her through and only hoped he would have the chance to make it up to her soon.

More shots rang out and one zinged the water not far from them. Someone was a good shot. He only wished they were closer to the ship. Suddenly, he heard someone yell out from the direction of the ship and he saw a few of his crew waving their arms at him. One of the men fired a musket toward the beach. The shot most likely did not reach the sand but it would make the soldiers think twice.

Tomás breathed a sigh of relief to know his men would cover them as they approached. More shots came from the beach, but none close to them. His arms were beginning to tire as he was sure Liam's were too, but they had to reach the ship.

"We are almost there. We can do it, Liam," he called out.

"Aye, Cap'n," Liam called out and pushed harder.

He had a good and loyal friend in Liam and knew he would never give up. Glancing down, he noted Gabrielle had tucked into the space between the planks and was staring up at him with wide eyes filled with fear.

"We are almost there. The soldiers cannot reach us with their weapons," he told her and hoped it lessened her worry.

While the soldiers continued to shout and fire at them from the shore, they rowed closer to his ship. Soon, he was able to hear several of his men on board shouting to them. He looked to the ship and saw they had lowered a rope ladder and one of his men was crawling down it in anticipation of assisting them once they were alongside the ship. He had a good crew.

He smiled and waved to them. Liam shouted to them in greeting. Curiosity even drew Gabrielle to lift her head from her hiding place to see what was happening. Now, she pulled herself into a seated position and watched as they approached the ship. As soon as they were within reach, one of the men grabbed the bow of the dinghy and pulled it close to the side of the ship. Another man took hold of the mooring rope Liam held out to him and secured it to the ship.

"Been on an adventure, Cap'n?" the man asked him in Spanish.

"Aye, you could say that, Jose," Tomás responded in like with a chuckle. "If you will assist our guest, we shall get aboard and make haste to leave the soldiers behind."

"Aye, Cap'n..." Jose held his hand out to Gabrielle, but she looked to Tomás as if questioning what she was to do.

"Tis all right, my sweet, Jose will assist you in boarding and then take you to my quarters," he told her with a nod.

She hesitated then faced Jose and placed her hand in his, stood, wobbled slightly under the rock of the small boat but balanced well before stepping out to grab the rope ladder. Tomás watched as Jose stuck close to her as she climbed the ladder. When she reached the top, she glanced over her shoulder and looked down at him with wide eyes then looked to shore.

Tomás followed her gaze and saw the soldiers arguing with each other and waving their arms about as if in frustration. He imagined they were quite frustrated as now the cave was completely filled with water and they would have to wait until low tide to return through to join the other men. It would be a long wait. He chuckled at the thought.

"Cap'n," Liam said his name and nodded toward the waiting ladder.

"You go on, Liam. I want to keep an eye on those soldiers."

Liam seemed surprised but glanced to the shore and nodded. He grabbed the rope ladder and stepped onto it. He quickly climbed the side of the ship and threw a leg over the railing.

"Bring the line with you and we'll pull up the dinghy, Cap'n," Liam called down to him.

Tomás did as suggested and looped the mooring line over his arm and began climbing the ladder. When he reached the top, he flung a leg over the railing and handed Liam the rope.

"If you will see to this, Liam, I will head to the bridge and get us on our way," Tomás told his second in command.

"Aye, aye."

~*~

Gabrielle followed the young man Tomás had called Jose across the deck keeping her eyes diverted from the men she knew must be watching her. She was grateful she was still wearing the captain's jacket so her scars were covered but it was warm and she knew she would have to remove it soon. Not to mention returning it to its rightful owner.

The young man directed her into a companionway. She hesitated. She could feel

93

the warm humid air greeting her from the dimly lit corridor. She glanced around her and was surprised to see no one was watching her except Liam as he stood at the rail directing a few men in retrieving the dinghy. He nodded at her.

Whatever had she been thinking to have agreed to this? Perhaps Cuddy could have persuaded the authorities she was innocent of any wrongdoing. She had not thought this through at all. She did not even have any change of clothing. Her skirt was still wet and scratchy with sand clinging to it. She had lost her shawl and now had nothing to cover her scars.

"Tis all right, Gabrielle. You are welcome to anything you need in my quarters," Tomás called down from above her.

She looked to see he no longer wore his hat and his long black hair blew free in the ocean breeze. He smiled at her.

"Jose will show you."

"Si, Miss, I take good care of the capitán," Jose remarked, once more directing her toward the dim corridor.

"I am sure you do...Jose, is it?"

"Yes, I am Jose," the handsome young man said with a big smile.

She doubted the young man had even seen twenty full years of life but he seemed happy enough. She could not help but think that such a charming and handsome young man should be attending parties and meeting eligible young women instead of living on a pirate ship with a bunch of men. But then she supposed the same could be said about Tomás.

"Thank you."

She heard Tomás calling out orders in both Spanish and English. She heard him call for them to weigh anchor and knew they would be on their way soon. But to where?

Stepping into the dimly lit companionway, Gabrielle put her hands out to each side to steady her steps since she could not see anything at first. Once her eyes adjusted a bit, she saw it was only a few steps to a level landing. She felt a hand, gentle on her arm. Jose was right there to assist her.

"Thank you, Jose."

"You are welcome, Miss," he said stepping up alongside her once they were fully in the corridor. "This way, please."

"Call me Gabrielle, please, Jose."

"Yes, Miss Gabrielle," Jose said with a big grin.

Gabrielle chuckled at his continuing to be so formal with her. She liked his version of her name, however. Tomás always made it sound melodic and so did Jose. She watched as Jose stepped to a doorway and pushing it open, he gave a small bow and with a sweeping motion of his arm, he invited her into the room.

"Thank you," she said in his native Spanish making his smile grow brighter.

She did not know much of the language but she could thank him well enough.

Stepping into the room, a fresh breeze from an open window greeted her and she was grateful for it had removed any stuffiness which might have normally filled the space. Glancing around, she saw a comfortable and well-organized room.

Jose made quick work to pull out a chair for her to sit in and bring a washbasin and pitcher of water as well as a clean towel.

"How long have you been with Captain Alvarez, Jose?"

He stopped what he was doing as if to think a moment.

"Almost a year now. I join La Bella Dama in Trinidad. The ship I traveled on from Spain sank in a storm off the shore. I was lucky to survive. I know how to swim." He grew quiet then added. "The others—not so lucky."

"Jose, I am so very sorry. You were very lucky, but skilled too. Knowing how to swim saved you." Her heart ached for the sadness she saw in the young man's eyes. "So this ship is La Bella Dama?"

"Yes, La Bella Dama...she is the beautiful lady," Jose said with a proud smile.

Gabrielle understood a captain's love for his ship. Her own brother had named his ship La Belle Femme—the beautiful lady—for their mother. She chuckled thinking how similar in thinking Tomás and her brother were, yet they would probably despise each other.

Suddenly, he was there—Tomás Alvarez. He seemed to fill the doorway.

"Jose, you may return to your other work," he told the young man who came to attention and quickly moved to exit the room.

When Jose reached his captain, he paused when Tomás placed his hand on the man's shoulder and nodded.

"You did a good job, Jose. Thank you," Tomás told him then stepped aside so the young man might leave.

Tomás stepped fully into the room and turned to look at her.

"We are on our way now, and I doubt the British shall follow," he told her as he began pulling at the laces which held his blouse together.

She had no idea what happened to his hat or the embroidered waistcoat he had been wearing when they boarded the ship. She could only imagine he had removed them because of the heat. She certainly understood wanting to remove some of her clothing because of the hot environment. It had taken her some time to even begin to get used to wearing a scarf so close around her neck and face in the heat of the tropical island. Even yet, she wanted to tear off the jacket Tomás had lent her and allow the cooling breeze to flow over her skin but she knew how others had no desire to see her scars.

Tomás proceeded to pull his blouse off over his head and that was when she saw them— white scars crisscrossing his broad tan back. She gasped in reaction and turned to look out the window.

"My apologies, Gabrielle, I was not thinking...please forgive me," she heard him say, and then he was quiet.

She glanced over her shoulder to where he had stood but he was gone. Looking around, she had not meant for him to leave. After all, these were his quarters. She came to her feet and started toward the door when he suddenly stepped out from behind a painted screen she had not noticed.

"Oh…I thought you had…uh…never mind," she stammered, feeling somewhat foolish for he had yet again surprised her with his considerate manners.

He had donned a fresh blouse. This one had no laces but instead lay quite open near the neck so a large swathe of tanned skin showed. He was rolling his sleeves up to above the elbows as he moved through the room until he reached his desk. He finished the second shirtsleeve and trained his gaze on her as she returned to her seat by the open window.

"Your scars?" She was hesitant to ask but it would be wrong of her to shy away from them as others did hers.

"Souvenirs of the English lash…tis one of my reasons why I have no love for the British who dominate life in the islands."

Tomás moved to the chest against the wall, opened a door and retrieved two mugs and a dark green bottle with a flat bottom. He set them on his desk, popped the cork out of the long neck of the bottle and poured a liquid into one of the mugs.

"Some ginger wine, Gabrielle? Tis mild but shall also help fortify your belly against any mareo—seasick ailments." He offered her the mug.

Standing, she walked to the desk and accepted the mug, taking a small sip because she did not know what to expect. She did not drink wine or any spirits, for that matter. She occasionally indulged in cider, but mostly tea.

This liquid was sweet with a sharp kind of bite but nothing harsh, and it did warm her insides as it slid down her throat. She smiled.

"Tis good. Thank you, Captain," she said with a nod and another tip of the mug to her lips.

"Please...Captain is so formal. I thought we had already settled on Tomás," he said with a slight frown.

"Yes, we did...but tis...yes, I am sorry—Tomás," she said with another quick nod then returned to her seat by the window.

She realized it would be rude to reject his informality between them. After all that he had done to protect her and of course, there was that kiss.

"So you were whip...the British punished you? Why?" she asked, keeping her eyes trained on the mug in her hands.

The sound of a chair scraping across the wood floor drew her gaze to his movements. He set his desk chair so he was sitting near but not next to her. He took a drink from his mug. She had not even noticed him pour himself some of the ginger wine.

"I was very young...sailing on my first ship. Unfortunately, the British sunk that ship. They fished me out of the sea, tied me to a mast and one of the crew used a lash on me while asking me questions I could not answer. My English was very little then so I was unable to tell them what they wished to know," Tomás explained looking out the window at the water settling in waves behind the ship. "It was not until Liam woke long enough to explain I only spoke Spanish—he explained how we were traveling to

Puerto Rico for the wedding celebration of our capitán's sister and we were carrying wine and other gifts for the celebration."

"Oh, my heavens...what happened to your captain?"

"He was killed when the Brits first fired on our ship. Liam and I were the only survivors. Liam was badly injured and barely conscious so they whipped me while asking me questions. I suppose they thought he would not survive it. To this day, I do not know how either of us did." He shook his head with a scowl as if the memory caused him pain.

Perhaps it does.

Her heart ached for what he must have suffered at their hands. She had never really thought about it one way or the other having been the daughter of an Englishman who had walked away from his family when they rejected her French mother as his wife. Having grown up in New Orleans surrounded by English, French, and Spanish people as well as the many people of color, both slave and free, she felt no ill will against any one group but hearing the British would do something so brutal without realizing the man did not understand the language was despicable.

"I am so very sorry. It must have been very frightening for you."

"It created a hate which made me stronger," he said without looking at her then his dark lashes lifted and she was staring into dark brown eyes which had her thinking how she could so easily fall in and never return. "Do you never feel angry over your scars? Over what happened to you?"

She stared at him as she thought about his words then shook her head.

"Anger—hate—none of those things will change what I live with now," she said. "I must simply accept what is."

He nodded but she knew his anger against the British and the man who scarred him was something very different from her situation. Who was she to blame for the fire?

"Your scars? You hide them. You are so beautiful, Gabrielle, you need not hide them," he remarked reaching his hand out toward hers as it lay on her thigh but she pulled it back.

She glanced away wishing her scars would disappear. His kindness had been great and she feared if he ever saw her scars in their entirety then pulled away, she would surely die.

"I was burned in a fire—a great fire in New Orleans, which took my parents as well as my skin. I was only fourteen and when I woke in the hospital, I was alone with no one to guide me."

"Such tragedy! You were so young. You had no other family?" Tomás asked taking her hand this time, setting aside his mug, and cupping her hand between his warm hands.

"I have a brother but he was not in New Orleans at the time. He might not know what happened even yet. He sails the seas as well and I have not heard or seen anything of him since the fire."

"How long?"

"'Tis almost eleven years now. For a while, a neighbor took me in, but then he died. I was working at a tavern when Cuddy found me and offered to bring me to Jamaica to be a companion and instructor to his daughters. They were with me today when I was arrested. I can only imagine how frightened they were," she said shaking her head.

She wondered if Cuddy was searching for her. Would he come after her? Would she matter enough for him to make the effort and if he did, would she be putting this man and his crew in danger?

"You know...if you might take me to New Orleans, you would be free of me and any chance of the authorities coming after you," she said in hopeful suggestion.

"What if I have no wish to be free of you?"

His question surprised her for she only thought him being kind. Anything more was too scary to consider. She had no experience with men other than the occasional grope by drunken men in the tavern before the look of horror which usually crossed their faces upon seeing her scars.

"What do you want from me, Tomás? I accepted your assistance in avoiding jail and possibly the hangman, but I cannot give you anything more. I have nothing. I only wish to return to my old life in New Orleans with the hope of finding my brother again someday." She would never admit she was afraid of him, the unknown, and the possibility she might have put herself into even greater danger by leaving Jamaica with him.

"For now, we shall head to a safe place to regroup then perhaps I shall consider taking you to New Orleans," he said releasing her hand, pushing to his feet and returning his chair to its place behind the desk.

"If it is ransom you seek, know I have no money and my employer will not pay you," she said then regretted it when his shoulders tightened and he turned to glare at her.

"Do you think me so criminal that I would kidnap you for ransom?"

"I-I—"

"Gabrielle, I have done some things polite society might call piracy but never have I harmed a woman nor would I ever. You are not a prisoner as long as you are with me. Keeping you from jail and harm was my only intention when I asked you to accompany us," he said with a scowl. "I thought I was saving you from such a fate."

"I am sorry. I just thought..."

Tomás shook his head. A look of disappointment crossed his handsome face and now she knew not what to say to change it.

"I have not much in the way of accommodations for you, Gabrielle, but I am willing to give up my bed to you for now," he said walking to the painted screen and pulling it back.

Behind it was a bed—a larger bed than she would expect on a ship with an ornate headboard and footboard. It looked very comfortable and large enough to accommodate him and more.

"I cannot put you out, Captain. Tis your ship and your quarters. If you have a cot or hammock, I can fit into any small corner for the time being," she said even as she wished to curl up into that big bed and go to sleep for a month with the hope of waking to discover her life for the past decade had all been a bad dream.

"Tomás...remember? And I was taught from my time as a little boy, a gentleman never allows a lady discomfort if he can make her comfortable." He gave her a quick smile then even as she remembered just how considerate he was of her needs, her safety, and his promise to protect her, the smile quickly faded. She had insulted him with her accusation.

"Perhaps I might be comfortable enough right here on the window seat if you have an extra pillow and blanket," she suggested as a compromise.

She had to admit, if only a private thought, she would feel safer on a ship full of men sleeping near the captain since he was already offering his quarters.

Tomás seemed to mull over her suggestion and frowned for a moment then shrugged. He moved behind the screen then returned a moment later with a blanket and a pillow.

"If you are sure you will not take my bed. I can sleep on the window seat," he said holding the blanket and pillow out of her reach.

She laughed and his dark brows shot up in surprise.

"I suspect you would hang off and be quite uncomfortable while I think I shall fit just so," she told him and to prove it, she stretched out prone on the seat and indeed, fit it just right.

When he chuckled, she knew she had won and sat up again. He handed her the blanket and pillow then shook his head.

"You are a stubborn one, Gabrielle. Smart but stubborn," he remarked as he moved to his desk and took a seat. "I have some charts to look over but if you wish, you may take advantage of the empty bed over there and rest a time."

She glanced at the bed and noticed he had opened a portal near the bed so a nice breeze blew through in there as well. She smiled and gave a small laugh. He knew how to tempt her. His attention was fully on the items on his desk. Gabrielle knew she had most definitely insulted him for he was using only her given name and did not react to her any further.

"I think I shall take you up on that offer, Tomás. Thank you."

He did not look up but simply nodded.

Chapter Five

Tomás watched her go beyond the screen, kick off her shoes, remove his jacket, which she draped over the screen, and then the scarf that she wore tied close around her neck. She stretched out on top of the bedcovers. She was a stubborn female for sure, but he liked that about her. Her lilting laughter had caught him by surprise because it was the first time she had seemed genuinely happy since he first encountered her. He imagined she had very little to find happiness in but he had hoped to be instrumental in changing that for her. Now he was not sure if she returned such a sentiment since she believed him only wanting her here for ransom.

Setting his charts out in front of him, he tried to concentrate but his attention kept returning to the quiet figure lying prone in his bed. She was in his bed and he wished he was there with her.

How could she believe me a kidnapper?

Why not? She knew him to be a wanted man.

He scowled thinking about how he had only ever been kind to her yet she thought the worst of him. This was not something he wished her to believe but what else could she think? He had taken her from the only home she had known in the islands. She did not know him, only that she was caught up in a web of lies and was now victim to false charges against him which could lead to her own demise if they are caught.

Raking his fingers through his hair, he returned his attention to the charts but he only saw her, the wind blowing her golden curls around her head, and the fear in her eyes when the soldiers had fired at them. She was beautiful but there was more to her. He knew Gabrielle Hawkings had lived more than most in a lifetime already at her young age. She had suffered pain, loss, and traveled alone to an island far from home with a man who had promised to care for her but in the end, would never have kept her from the noose. That deed now fell to him instead, for he was the one who had caught her up in this dangerous situation. Had he not come to her aid, she would not have been seen in his company but then again, she might have fallen to a worse fate.

No. He had done the right thing in coming to her aid but only wished she had not been caught in the snare the British planned to use to capture him. Tomás had no doubt they arrested her to use as bait to draw him out. Had he not rescued her would her protector, this man Cuddy, have been able to convince the authorities she was innocent?

Possibly.

Tomás looked to where she was sleeping. No, he was not willing to chance it for there was something special about this innocent soulful girl who had already captured his heart. He was not one to fall for just any pretty face except long enough to satisfy his needs, but Gabrielle was different. First, he doubted she was the type to toss her skirts for a man, any man. No, he suspected she was far too inexperienced. Her kiss was tentative yet eager once she relaxed. Her thinking he was only seeking a bed partner when he offered his bed told him she was innocent of more than criminal activity. She was innocent regarding life as a whole.

"You are safe with me, my sweet. I shall not allow anyone to hurt you," he whispered to the room. "Not even me."

Returning his attention to the charts in front of him, he did his best to ignore the beautiful girl in his bed and plan their next move. He believed they were safe returning to his home on the small unclaimed island nearby the larger island of Cuba. Very few visited the island for it served better as a haven for those called pirate such as himself. The British usually left the inhabitants of La Isla alone and unbothered so he hoped the British would not think to look for him there. This man, Cuddy, she had told him he was a sea captain so he might have a ship of his own to search for her.

Perhaps taking her to New Orleans might be a better idea. It would prove to her he was no kidnapper. No, he was not ready to give her up yet. He wanted more time with her, perhaps to persuade her to stay with him. If she did not like his home, he would happily build her a home on whatever island she wished, dress her in finery, and give her babies.

Babies!

Whatever was he thinking? Although, sharing such a normal thing as a family with Gabrielle was not a wholly distasteful idea. Tomás pushed such strange thoughts from his brain and returned his attention to the charts.

~*~

The light had dimmed in his quarters so Tomás lit a lantern. He glanced at the sleeping figure in his bed and wondered if he should wake her. Cook would be bringing a meal soon and he was sure she would be hungry.

As if hearing his thoughts, there came a knock on his door.

Pushing out of his chair, he stretched his back a moment then walked to the door and opened it. Cook stood there holding a tray and looking surprised probably because Tomás had opened the door instead of calling out for him to enter as he usually did.

"Supper, Cap'n," the old salt said, his Irish accent still heavy even after a couple of decades away from the island on the far side of the Atlantic.

"Yes...thank you, Cook. Set it out as usual, but quietly," he remarked nodding his head toward the sleeping area.

"Aye, I bring enough for both of ye, sir."

"Good. I think she shall be hungry."

"Something smells delicious," Gabrielle announced from behind them.

Tomás turned to see her emerge from the darkened space wiping sleep from her eyes. Her hair tousled from sleep made her look even more beautiful but in a completely different manner, one he doubted she would appreciate if she was as innocent as he suspected. He cleared his throat pushing such thoughts from his head.

"Cook has brought food and I am sure you must be hungry," he told her. "Come, have a seat."

He watched as she started forward then suddenly her hands went to her neck and she turned, hurried back behind the screen and when she returned, she was wearing her scarf draped across her like her shawl would have and tucked up under her chin. He shook his head.

"Gabrielle, please, I speak the truth when I say you are beautiful. Tis far too warm to bundle up in such things," he told her, waving his hand at the scarf. "You are among friends here who do not judge you. We all bear scars of some sort. Do we not, Cook?"

The older man nodded then turned and pulled up his old shirt. There on his back was a serious of scars much like those on his own back. Tomás knew the man had been the victim of a lashing just as he had.

"I am so sorry, sir." Gabrielle lowered her chin and looked to the floor.

His intention was not to make her sad but to show her everyone carried scars of some sort, and not all were visible.

"Tis all right, Miss," Cook said tucking his shirt in over his round belly. "I lived with 'em a long time now."

"Come, Gabrielle, eat," Tomás said motioning to a seat at the table where Cook had set two places. "Thank you, Cook."

The man nodded and retreated from the room, closing the door behind him. Tomás waited for Gabrielle to reach the table then he pulled out her chair so she might sit then he took his seat.

"Cook does not do fancy so I hope Irish stew is to your liking," he said with a chuckle.

He watched as she lifted a spoon then dipped it into the bowl in front of her. After taking a mouthful, she smiled and nodded. "Tis very good...even better than Siobhan's, I think."

"Who is Siobhan?"

"She is...was—" She cleared her throat. "Never mind, tis not important. She was an old friend. Someone I shall never see again."

He suspected she was someone Gabrielle knew in Jamaica. It was his fault she had left everyone she cared about behind but they would not have been able to do anything for her once she was in the hands of the British.

"I am sorry," he said. "Ginger wine? Or perhaps some rum?"

Gabrielle laughed. "Rum? No...I think not. I have never tasted it. I served enough of it but never indulged."

"Then you will taste some. I believe you will like it." He pushed his chair back, stood, walked to the chest, opened a door, and retrieved a bottle of rum. He grabbed two mugs and returned to the table where he poured some liquid into each of them. "Tis strong, so go easy," he said handing her a mug.

She nodded and accepted it, lifting it to her mouth. First, she sniffed it and smiled.

"Tis sweet-smelling," she said with surprise then tasted it.

He watched her eyes grow large then she pulled the mug away, her pink tongue stroked along her lips sparking his imagination as to other things he would like that sweet flesh to do. Clearing his throat, he took a long swig of the rum and welcomed the burn. Perhaps her sleeping in his quarters was not such a good idea after all. When he glanced at her, she was smiling.

"I like it. It burns a little but it tastes good." She took another sip and smiled again. "Will it make me intoxicated?"

Mother of God, I hope so! No, you fool. Tis not how you wish to have her.

"Yes, possibly, so go easy on it," he told her even as his attention begging cock was telling him to encourage her.

"So where are we going?" Gabrielle asked suddenly setting her mug down.

Her scarf slipped from her right shoulder and the lower part of her upper arm came into view. The skin was marred with harsh scarring which made his heart ache for her, but did not offend him. How could it when his own back looked like raw meat at one time and was still the furthest thing from smooth. She snatched the scarf up and pulled her arm into her lap.

"Do not hide from me, Gabrielle," he said reaching his hand out with the palm up encouraging her to give him her hand. "Please."

She looked at him with a deep sadness in her eyes, which tore him to the core. Her hand appeared above the table's edge and slowly slid forward until she put her hand in his. When he squeezed it gently, she gave him a small smile.

"You are safe among us on La Bella Dama. We are a ragtag group of men who have experienced pains, losses, and misfortunes of our own. We do not judge others for we are not perfect either." He squeezed her hand again and smiled at her.

In return, she smiled then pulled her hand back.

"I have not met many people who have not been offended by my scars. Cuddy understood for he has scars as well, even more evident than yours or mine for his cuts across his face for all to see," she remarked tucking her chin again. "I thank you for your kindness. I do."

Her words clicked in his head. So t*his man, Cuddy, he has a scar on his face.*

He wished to ask her more about his scar but did not wish to press. After seeing the big man with darkish hair and the same build as the man he sought, he had wondered if it could be him but now he wanted to know for sure. He needed to know.

"Your friend, Cuddy, he has a scar?"

"Yes, across his cheek. He wears a beard most of the time since like you, he spends much of his time on the open sea but you can see it even through his thick scruff," she explained before taking another drink of rum.

She must have taken in too much for she suddenly coughed.

"Go easy, Gabrielle."

She nodded and cleared her throat.

"When Cuddy first saw my scars, he felt sorry for me but then told me he understood my pain. He said only someone who had suffered something similar can understand and look past it," she said then looked up, her eyes meeting his. "As you understand, I suppose. Thank you."

He smiled and was about to tell her he did more than simply understand. He saw past them so much so he did not see them at all— only her beauty but a knock on the door interrupted him.

"Si...enter," he called out.

The door opened and Liam poked his head inside.

"Do not wish to interrupt but we are close to a shoreline. Do you wish to anchor here or continue?" he asked.

"I shall be right there. Thank you, Liam," Tomás said then looked to Gabrielle. "I must away for a bit but please, finish your meal and help yourself to any of my books if you wish. I trust you read."

She nodded and smiled. "I do read, thank you."

"Good, they are all in English as I use them to assist my learning of the language," he told her. "Go slow on the rum. I do not wish to return to find you passed out from drink."

He winked at her and delighted when she laughed in response.

"I promise." She tucked her chin again.

Pushing away from the table, he walked past her to the door. Stepping into the passage, he closed the door behind him.

"How is she?" Liam asked.

"She rested a while but I suspect she wishes none of this ever happened," he told his friend as they walked toward the doors to the main deck. "She thinks we have kidnapped her for ransom. She is a sad young woman."

"Did you tell her we are not kidnappers?"

"Yes, but I do not think she believes me."

As they entered the main deck, the fresh sea air soothed his skin. It was much more comfortable out in the open air than in his quarters. Many a night, he slept on deck for that very reason but he could not ask Gabrielle to sleep on deck with the men. Perhaps he would sleep on deck tonight and give her the bed. The thought of her sleeping on the window seat went against the grain as a man who only wanted comfort for the women around him. His father had taught him well in that regard.

"The island is uncharted and the cove on this side is quiet. I believe we will be secure here tonight unless you wish to continue," Liam remarked pointing out the empty beach and quiet jungle on its edge.

"Good, this will suffice to rest us. We will continue home at daybreak. We must stay alert all the same," Tomás said as he turned to scan the horizon on the seaside of the ship. "And Liam—"

Liam paused in his steps.

"Good work, my friend, thank you."

"Any time, my friend." Liam started to walk away again.

"Liam?"

"Aye," he said turning back.

"What did you think of that man she calls Cuddy?"

"I don't know. It has been a very long time but there was something about him..." Liam shook his head. "He could be the one," he said stepping up alongside Tomás. "Did she say any more regarding him?"

"Yes...she said he has a scar on his face," Tomás remarked then looked at Liam.

His friend wore wide eyes and his brows had disappeared up under his hat.

"Interesting," Liam remarked. "Do you suppose it could be him?"

"There is always the possibility but..."

"But if he is the one and she cares for him? What then, Tomás?" Liam asked with a frown.

"I do not know. My head tells me one thing and my heart says another," Tomás said with a deep sigh as he stared out at the water not seeing it, but only seeing the smiling face of the sweet angel in his quarters. He wanted to make sure she always had a reason to smile.

"Might I suggest...take her back home."

Tomás turned to stare at his friend, his eyes narrowing on him.

"No. No. Tis not an option," he exclaimed.

He could not believe his friend had suggested such a thing. Take her home—to what? Certain death or possibly life imprisonment. No, he would not. He could not.

"I did not mean to the authorities, Tomás. Perhaps we could sneak her back onto the island, check out this man, Cuddy, and if it is not him, perhaps he will protect her," Liam said with a shrug.

Tomás stared at him. It was an intriguing thought and he was curious about this man, Cuddy, who had a scar just as the man he sought had.

"No, not now, Liam...perhaps later but right now the Brits are probably watching for us, and for her, so it is too dangerous. No, we shall take her home with us. Perhaps she shall not be so sad there."

"Aye, tis true. The Brits are probably watching the house where she lived. She will be safe with us and maybe after things calm down, she can go home or wherever she wishes to go," Liam said with a shrug. "If she wishes to go somewhere else, that is."

"Very true, Liam, very true," he said. "I think Felicity would like her too, do you not think so?"

"Aye," Liam exclaimed. "If that little sweetheart cannot win her over, you do not stand a chance in hell with her." He laughed and slapped Tomás on the back making him laugh too.

"I think you are right, Felicity is my sweet little flower. No one can resist her charms," Tomás said with a nod. "As soon as we are prepared in the morning, we shall go home."

"Good. I shall inform the men. At first light, I shall send them out to scout for fresh fruit and then we can set sail," Liam said with a smile then walked away.

Tomás looked out over the water and wondered if what he was doing was the right thing. Was it possible Gabrielle's protector might have freed her from the authorities and now he had stolen her away from the only home she felt safe in? Was he being selfish because he wanted to be the one to protect her?

"Capitán," Jose spoke from behind him.

Tomás turned to look at him in response and the young man gave a nod toward the companionway leading to his quarters. Following the direction he indicated, Tomás looked past him. Gabrielle was standing near the opening looking around with his jacket closed tight around her. When her gaze fell on him, she smiled shyly and tucked her chin.

"Gabrielle, you should not be up here," he said as he approached her. "Are you all right?"

"Yes, I just—the lantern went low then it went out. It started getting very dark in there." She glanced around then lowered her voice. "I was a little frightened."

He chuckled and pulled her close. Tucking his fingers beneath her chin, he lifted her face until she was looking up at him.

"Tis fine, Gabrielle," he told her and received a small smile in return. "Tis very nice out here. Please enjoy the fresh air. I believe we shall be blessed with a beautiful sunset."

He walked her to the rail so she might look out over the water. A stiff breeze blew her hair back from her face and lifting her chin, she closed her eyes.

"Ahh...that does feel so nice." She opened her eyes and looked up at him. "I fear tis rather warm in your quarters."

"Yes, it can be, which is why I have decided to sleep on deck tonight so you may have my bed tonight. Tomorrow, we shall be at my home and you may have a bedchamber of your own." He smiled at the thought of showing her his home and introducing his sweet daughter to her.

Felicity was the orphaned daughter of the woman he had planned to marry before she and Felicity fell ill to measles. Mary had succumbed to a high fever. He had not been in love with Mary but he had wanted to make sure she and Felicity were safe. Mary's husband had been a member of his crew and the man had sacrificed his own life for his when another had tried to stab him in a tavern. The man, drunk and angry with Tomás because one of the tavern wenches had preferred him to this man, came at him with a knife when his back was turned. Luis had stepped between them taking the knife to his chest. Tomás had promised him as he lay dying that he would always take care of his family.

After Mary died, he took Felicity in and became her family. Since the girl was only two at the time and had suffered blindness in one eye and a limp from her own battle with the measles, Tomás had hired a woman to watch over her and care for her. She was a sweet child with a big heart and he had come to love her as if she were his own. He hoped Gabrielle would attach herself to the girl as easily as he had.

Watching Gabrielle at the rail, he reveled in how easy she stood on deck. She was a natural for sea travel.

"Have you traveled by ship much, Gabrielle?" he asked her.

She turned and smiled at him as if suddenly pleased about something. She chuckled then looked back at the water.

"Actually...no. I was born in New Orleans and until I traveled to Jamaica, I had never been on the open water. I do love it though. I think it must be in my blood for my father was a sailing man as is my brother. My brother has a ship named similarly to yours—La Belle Femme."

He grinned and nodded.

"I know this ship. My God...your brother, he is Capitán Hawke?" he asked with surprise.

"Yes. You know him?" Gabrielle gave him an eager smile.

"Yes, we have crossed paths. He is a good man," he told her then frowned. "I am not sure he would be pleased with the current situation. I fear he might have my neck stretched faster than the hangman if he knew how I had compromised your safety."

"Perhaps, but I think he would be pleased you saved me, Tomás," she said with a nod. "I am. Thank you." She sighed and looked out over the water. "You have yet to say where we are going."

"We are going home for now. We have our homes on a small island of little consequence to the British where we live quietly, and in safety. I believe you shall like it. I hope, anyway," he said and grinned when she looked to him.

"I would like to see where you live," she said before turning to look back at the beautiful colors beginning to fill the sky and reflect off the water.

This young woman surprised Tomás with her willingness to accept things and try something new, even if she thought him a criminal and kidnapper. He believed the blood of sailors did flow through her veins, and her brother would be proud of her.

Frowning, his thoughts went to her brother. He did know the man, not well but knew him well enough to know he would not be pleased with her being with Tomás and wanted by the authorities. He only hoped he could resolve all of this before Captain Hawkings discovered with whom his beautiful young sister was now keeping company. He knew the man to be fair, however, he also knew him to be fierce in loyalty.

He stepped up next to her at the rail and leaned his forearms on the wood. This was his favorite time of day when the sun slowly dipped beyond the edge of the sea casting colors of pink, orange, and red across the sky and reflecting off the waves like sparkling jewels. Life on the sea was dangerous, filled with unknowns, bad weather, and humans who would just as soon slit a man's throat as assist him from the water. However, life on the sea was also simple and pure. The sea was a fickle companion who would make love to a man onc day then toss him to the sharks the next. But the sea was also generous to those who respected her.

"Do you have a family, Tomás?"

Her question caught him off guard since he had only just been thinking about Felicity.

"My blood family is gone but I have a little girl I think of as a daughter," he told her smiling with fatherly pride.

"She is not your daughter?" Gabrielle asked with wide eyes.

"Felicity is the daughter of friends who both died and I promised to watch over her. She is a joy, a blessing actually. Always, she is teaching me there is much more to life than anger or revenge. Much like you do, my dear," he told her capturing her gaze with his and holding it before his own dipped to her mouth.

He almost laughed when she blushed.

"You do not think you have such an influence on me?" he asked her.

She shook her head and tucked her chin before looking out over the water again.

"The sun is gone," she commented, perhaps in an attempt to change the subject.

"Yes, it sleeps so it might shine on us again tomorrow. Tis time you rest as well, Gabrielle. I am sure you are tired from all that happened today," he said, smoothing a stray strand of silky hair from alongside her face to tuck it behind her ear.

She turned to look at him.

"I am tired but I do not wish to put you out of your bed. Tis important for the captain of the ship to be rested too," she said with a shake of her head. "I shall be fine on the window seat."

"No, no...tis fine you sleep in my bed. I shall sleep out here and enjoy it. Please, be comfortable."

He turned to look for Jose. Spotting him, he called out and motioned the young man over to them.

"Jose, please see fresh water is brought to my quarters," he requested.

"Aye, sir, right away," he said with a smile and a nod to Gabrielle then hurried away.

Tomás laughed drawing a frown from her.

"I think perhaps Jose is rather smitten with you. Tis something I completely understand for I was the first moment I saw you," he told her drawing yet another blush from her fair skin.

"You flatter me so, Tomás...I do not know what to believe," she said with a low chuckle then turned toward the doors leading to his quarters. "Might I ask for your assistance in relighting the lantern?"

"Of course, yes, I shall take care of it personally," he said leading her back to his quarters.

Once there, he noted the room was completely dark aside from a bit of moonlight shining through the window in the area of the bed.

"Stay here, Gabrielle, I shall have the lantern lit in a moment," he told her.

Light from the lanterns in the passageway lit the room enough to allow his eyes to quickly adjust so he found and lit the lantern where it sat on his desk. He checked the level of oil in the lantern and it was plentiful. He wondered why it failed to stay lit then turned to face Gabrielle. She stood just inside the doorway, her chin tucked as she did when she was self-conscious. Had Gabrielle dimmed the light until it went out? Why would she do such a thing?

Perhaps she does not wish to be alone.

Why had he not thought of such a reason? She was alone on a ship with strangers, including him. She had not wished to remain alone in his quarters. Perhaps she did not wish to be alone to sleep either. He had not considered such an idea.

"Tomás, I know you are only being considerate but I wish you would reconsider keeping to your bed. I truly shall be quite comfortable on the window seat. I shall have a fresh breeze from the open window," she said strolling across the room and taking a seat by the window.

"Would you feel safer if I am sleeping here with you rather than on deck?"

Gabrielle did not answer but seemed to be thinking about it. She glanced around the dimly lit room then nodded.

"Yes, I understand. I shall stay here then, but will you not reconsider taking the bed?"

She shook her head again so he relented.

"All right, but if you change your mind—"

"I shall not."

He walked to the bed, grabbed a couple of pillows and a blanket then returned to her. He handed her the items and she took them with a smile.

"I shall be quite comfortable. Thank you, Tomás," she said.

A clearing throat drew their attention to the doorway. Jose stood there with a pitcher of water and a grin.

"Put it on the wash table, Jose," he told the young man then looked back at Gabrielle. "So you might refresh yourself if you wish. I shall be out on the deck for a while yet. Please make yourself comfortable and try to sleep. I shall be quiet on my return."

"You shall return though?" she asked with worry in her eyes.

"Yes, Gabrielle, I shall," Tomás told her and stroked her hair back from her cheek. "I shall make sure you feel safe—always."

~*~

Gabrielle watched the two men leave then sat staring at the empty room. She thought about her two young charges, Siobhan, and Cuddy. Were they searching for her? Cuddy might have convinced the authorities to release her. He had always said he would take care of her, protect her.

Then again, Tomás had promised her the same. He had promised a little girl's parents the same and kept that promise so perhaps he meant his words. Should she put her trust in him? She wished she was more trusting of him, but she could not ignore he was a wanted man. So perhaps he had not kidnapped her but all the same, he had taken her away without enough time to truly consider the situation. Now the authorities would be seeking her for fleeing them. And worse, she had fled in the company of a known pirate. How she wished she had never left New Orleans.

Standing, she set the blanket and pillows down, spread them out to make a bed for the night, and then removed his jacket and her scarf. It was a relief to get the cloth away from her damp skin. Moving to the wash table, she loosened the top of her dress, soaked a cloth she found in a stack on the table, and ran the cooling cloth across her neck, under her hair, and over her face. Wetting it again, she ran the cloth down her left arm reveling in the sensation of the coolness evaporating off her skin then moved to her right. The cloth dragged across the raised scars extending from her shoulder down to nearly her wrist. Even after all these years, the area seemed to burn as the water evaporated. Would she ever feel normal again?

It was true so many others carried scars, but they were men and so not judged by their appearance the way a woman was. When others saw her scars, they cringed away and said cruel things. She doubted others drew back in horror and disgust when men revealed their scars. She knew no one would ever wish to have her as a partner in life for she was so disfigured and unappealing. Even drunks drew back and discarded her when they discovered her scars.

Tomás claimed they did not offend him, but he had not seen the extent of them as they stretched along her arm and down the side of her body. Tears filled her eyes as she continued to wash. He was so handsome, so charming. He could have any woman he wished. He would never want her. No man would ever want her.

Once cleansed and feeling more comfortable, Gabrielle took a seat in the window to enjoy the fresh air flowing through the open panes. She had removed her wet shoes hours earlier and set them on the sill to dry. She tested them and indeed, they were dry enough. She set them on the floor, drew off her stockings then plumped a pillow against the window frame and closing her eyes, she allowed the cooling sea breeze to flow over her.

Chapter Six

Gabrielle came to an alert state with a start and a gasp. The room was dark but for a sliver of moonlight entering the space through the window. She wiped the sleep from her eyes and wondered what had awakened her. A sudden rustle of cloth caught her attention. She moved to stand and found someone had covered her with a blanket and it had tangled around her legs. Pushing it aside, she stood, settled her stance to the gentle rock of the ship and looked around the room. The screen had been pulled to its open state so she peeked around it. It was then she heard a soft snoring sound.

As her eyes adjusted to the darkness, she could now make out the figure of a man lying on the bed. He was on his belly with only britches covering his lower half and his dark hair a swathe of inkiness across part of his back and the upper part of an outstretched arm. His skin seemed to glow against the blackness of his hair. Her gaze fell on the scars which crisscrossed his back and tears stung her eyes thinking of the pain he had endured as they healed.

She wished she had met Tomás before her injuries when her skin was still smooth and silky. Would she have attracted him then? Her gaze slid along his back to the area covered by the dark cloth of his britches and she smiled taking note of what an attractive bottom he had. A blush of heat filled her cheeks and a shimmer of excitement pooled low in her belly as she stared at the man sleeping on the bed.

He suddenly groaned and rolled slightly to the side. His movement startled her making her flinch back nearly knocking over the screen. Correcting it as quickly as possible and then being as quiet as she could, she hurried back to her makeshift bed by the window. Pulling the cover over her, she closed her eyes and tried to calm her breathing even as she heard the bed creak under his weight. She knew he was up and her heart pounded in her ears knowing he was looking at her.

Why was she so embraced by guilt? She had done nothing offensive, only watched him sleeping for a few minutes. She nearly laughed at her own foolishness even as she knew she had been thinking and feeling things completely inappropriate.

"Gabrielle?"

She heard him speak in a soft whisper but she continued to feign sleep. Perhaps he would think it was simply the wind causing the screen to waver. A moment passed in silence. Tempted to peek to see where he was, she forced her eyes to stay shut. When she heard a sigh, she knew he had been watching her just as she had watched him. She wondered what he had been thinking as he did so. She was about to open her eyes when she heard the creak of the bed again. He had returned there and had left her to sleep.

Opening her eyes, the room was quiet with the screen in place. Listening, she did not hear his snore so he was probably still awake. A yawn grabbed her and she decided sleep was a stronger need than thinking about the handsome man stretched out on that comfortable bed. She turned on her side, closed her eyes, and hoped she would meet him in her dreams. In her dreams, she always had smooth skin, fine clothes, and had not the fear of baring her arms.

When she woke again, it was day and she discovered she was now in that comfortable bed. She rolled onto her back and stretched. Somehow, Tomás must have carried her to the bed without waking her. A cool breeze flowed over her but the room was already stuffy from the day's heat making her wonder the time.

She sat up and noted the screen had been tucked away so air moved more easily throughout the room. Tomás certainly did seem to think of her comfort. Her gaze fell on the desk. On it was a tray and on the tray was a bowl covered by a cloth. Intrigued, she stood, smoothed out her dress which had seen better days after being worn in the surf then slept in, and walked barefoot to the desk. Pulling aside the cloth, she smiled seeing fresh fruit filling it.

Taking a seat, she marveled at the delights in front of her. Someone had taken the time to cut open guava, coconut, and even a pomegranate for her. There were gooseberries and star fruit also. She popped a couple of gooseberries into her mouth and stood to look around the room which held so many interesting items belonging to her host. There was an ornate mirror on the wall near the wash table and when she glanced at her reflection, she groaned.

Her hair was a tangled mess. She pushed her fingers through it as best as she could but the tangles were not letting go. She dropped her hands to her sides with a frustrated groan when her gaze fell on a beautiful silver-handled brush with lovely and very fine bristles. She glanced around and saw a plain brush, which must belong to Tomás for it contained long strands of his black hair. He must have left out this brush for her personal use.

She met her gaze in the mirror and smiled. His kindness and consideration for her comfort and well-being continued to surprise her. Perhaps he was as good a man as she first thought him that day in town when he had rescued her from the clutches of the drunken man.

Picking up the brush, she marveled at the intricacies of the designs in the handle. The bristles were soft, but would surely do the job. Where had he come across such a fine item? She glanced in the mirror once more. *Silly girl, he is a pirate.* It was rude to ask where a gift came from and she was certainly not going to be such by asking.

She began working the brush through her hair and it took some work and more than a few pains but eventually, her hair was smooth and shiny again. She had no pins or ribbons so she simply plaited it down her back and allowed the front hair which wasn't long enough to stay back to curl around her cheeks.

Returning to the desk, she sampled more of the fruit until she was full then returned to the window seat, pulled on her stockings and shoes, grabbed her scarf and pulling it full open she wrapped it around her shoulders. Her neck might be exposed but the burn scars were less there than down her arm so she hoped none of the men would object.

Gabrielle made her way through the dimly lit companionway to the steps leading up to the main deck. When she came into the bright sunlight, her eyes closed in reflex. She shaded her eyes with one hand and looked around. Soon her eyes adjusted and she was able to relax her arm.

"Hola, Miss Gabrielle," Jose said from his seat on a barrel where he sat tying a rope. "Is a beautiful day, do you not think so?"

She smiled at him. "Yes, tis a beautiful day, Jose."

"Did you sleep well, Gabrielle?" Tomás called down from the bridge above her.

"Yes...yes, I did, and thank you," she answered, shading her eyes so she might see him.

"Thank you? For what exactly are you thanking me for?" he asked as he descended the steps toward her. "We all had fresh fruit this morning. The small island was quite generous."

"The fruit was delicious...but I mean for putting me in your bed," she said in a low voice not wishing to announce to the entire crew how she had slept in his bed.

"Yes, I was no longer using it so I lifted you and put you there in my stead. You were very much asleep, and I promise...I took no liberties," he said in a near whisper near her cheek.

She gasped. She had not even considered the possibility.

"Well, I appreciate it very much. Thank you," she said looking away because she knew her skin was flushing red at the thoughts she had had about this man during the night.

She pulled her plait around to the front so it curled around her neck. With him so close, she was very self-conscious of her scars.

"You are most welcome, Gabrielle."

"Oh, and thank you for the lovely brush, it was put to very good use. Trust me," she said with a laugh without looking at him.

"You are welcome. Now, what brings you on deck?"

"Tis rather stuffy below. I thought it would be nicer to be out in the fresh air. If that is all right with you, Captain?" she asked him tucking her chin to avoid his eyes.

"But of course. I only ask that you stay out of the way of the men as they work. Please, you may sit over here and still have a good view without getting stepped on," Tomás said taking her arm in a gentle hold and leading her toward the rail then rolling a small barrel close for her to sit on.

"This is nice," she said taking a seat and pulling her scarf up around her. "Thank you again."

"You are welcome...enjoy," he said with a smile and a tip of his head. "Call out if you need anything."

He quickly walked away and returned to the bridge.

Gabrielle leaned against the rail and watched the water below rushing past the ship. The wind was brisk and the sails full. She had no idea the distance they must travel to get to their destination but she didn't mind the time spent in the fresh sea air. It was true she had taken to travel by ship without incident. If it was possible for the sea to be in a person's blood, it swelled rampant in her family's blood. Now she wished she had begged to travel with her brother, even if only a short distance. She envied him traveling to new and different places. She had heard him talk many times about traveling to the Far East and wondered if that was where he had been these many years.

A sudden sadness overwhelmed her thinking of Beau and whether or not he was safe or even knew of the death of their parents, or her injuries. Her fingers gently stroked over the scars on her arm. Would he be as disgusted by her disfigurement as others were?

"Miss Gabrielle?"

She turned her head to find Jose standing nearby. He was holding a rather dilapidated looking straw hat.

"Tis not right for such a pretty lady to sit in the sun. I wish you to wear this," Jose said holding the hat out to her.

She took it and smiled at him.

"The sun does feel wonderful but you are right, Jose, my skin will suffer from it all too soon if left uncovered. Thank you."

"Yes...if you need anything, please...you ask Jose," he said pointing to his chest with a big grin and throwing his shoulders back in pride.

"Thank you, Jose," she said with a nod and placed the hat on her head.

Gabrielle had to hold it there to keep the wind from stealing it but it provided nice shade for her face. All of these men seemed so considerate. *Pirates...pshaw!*

~*~

Tomás watched as his young crewman offered his hat to Gabrielle. When she smiled up at him and took it, a pang of jealousy stabbed his chest. He wished she would smile so freely with him. He noted how she did not tuck her chin when she talked with Jose. Perhaps she held no attraction for him but did for Jose.

Slamming his hand on the railing, he gave a low growl.

"Captain, is there a problem?" his helmsman asked from behind him.

"No...no, I just thought of something which displeased me," he told the man over his shoulder.

He spoke the truth. He did not like the way Jose looked at Gabrielle or flirted with her. Perhaps the man needed other duties rather than looking after him and his needs. Looking over the men working on the deck and in the rigging, he knew he had no desire to have any of the men in such close vicinity to Gabrielle.

He released a hard sigh. The sooner they reached La Isla the better. He had hoped to reach the island by the evening since the wind was in their favor but they had set sail later than he had planned since he had sent the men back to retrieve more of the fruit growing in plenty on the island. He wanted to make sure Gabrielle had enough.

"I had hoped with such a favorable wind in the sails we would be home by nightfall," he said turning to look at the helmsman, and hoping it was a good explanation for his bad humor.

"Yes, sir, but the weather is fine and perhaps if we sail through the night, we will be home for the morning meal," the helmsman replied with a grin.

"Yes, I agree. I think we shall do just that," Tomás said with nod turning his attention once more to the girl seated at the rail. "It shall be good to be home and sooner is better than later."

~*~

The day was long but Gabrielle had enjoyed every bit of it watching the goings-on as the men around her worked. She had taken the occasional break to return below to rest and take relief but had spent most of the day on deck in the fresh air and sunshine. Cook had even brought her more fruit and brown bread when the captain and others had taken a quick meal. Now the sun was setting in front of them but they were nowhere near land.

Glancing up at the bridge, she saw Tomás talking with Liam and the helmsman. Liam stood with his arms folded across his chest and did not seem very agreeable to whatever it was his captain was explaining. He shook his head then his gaze slid to her. Not wishing to be caught watching, she tucked her chin. When she peeked back at the bridge, Liam was no longer there and Tomás was leaning on the railing and calling out orders to some of the men in Spanish.

"We are sailing through the night to reach home by morning, Miss, so Tomás suggested I escort you back to his quarters. Cook will bring you an evening meal and I will bring you some fresh water so you might freshen up," Liam said after he stopped alongside her.

His sudden appearance had surprised her but she tried not to let him know that. She pulled her scarf tight around her and peeked up at him from under the straw hat she had worn most of the day. She wondered why it was Liam instead of Jose bringing her water and accompanying her to the captain's quarters. It was not Liam's usual duties, she was sure.

"You do not seem happy about that," she remarked when she noted how his mouth had drawn tight as he spoke.

"Not happy at all. The crew is tired and eager to get home but we could still be there by mid-afternoon if we slow down and rest for the night."

"Then why are we not doing so?"

"It seems Tomás—" Liam began then glanced up at his captain standing on the bridge.

She followed his gaze but when Tomás saw them looking at him, he braced his feet and folded his arms across his chest.

"He just wishes to get home as soon as is possible," Liam said with a scowl.

"Oh," Gabrielle uttered.

He probably wishes to be rid of me. The sooner, the better.

She stood.

"I can find my way to his quarters, Liam. Thank you," she said starting past him.

"I was ordered to escort you, Miss, and so I will," Liam said placing his hand at her right elbow.

When she flinched away, she sighed in reaction to her rude reaction.

"I apologize. I prefer not to be touched on that arm. I am sorry."

"Tis all right, Miss, I understand," Liam replied then grinned at her. "I got a scar down my left leg that still pains me at times."

"You have scars?"

"Aye, quite a few, Miss. Some from lashes...some from my own stupidity, like the one on my leg. Foolish me, I caught it on a nail while climbing over the rail. Damn near lost the leg and probably would have if not for Mikaela's skill with herbs," he told her with a guffaw.

She wondered who Mikaela was but did not ask.

"I even has one from being shot," he continued with a boisterous laugh as they approached the companionway.

"You were shot?" she asked with a gasp and halting her steps.

"Aye, before I left Scotland. An angry father wanted me away from his daughter so he came after me with a pistol. Caught me in the arm as I rounded the curve in the road," he explained then pulled up his sleeve to show her the scar on his forearm. "Just a scratch really but it impresses the ladies when I say I was shot." He winked at her making her laugh.

"I am sure it does, Mister Campbell," she said smiling and appreciating how he was trying to make her less self-conscious of her scars.

"None of this, Mister Campbell shite, Miss...you call me Liam," he announced. "Pardon me language."

"No pardon needed, I have heard far worse in the tavern where I worked in New Orleans," she remarked as she stepped into the companionway.

Someone had lit the lanterns in the passageway and it made it far more welcoming than the darkness she had expected.

"It seems you have led quite a life already for such a young lady," Liam remarked as he pushed open the door to the captain's quarters then waved an arm for her to enter.

"I have been on my own since I was fourteen. It is not easy for a woman on her own to make her way without compromising her virtue or turning to crime."

Liam cleared his throat uncomfortably.

"I did not mean to insinuate you had done anything—"

"Tis all right, Liam. I understand your meaning and I suppose I have experienced a lot in my short life but there is much more that I have yet to experience most of which, I doubt I ever will," she replied as she took a seat by the open window where she had slept the night before.

"You have a long life ahead of ye, Miss...and you have a very pretty face and figure," Liam said as he pulled the screen open and partially hid the bed.

Gabrielle swore the man was blushing. She suspected he was not used to being alone with a young woman and attending to her...at least not in the fashion of which he was at the present. She hid her face so he wouldn't see him smile.

"A pretty face is only worth so much especially when the rest of you is disfigured and ugly," she said with a frown.

Liam looked at her and seemed unable to find words to respond.

"Real beauty is far deeper than skin and good looks, Gabrielle," Tomás said from the doorway.

"Aye, Miss, he is correct about that," Liam said with a grin. "I know some beautiful women with hearts of evil and once you glimpse that bad, the outside beauty disappears."

"Thank you. Thank you, both for making me feel a bit prettier," she said with heat filling her cheeks.

Feeling self-conscious, Gabrielle turned to look out of the window.

~*~

"Might I say, Miss," Liam said, making her turn to look at him over her shoulder. "All I see before me is a beautiful woman with a beautiful heart. I know this because you were willing to protect my foolish friend here."

Tomás cleared his throat at his friend's insinuation. "Foolish?"

"Aye, *foolish*. If you had not been so hell-bent on seeking out this pretty lady, we would not be in this pickle, now would we?"

Tomás saw Gabrielle dip her head again but not before a smile lit her lips.

"Yes, I suppose this is true. If allowing my heart to rule my head makes me a fool, I claim the title proudly," he said slapping his friend on the shoulder. "What does that make you for following me into such a folly?"

A laugh burst from Liam and drew Gabrielle's attention back to them. He smiled when he saw her tuck her chin and turn away but not before a small bit of laughter slipped passed her lips.

"I shoulda known better, tis true," Liam said with a shrug. "I guess that possibly makes me a bigger fool than you. Best we learn something from this, my old friend."

"And that is?"

"The next time one of us wants to chase after a pretty girl, the other needs to knock him on his arse."

Tomás burst out laughing at the man's remark and was soon joined by Liam. Out of the corner of his eye, he noted how Gabrielle's shoulders moved up and down even as she covered her mouth. She was laughing as well and knowing they had brought her a bit of humor to brighten her situation pleased him very much.

"Well, my very clever friend, what say you check with Cook about a meal and tell him to bring enough for the three of us," Tomás said with a grin.

"Aye! I am glad to join you both for supper. Thank you," Liam said with a happy smile. "I shall check on the heading then be back soon. Ready the rum, my friend,"

After Liam left the room, Tomás stepped to the door and closed it.

"If you wish to, I brought fresh water so you might wash a bit of the sea spray off of you," he said picking up the pitcher of water he had set by the door before either of them had noticed him.

Gabrielle turned to look at him.

"Considering all of me is quite covered in sea spray, it probably is not worth the bother, but thank you," she said without moving from her seat at the window.

"Yes...I wish I could provide you with a proper bath, but we will be home by morning and then you may have every comfort you desire," he said setting the pitcher on the wash table. "I have no change of dress for you but you are welcome to any of my things which might fit you."

This gained her attention. She turned in her seat and glanced at the sleeping area.

"Perhaps you have a blouse I could borrow," she said in a quiet voice.

"Yes...I do and since you are so tiny, it shall cover you well," he said.

"I am not very tall, tis true, but I never thought of myself as *tiny*," she exclaimed standing and wrapping her scarf around her.

"Yes, but you are, Gabrielle, next to me and most men, you are quite tiny," he said stepping close to her and noting how she had to tip her head back quite a bit to look up at him. "Perhaps you are like the enchanted infantina in the old Spanish ballad and you wish me to free you so you might become my love."

Gabrielle laughed.

"I doubt I am an enchanted...what was it?"

"La infantina...a princess," Tomás explained as he brushed a golden curl away from her cheek.

She laughed again and tucked her chin.

"I am certainly no princess."

He tucked his finger under her chin and lifted it until her eyes met his.

"But you are, my sweet, only I am the enchanted one," he said as he dipped his head and touched his lips to hers.

He was about to pull her into his arms and kiss her until she believed she was as beautiful as he knew her to be when a knock sounded on the door. He released her and stepped back.

"Come!" His voice sounded harsh and cracked a bit so Tomás cleared his throat. "Come!"

~*~

Lying in the comfortable bed because Tomás had insisted with a cool breeze blowing over her bare legs where the large blouse she had borrowed from Tomás did not cover, Gabrielle traced her fingertip along her lips. Cook had interrupted them with the evening meal and Liam arrived moments later. She could not stop thinking about what might have happened next had the two men not chosen that time to arrive at the captain's quarters.

Admittedly, she wanted Tomás to kiss her again but they had been alone with the door closed. She knew no one would enter the room without expressed permission from the captain so had he ordered them away they would have obliged, but what then?

She was a grown woman—one of an age when most women she knew were married and already had children. Had her life gone in a different more normal pattern, she would most likely be married, have a couple of children, and be living a quiet life in Louisiana, but it had not. Instead, she was here, so near to a handsome, desirable man who made her blood heat, her heart race crazily, and had her thinking of doing disrespectable things with him. But she was inexperienced—a virgin. Before the other day, she had never even been kissed. She had no idea what she was doing. She was sure it was simply lust driving her thoughts and even if she succumbed, she doubted Tomás would continue his seduction once he saw the horrific and disgusting-looking scars along her body. Even in the dark, he would feel them and the sensation alone would discourage any lustful thoughts or actions he might pursue.

Slamming her hand to the bed, she squeezed her eyes shut against the tears burning her eyes. She was a fool to think he would ever desire her in any such manner. Most likely, he was simply trying to make her feel better about her scars and her situation. She still was not sure he had not tricked her into accompanying him with some ulterior motive. He was a pirate and criminal after all.

Turning on her side, she tucked her arms in and wished again as she had so many times over the years that she could turn back time and escape the fire which had disfigured her and sent her life spiraling out of control. She wished she had never left New Orleans but had waited for her brother to return. Beau would have taken care of her, protected her, and loved her despite her scars. She hoped.

Tears rolled from her eyes thinking of her brother. Gabrielle missed him so much her heart ached. Why had he never looked for her? Why had she never received a response from La Coeur de la Terre? Had no one cared enough to look for her or wish her to come home? Were they all gone? Was she completely alone in this world?

Gabrielle had suffered a feeling of loneliness over the decade since being thrust into the world alone, scarred, and devastated but never had she felt so completely alone and lost as she did right now.

Chapter Seven

Gabrielle must have finally fallen asleep after lying awake for far too long. Neither the delightful comfort of the bed nor the scent of Tomás on the pillow could be denied. Despite her sad feelings, the smell of him close was as comforting as the softness of the bed. She had heard him return but sleep had captured her even while knowing he was nearby allowed her to sleep in peace.

Opening her eyes, she squinted against the bright sunlight shining through the open window near the bed. There were sounds of activity and voices. Was that the sound of children, she heard?

Climbing from the bed, she stretched then crossed the room to the wash station. When she glanced in the mirror hanging on the wall nearby, she noted how crying herself to sleep had left her eyes puffy and red. She poured water into the basin, soaking a cloth then held it to her face. It felt cool and refreshing on her eyes and skin.

A sudden knock came on the door then it slowly opened, but only a slight bit.

"Dearest, are you awake?" It was Tomás and relief flowed over her.

"Yes...I am," she replied.

145

When he poked his head around the door, he groaned and retreated.

"You are not dressed. I am sorry," he said through the door.

She laughed. Her legs had not been burned and scarred so even as it was improper for him to see them, she did not mind.

"Please, I am decent enough."

He opened the door and stepped inside but kept his eyes averted. She chuckled at the thought he was still playing the properly mannered gentleman even though he had stolen kisses from her. Perhaps he truly was sincere in his words and actions.

"We are home, Gabrielle," he said moving to the window and looking out. "As soon as you are dressed, I shall take you to my home where you can have a proper meal and a bath."

"That would be very nice, Tomás," she said running a brush through her tangled hair. "May I continue to wear your blouse, for now at least. It covers me well and since I don't have my shawl..."

"Of course, anything of mine is yours, please do," he said with a smile and finally looking at her.

She noted how his eyes traveled the length of her and paused on her naked legs and feet. When she heard him give a small groan, she turned away so he would not see her pleased smile. Perhaps he truly was attracted to her. When her eyes met her reflection traveling directly to the scars on her neck, she knew it would not last and her smile fell away.

"Please, finish dressing and I shall return to take you ashore," Tomás said and quickly left the room, closing the door behind him.

Gabrielle knew there was no future for her with Tomás even if the authorities never caught up to them. The sooner she found a way to leave this place he called home and returned to New Orleans the better.

~*~

Standing on the deck, Gabrielle watched several people milling around on the beach before her. The island was small but beautiful with lush vegetation, palms, and flowering vines. Women in brightly colored skirts and blouses herded children to calm down as they ran in and out of the gentle surf and called to the men on the ship. She could only think these were the men's families. This was wholly unexpected.

Turning to look toward the bridge, she now wondered if Tomás might have a wife to go with the adopted daughter he had told her about earlier. She watched as he gave orders to one of the men. When he was done, he looked down at her and smiled. He had such a wonderful smile.

"I hope you will be content on our little island, Miss," Liam said from alongside her drawing her attention.

"Do you have a family here, Liam?"

"Family? No...not here," he said with a sadness filling his eyes. "I had a wife many, many years ago but she died in childbirth along with my son. Then again, I guess the crew is my family. Tis all I need."

147

"Oh, Liam, I am so sorry," she said feeling tears swell and reached out to squeeze his forearm.

"Do not fret, Miss, tis a long time ago...before I left Scotland."

"It seems this ship is filled with stories of sorrow."

"Aye, I had not thought of it that way, but nearly everyone aboard has lost someone dear to them," he said glancing around. "Even the youngest of the crew has seen sorrow. You are most observant and compassionate. Perhaps I see why Tomás wished so to find you."

"Are you ready to go ashore, Gabrielle?"

She turned to look at Tomás who had joined them without either of them noticing. She wondered about Liam's words. Had Tomás truly been so eager to find her? And if so, why? The thought of using her for ransom slipped into her mind again. If it was the reason, he would not benefit at all for she was of no value to anyone anymore. Although, she was beginning to believe ransom was not the reason at all.

"I am, yes," she replied then followed him to the rail.

When he climbed over the rail, she sighed and looked around.

"Is there not an easier way to get off the ship?"

Liam laughed.

"I am afraid not, Miss. We have no dock and unless you wish to dive over the side, it is the rope ladder or you will forever live on this ship," he said with a chuckle and taking her hand to assist her. "Come."

Gabrielle shook her head.

"Well, as much as I enjoyed my time aboard, I do not wish to live here forever," she said then after tying her scarf tight around her and with Liam's assistance, she began to climb the rail.

Groaning when her skirt caught on a nail, she hesitated then yanked the cloth. Hearing it tear, she shrugged. Her appearance was already one of a street urchin so what was a tear in her dress going to matter now.

"Are you all right, Gabrielle?" Tomás asked from beneath her.

She glanced down at him and a dizzy sensation grabbed her.

"I was until I looked down. Now I am not sure I can do this," she said looking to Liam.

"No problem, I shall carry you down," Tomás said with a chuckle then suddenly, he was there with her at the top of the ladder.

"Liam, swing her onto my back," he ordered.

"Your back," she exclaimed but before she could argue against the idea, Liam had grabbed her beneath her arms and swung her out so she landed against his captain's back.

She landed there with a groan and grabbed hold around his neck and hung on fearing she would fall.

"You are fine, Gabrielle," Tomás said turning his head and pressing a kiss to her cheek. "Wrap your legs around my waist and loosen your hold on my neck just a bit so I might breathe a bit better."

Fearing she would strangle him, she did what she was told and hooked her hands in a tight

149

hold further down his chest while she squeezed her legs around his body.

"That is good. You shall not fall. As tight as you are clinging to me, we shall go together if it happens," Tomás said with a laugh.

"Please do not fall, Tomás," she said with a shaky voice. "And do not drop me."

"Trust me, dearest, trust me."

Trust. That was a hard thing for her to do. She had been abandoned and forsaken far too many times to freely put her trust wholly in any one person. But for now, she must trust Tomás or they would both end up in the water below.

Hanging tight as he climbed down the rope ladder, she was suddenly pleased she had donned one of his over-large blouses for the sleeves covered her arms completely. However, as she bounced a bit on his back as he moved, her skirt began to hike up in a most unladylike manner. The entire situation suddenly struck her as completely ridiculous and she began to giggle like a child. Whether from fear or just embarrassment, she was not sure but it was enough to make Tomás halt his descent.

"Gabrielle, as much as I am enjoying have your arms and legs wrapped around me, please try to limit your movements for they are causing my body to react in a manner which could cause great embarrassment to us both when we reach the bottom," he said in a tight, low voice which sounded a bit strangled and not by her arms.

Heat filled her cheeks when she thought of how her breasts and lower body were pressed against his hard body.

"I am sorry, Tomás...I did not...never mind, I am just nervous, I guess," she said with a smile then hid it when he peeked at her over his shoulder.

"As I said, Gabrielle, I am enjoying it. Although, I would much rather it be done in a much more private setting," he said with a smile sending a shiver over her which she definitely knew was not from fear.

With a deep exhalation, Tomás continued his descent and she clung tight trying not to bounce against him. She had to admit she was enjoying holding him so close as well, only she wished she was facing his front rather than his back.

Suddenly, hands grasped her waist from behind making her give a small squeal.

"You can let go now, Miss," a man's voice said. "I got ye."

She released Tomás and those hands lowered her into the waiting dinghy. She tried to stand but her legs felt strangely wobbly so she plopped her bottom onto a plank seat and watched as Tomás stepped confidently into the small boat followed by Liam.

She watched as Liam used an oar to push them away from the ship then the man who had caught her at the bottom of the ladder settled into a seat and began rowing them toward shore. Tomás took a seat across from her and smiled at her.

"I hope you shall like our home," he said.

Gabrielle turned slightly so she might watch as the shore came closer. The people who had gathered on the beach moved closer to the water and most of the children were splashing about

151

in the gentle surf. She noted one little girl was waving her arms and hopping up and down, but in a strange manner. She stood almost knee-deep in the water but her right leg seemed shorter and thinner than the other. As her gaze moved over the others gathered, she took note of others with imperfections. One woman was missing an arm, another wore a patch over an eye, and there was a young boy missing part of a leg and leaning on a crutch. Had she fallen in with a band of misfits?

She looked back to Tomás. He was grinning and waving. There was something beyond kind about this man and her heart gave a little jolt watching him smile and greeting those awaiting him. The sound of children laughing and someone calling out brought her back to the moment.

Tomás stood, jumped out of the dinghy, reached for her and when she put out her arms, he pulled her from the boat to cradle her in his arms. He walked the remaining distance through the shallow water and when he reached the sand, set her on her feet. She quickly smoothed her skirt and tugged at her sleeves.

The little girl she had watched hop and down in the water with the strange gait and looked to be about five years of age gave up a loud squeal. "Papa!"

Tomás bent with his arms extended and swept the little girl up into his arms when she stumbled to him. He spun her around as he hugged her to his chest. The little girl showered his face with kisses and he laughed. Then he planted a kiss on her lips and she cupped his face in her small hands.

"Papa, where have you been? I have been worried," she said with a frown.

"Little one, I told you I had an errand to do and would return."

Gabrielle saw him glance around.

"You came here alone?"

"No, no, Papa...Maria brought me," the little girl told him, turning her head so she might see the beach better with her good eye since the other was heavily clouded. She pointed to a young woman who was standing nearby talking to Liam.

Tomás nodded and waved to the girl then he gave the little girl another quick kiss, set her down, and took her hand leading her to stand in front of Gabrielle. She had a distinct limp and moved slowly in the sand.

"Felicity, I wish to present our new friend, Gabrielle. She shall be staying with us for a while. I want you to make her feel welcome." Tomás smiled at Gabrielle. "May I present my daughter, Felicity," he said then drew the little girl to his side before setting her in front of him, his hands resting on her small shoulders. "She worries about me when I am away."

"Greetings, Señorita Gabrielle," Felicity said with a smile and a small curtsy.

"My pleasure to make your acquaintance, Miss Felicity," Gabrielle said in return and presented her a curtsy in return. "I understand your worry, for your father's actions...well...they give me concern as well."

What was worrying Gabrielle more than anything else at the moment was whether or not Tomás had a wife to go with the daughter? However, she appreciated how Felicity turned to hug her adopted father's leg and reveled in the gentle manner of how Tomás stroked the little girl's hair. He was a good and loving father to the little orphan and there was no better quality in a man than that.

Felicity turned to look at her with a smile. She had an angelic face but where once the little girl had had two large expression-filled dark brown eyes, one was now cloudy and dull from blindness. Her heart ached for her and tears began to burn at the backs of her eyes. She quickly glanced at Tomás but he simply smiled.

"I am surrounded by beautiful women today," he said before leaning down to press a kiss to the top of Felicity's dark-haired head.

"Come, Miss Gabrielle," Felicity exclaimed grabbing her hand and leading Gabrielle along the sand toward the lush vegetation at the edge of the beach. "You must meet Mikaela too."

She glanced at Tomás and he nodded with a grin.

"Go...she surely will insist until you do," he said with a laugh. "I shall follow in a moment. She knows the way. Tis only a short distance."

Wondering again about this person named Mikaela, she followed the little girl into the jungle and was surprised to find there was a very well-structured path. The air was cooler in among the wide-leafed plants and under the towering palms. There was an earthy scent mixed with florals. Birds twittered and called out, and occasionally set to flight when disturbed.

Felicity was chattering away as she tugged Gabrielle along and she had not truly been paying attention until she heard the girl mention a waterfall.

"There is a waterfall here?"

"Oh si," Felicity said turning her head completely so she could see Gabrielle. "Papa can take us. I am not allowed to go alone and Mikaela does not like the juju there."

"Juju?" That was a term she was quite familiar with for Mama La Rue used to scare her with stories of bad juju if she misbehaved.

Suddenly, they came into the open and there before them was a collection of lovely homes built from sunbaked clay in various colors. Each had a stone chimney and an elaborately tiled roof. She had expected something far less sophisticated. Now she was not sure what to think of Tomás Alvarez and his band of pirates.

Felicity led her to the largest structure which seemed to be centrally located in the small village. The house was far grander in comparison to the others while the others were quite nice already. There was a stream of smoke rising from one of three chimneys, this one near the back of the structure. Beautiful flowering vines framed the arched doorway and more flowering bushes lined either side. Felicity threw open one of the double doors which were painted a color reminding her of a freshly cooked crab's shell, but somewhat paler.

"Mikaela, come see," Felicity hollered once they were inside and wobbled off down a hallway.

Gabrielle had entered a large foyer with tiled floors, lantern sconces enough she was sure it was very bright at night and walls the color of the sand on the beach. There were two large archways. One led into a room to the left which she suspected was a sitting room, and the other down a hallway toward another open area lit by sunlight. The house was amazingly cooler than outside. Off to her right were double doors. One was open enough to see inside. It was a large room containing a beautiful wooden table with carved legs and surrounded by six chairs with tall ornately carved backs. She noted the fine embroidered cushions on each seat and the ornate black iron candelabra hanging above the table

She stood staring at the space around her with awe. Never had she expected anything so grand. It surely rivaled even her home at La Coeur de la Terre. Stepping to the archway to the left, she entered a large lovely room with more fine furnishings but which also had a relaxed lived-in feel to it. A large carved arching fireplace took up most of the wall facing her and set before it was a divan and two chairs with side tables. Along the front wall, a desk and chair sat before a window with paned glass. On the opposite side of the room sat a small table surrounded by four chairs. As her gaze traveled the room, her eyes took in one thing, which was most surprising to her. On the wall where she stood, lining both sides of the archway, were shelves, and the shelves contained books—many books. This house was comfortable yet grand. It was surprising for she had not thought of Tomás having a home such as this. He must be very wealthy. He must be quite successful as a pirate.

A tall woman emerged from the hallway leading from the back where Gabrielle had thought the kitchen might be located for the woman was wiping her hands on a cloth. She was very beautiful and Gabrielle had to bite back a gasp of surprise—and disappointment. Felicity was hobbling alongside her chattering away but the woman's attention was on Gabrielle.

The tall, slender woman with smooth dark skin which held a creamy golden hue raked her stunning light hazel colored eyes over Gabrielle and wore an expression of disdain on her fine features before she quickly hid it. Unfortunately, Gabrielle did not miss it and suddenly felt even more inadequate in her dirty, atrociously mismatched clothing, short stature, and wild untamed hair. She dipped her chin to hide her scars which she felt were glowing like the moon in a dark sky at that moment.

The woman draped the towel over one shoulder covered by a sleeveless blouse of crimson red which matched the same red mixed with a multitude of colors in the wrap encircling her head. Whereas Gabrielle kept her scarred appendages covered this woman easily flaunted long elegant arms covered in smooth beautiful skin. Under a surprisingly clean apron, a multicolored skirt flowed casually around her legs and bare feet peeked out from beneath it.

"Mikaela, meet Gabrielle," Felicity exclaimed clapping her hands as she came around from behind the woman.

"Welcome, Miss Gabrielle...may I fetch you something to drink?" Mikaela asked with surprising politeness.

The woman had a lovely voice accented in such a way so it sounded like a melody. It had a familiar sound to the accents of the slaves and bayou dwellers back home in Louisiana, but slightly different. Gabrielle liked it. It reminded her of home.

"Thank you, Mikaela, yes, please," she responded and attempted to smile.

Mikaela motioned her to a seat in the drawing room then turned and walked away disappearing into the back of the house, presumably to the kitchen. Gabrielle looked around the room and when her gaze fell on a mirror hanging on the wall near the front window, she gasped in horror at her reflection. Her hair was wild with strands hanging loose from what was left of a neatly tied plait. Her scarf was torn and her neck had been exposed to everyone's view for who knew how long.

Trying to cover the scars on her neck, she tied and retied the scarf until nearly in a panic for she could not get it to settle the way she needed. Still wearing the blouse Tomás had lent her at least meant her other scars were covered but what was she to do without her shawl. She glanced over her shoulder to see Mikaela coming toward her with Felicity bouncing around in front of her. She envied the beautiful woman her long smooth neck, and elegant arms free of blemishes.

She turned back to the mirror and tried to correct the mess the sea air had made of her hair and retied the scarf yet again. When she turned around, Mikaela was standing near a side table alongside the divan. She had set a tray on the table and on it was a pitcher and a glass. Gabrielle did her best to smile but she was wholly intimidated by this beautiful woman.

Just then Tomás burst into the front foyer and stopped in the archway.

"Mikaela...ah, you have met our lovely Gabrielle," he said with a big grin even as he scooped Felicity up into his arms when she ran to him. "I hope you shall be fast friends."

Gabrielle looked to Mikaela who simply nodded then turned away and returned to the kitchen through a door she had not noticed.

"I do not think Mikaela likes Gabrielle, Papa," Felicity said with the open innocence of a child.

Gabrielle dipped her chin and turned away but sensed Tomás looking at her. She wished she had taken her chances with the authorities and not come here.

"Ridiculous, little one, Mikaela is just...how do you say? Shy," he said making Gabrielle glance at him. He smiled at her. "She shall come around and you shall be friends in no time."

She nodded and where she hoped she and the beautiful woman would be friends, she had doubts for she sensed Mikaela wanted Tomás and Felicity for her own.

"Mikaela has been with us since this little one came to be with me. Is this not so?" He tickled Felicity so the little girl squealed and giggled then squirmed to be released.

She hobbled back through the foyer and disappeared. Tomás laughed and motioned Gabrielle to take a seat with him on the divan.

"I believe she likes you," he said as he waited for her to sit.

"Felicity was only two years old and far too much for me to handle alone. Since I am gone sometimes for months, Mikaela has been an angel to care for her, as well as me, all these years," he told her taking his hand in his.

When his fingers slid beneath the sleeve of the blouse she still wore, she pulled her hand away and curled it into her lap beneath the other.

"Forgive me, I do not wish to make you uncomfortable. Speaking of comfort, tis quite warm...I am sure Mikaela has a few items of clothing she can share which will be far more comfortable," he said standing and looking toward the door she believed led to the back of the house.

She grabbed his hand to still him. Tomás cupped the side of her face as she looked up at him and she swore he claimed her heart forever in that moment.

"I do not wish to be a bother. I am quite comfortable," she told him.

Of course, it was a half-truth for she knew she looked like some homeless waif and was in desperate need of a thorough cleansing. He chuckled and shook his head. She suspected she was not fooling him.

"At least have something to drink," Tomás said picking up the pitcher and a glass, filling it with a pretty pink liquid and handing it to her then taking a seat again. "Tis Guava juice...one of our favorites here."

"Thank you, tis one of my favorites as well. You were telling me about Felicity," Gabrielle said before sipping the flavorful juice. "Might I inquire about her leg and eye?"

"As I told you, she was the daughter of very good friends. Her mother died when she was but only two years old. Her father, one of my crew, died before she was ever born. One summer, measles visited us here and her mother and Felicity both came down with fever. Mikaela is a genius with herbs but even she could not save Mary. I had gone to Jamaica to retrieve Mikaela's mother who knows medicinal ways even more but by the time we arrived, Mary was gone. Working together, they managed to save Felicity as well as several others." He shook his head and she felt his grief.

"As Mary lay dying, she made me promise to always see after Felicity. I could not refuse. I already adored the child and she needed someone to care for her. Of course, I had not thought it through for I was ill-equipped to care for a little girl so young. And then there was the damage her fever had done. It left her blind in one eye and although we do not know why, her leg has never kept up with her growth. But I still think her beautiful, smart, and absolutely charming."

He sat back with a grin and sipped from his glass of juice. She could not help but think what a truly kind man he was and what a big heart he had as well.

"I do not know what I should have done had Mikaela not volunteered to be everything to us," Tomás said with a smile. "At first, she would not take payment but I soon convinced her to take a small amount plus she always has a home with us."

As if answering a silent summons, Mikaela entered the room carrying a tray containing two plates of fruit, bread, and smoked meats. Tomás stood, set his glass on a side table and reached out to take the tray. He carried it to the small table set at the back of the room before taking Mikaela by the hand and stepping closer to the hallway leading to the back of the house. He spoke to her in a low voice. She listened then suddenly glanced at Gabrielle and smiled. As if she was not gorgeous enough, she was even more so when she smiled. Whatever Tomás had said to her, it had brightened her disposition for she nodded, and still smiling retreated down the hallway.

"Gabrielle, come...we shall eat at the table," he said motioning her to join him.

She picked up his glass as well as her own and walked to the table. He held a chair for her as she took a seat after setting the glasses down. Before sitting, Tomás retrieved the pitcher of Guava juice and topped off the glasses.

"Whatever you said to Mikaela seemed to brighten her spirits," Gabrielle remarked and almost immediately realized how catty it sounded.

"She is always cheerful but tis like I reminded Felicity, she is shy," Tomás said pulling the skin off of a slice of mango and presenting her with a piece. "I requested she prepare a spare bedroom and draw a bath for you. She is always willing to assist."

Men. Now Gabrielle understood the reason for the smile on the woman's face for if she was to make up a bed in a separate room for her then she knew Gabrielle would not be bedding down with Tomás. Knowing so surely pleased Mikaela immensely for the woman was jealous and Tomás had not a clue.

"...has need of a real family for even though I have tried to be a good papa to her, Felicity needs a mother figure more," Tomás said as he bit off more fruit, licked his fingertips and laughed.

So intent on Mikaela, Gabrielle had missed some of what Tomás had said, but she understood the idea behind it.

"Do you not worry she will fall to a worse fate if you are apprehended? What makes you think we are safe here? Would it not be wiser to leave the island? Perhaps we could take her to New Orleans." She knew she was asking too many questions but her worry over what might happen next had her on edge.

Tomás laughed and leaned back in his seat.

"Do not worry, Gabrielle, we are quite safe here. You see, for whatever reasons, both the British and the Spanish have ignored this island. Everyone knows it is here yet no one

163

comes...well, except those hiding from others. There are a few small communities on the island and I have to admit, they are mostly inhabited by the less lawful."

"And if the British decide to investigate whether or not you are hiding out here...then what?"

"We retreat into hidden caves where they shall never find us. Trust me. We are quite safe, I promise you. We have lived here unnoticed and unbothered for nearly a decade and believe me they have sought my neck for nearly as long."

She sighed and dropped the piece of fruit she had been nibbling.

"Gabrielle, trust me...you are safe here," Tomás told her but she could not push away the sense she should never have left Kingston.

"I worry Cuddy may come searching for me. If he does, he will bring others with him," she said wiping her hands on a cloth. "If he does, you and your friends shall be compromised."

"He will not find you," Tomás told her.

Shaking her head, she still worried. "But if he does seek me, he will not stop until he finds me. I am worried for you—and Felicity. Perhaps tis better I return to Kingston and face the authorities—alone."

"No...Gabrielle, they intend to use you to draw me out. I am sure of it," he remarked in a low voice. "I shall not allow them to do so or to harm you because of me."

"And if my being here puts Felicity at risk?"

"If I thought it so, I would not have brought you here," he said wiping his hands on a cloth. "I do not wish to discuss this any further. You are welcome here and I have promised you are safe. If you wish to leave, I will find someone to take you where you wish to go."

He stood, stared at her a moment as if he wanted to say something more then turned and stalked from the room. Alone, Gabrielle sat staring at the chair where he had once sat and realized she had angered him by continuing to question what he believed was the best for her as well as Felicity. Her being here was a huge mistake and it was obvious now he no longer wished her with him. Perhaps she should find someone to take her elsewhere...New Orleans, maybe.

Chapter Eight

Tomás stayed busy the rest of the day along with his crew unloading supplies from the ship as well as visiting with his friends throughout the small village. He always made sure they all had what they needed and were well. He felt responsible for every person living in their little space on the island. There were others on the island living in small communities but each group kept to themselves and only if in need, did they ever ask for anything.

As he wandered slowly back toward home, he thought about what Gabrielle had said regarding her friend, Cuddy coming to find her. Not that he wished the man to do so, but he half-hoped he would so he might know for sure if he was the man who had lashed him almost to death. If it was him, he knew he would kill him no matter what he meant to Gabrielle.

The bastard Englishman with the scar down the side of his face had nearly killed him and left his back scarred. He had sought the man ever since the day he awoke on the shore of a small island where the crew of the British ship had abandoned him and Liam. They knew they had killed good men and stolen the goods meant for their captain's family celebration. Liam had always said they needed to count their blessings the Brits had not killed them and fed their remains to the sharks but Tomás was unable to let it go. He figured they had only allowed them to live because Liam was Scottish and as for Tomás, they probably assumed since he did not speak English well, he could not identify them.

This was probably true of his memory of the rest of the men aboard that ship, but he would never forget the face of the man who had whipped him until he passed out. That face had haunted his dreams since that time and continued to do so. Liam had suggested many times the man might not even be alive anymore but until Tomás knew it for sure, he would never stop searching for him.

His gaze shifted to where Liam sat on a wooden crate while Maria trimmed his wild red hair and beard. He smiled watching the girl for he suspected she was quite smitten with the gruff Scot, but his foolish friend was oblivious to it. What the pretty young woman saw in him he could not comprehend, but love had reasons of its own.

Liam was a man with a big heart and kind demeanor and perhaps that was what drew her to him. He wished his old friend would open his eyes to the girl's attraction for he could do far worse than to take her as a wife. At not even twenty years old, Maria could give him the children he knew his friend wanted and she would be strong for many years when Liam became old and needed care. He laughed when Maria tugged on his hair to make him sit still and Liam squawked like a chastised child. Yes, she would make the grumpy Scot a good wife.

As for his own future, his thoughts returned to Gabrielle as he approached the front door of his home. He had not liked what she had implied about his wanting her here for nefarious reasons but he hoped she would come around and find a home with them. He looked at his home. It was not grand but comfortable. He hoped she liked it. It was a good house, large enough for a family and well-furnished but he believed it far more comfortable than even his father's home had been.

He had accumulated a large cache of wealth over the years and even with the large amount he had spent to build the homes for his crew and their families, he had plenty more for the future. Part of it, of course, was Felicity's inheritance and he would make sure she had it when she came of age. It was her father's share of the bounties they had taken over the years and it belonged to his daughter. Tomás kept a clear accounting of his adopted daughter's inheritance. Of course, if he never fathered any children of his own, she would inherit the entirety of his wealth minus enough to keep Mikaela comfortable into her old age.

There was a time when he had considered taking Mikaela as a wife, but he knew he could never love her the way she deserved. Not long after she came to live with him and Felicity, she had offered her body to him and having gone far too long without a woman, he had accepted her. Unfortunately, in the aftermath, she believed she was then the woman of the house and tried to move into his bedchamber. He had no other choice but to rebuff her. Now he pondered

Felicity's comment that Mikaela did not like Gabrielle.

It was possible she was jealous of Gabrielle and probably the reason her mood changed after he asked her to ready a bedchamber for their guest. She knew if Gabrielle had a bed of her own, she would not be sharing his. However, what she did not know was he intended to eventually change that arrangement. He hoped to make Gabrielle his wife someday if she would have him. He wished only to make her happy and build a life with her. If only she would put her trust in him.

Opening the door, he stepped into the foyer and reveled in how much cooler it felt on his skin. He had the homes built in the traditional Spanish manner because the clay walls kept the heat out and with windows situated throughout the rooms, the tropical breezes allowed for a delight movement of air which helped cool the house.

Mikaela stepped into view at the back of the house, so he walked down the hallway splitting the home into two halves. Where she stood there was another hallway perpendicular to the main one which led to bedrooms on each side of the home. Mikaela and Felicity had rooms off the hallway to the left and his grand room, as well as two other smaller ones, was located to the right. At the center of the very back of the house was the large kitchen with a huge clay fireplace equipped with cast iron pots, grills, and skillets of every size and configuration Mikaela would ever need to cook them delicious meals.

He had worried it was too much for Mikaela to handle on her own, so he had arranged for a young girl named Stella to come most days to assist her with chores and meal preparations. Stella was only twelve but was learning quickly how to cook meals and keep the house in good order. In return for her working for Mikaela, he paid her a salary but insisted she continued her lessons at the small school he had built when one of the men brought home a new wife who was a governess at one time.

Thinking of the school gave him an idea. Perhaps Gabrielle would enjoy helping teach the children and Felicity. It would probably benefit Felicity greatly to begin her education in manners and society now rather than later. He hoped to someday take her somewhere with more society to find a husband. With her disfigurements, he knew it might be difficult but if she was fine in her manners and came with a large dowry, finding a husband for her might not be impossible.

"Something smells delicious, Mikaela," he said with a smile.

"Thank you. The garden yielded some nice vegetables and avocadoes today so I thought I would do a gumbo with shrimp and a fruit salad. It might be one of my best," she said with pride.

"Good. I am hungry," he said glancing about the kitchen behind her. "Where is Felicity...and our guest?"

He looked toward the large porch outside the wall of windows which helped keep the kitchen from becoming too warm.

"Felicity is in Miss Gabrielle's room. She took a short nap but then woke and sought out our new guest. I believe she wants to go to the waterfall," Mikaela said with a frown. "I tell her she has to wait for you. You know I do not go there."

"I know...bad juju...a trip to the waterfall sounds good. I can take a swim and refresh myself rather than making you heat water for a bath."

"Thank you for that. I already did it once—for Miss Gabrielle," she remarked, and he did not miss the sneer which lifted her lip slightly.

"Good, she had a bath. I had promised her one when we reached home. She hasn't a change of clothes—"

"Already seen to that too," Mikaela said with a huff. "I give her a skirt and blouse to wear for now. All too long on her short body but I sent Stella to borrow some things from the other women—the short ones."

Tomás turned away to keep her from seeing him laugh. There was no doubt in his mind Mikaela was green with jealousy.

"Thank you, Mikaela, I knew I could count on you to make her welcome." He hoped the sarcasm he was feeling did not show too much in his tone. "I shall retrieve my wayward daughter so we might visit the waterfall before your delicious gumbo is ready to eat."

Mikaela nodded and retreated into the kitchen. Suddenly, it dawned on him he had no idea which room Mikaela had put Gabrielle in.

"Mikaela," he called out.

She turned to look at him.

"Which room?"

"The one at the far end across from yours," she answered. "It has a tub, remember?"

"Right...it does," he said with a nod.

Mikaela could have put Gabrielle on the opposite side of the house from him but her good heart knew the room she chose was best. It had a large comfortable bed and a tub so Gabrielle would have privacy—except when his nosy little Felicity decided to bother her.

Tomás walked down the hallway toward his room but when he reached his doorway, he continued to the end of the hall. He knocked on the closed door and waited. A moment passed before the door opened. Gabrielle smiled at him and stepped back to allow him entry. Felicity was sitting in a chair at the dressing table and smiled at him in the reflection of the mirror above it.

"Papa," she said turning to look at him. "Gabrielle is making me beautiful."

"I am sure she is but she is simply improving on the beauty I always see before me when you are around," he told Felicity making her giggle.

"I was just putting some ribbons in her hair. She has such lovely dark hair. I am quite jealous," Gabrielle told him then returned to stand behind Felicity and continued working on her hair.

"I was told you want to go to the waterfall, little one."

"Oh si, Papa, can we?" Felicity asked bouncing in her seat.

"Yes...we can visit for a short time before supper. Mikaela has made a gumbo which smells delicious so we do not wish to miss it," he said with a chuckle then laughed aloud when Felicity begged Gabrielle to finish faster.

"Can Gabrielle come too?"

"But of course, if she wishes," Tomás said with a smile at Gabrielle when she looked at him.

He had hoped she would accompany them. It was a beautiful waterfall and swimming hole.

"I would love to come. Hold still, little one, while I finish this last bit," she said with a scolding tone only to quickly chuckle and give Felicity a quick squeeze.

Once she was finished decorating Felicity's hair with ribbons woven into some of the hair while others became bows, he and Gabrielle were left to follow the excited little girl as she limped from the room at her fastest speed. Tomás noted Gabrielle was still wearing his blouse from the ship but belted with a brightly colored sash over a skirt of varying shades of blue. Her hair was damp but plaited and she had one of Mikaela's colorful headwraps draped around her neck.

"You look lovely, my dear, but are you sure you would not rather wear a cooler blouse," he asked.

"Mikaela offered me a beautiful pink blouse but it left my arms bare and I would rather leave them covered. Your blouse is fine...if you do not mind me borrowing it a bit longer until I can see about something else," she said with a pleading in her eyes he could not deny.

"But of course, you are welcome to anything I have," he replied with a smile.

173

"Your home is beautiful and my room is far grander than I need," she said.

"Tis yours for as long as you wish." He hoped she would choose to move across the hall into his one day.

As they passed through the kitchen, he smiled at Mikaela.

"We will return shortly...I believe Felicity has already told you we are going to her favorite swimming hole?"

"Do not be too long? Supper will be ready very soon," she said with a smile.

"It smells delicious, Mikaela," Gabrielle said peeking into the large pot simmering over the heat of the fire.

He noted how Mikaela's smile faded and she simply nodded in response to Gabrielle's friendly comment. He might have to speak to Mikaela about her attitude. He would not tolerate unrest in his home. It set a bad example for Felicity.

He directed Gabrielle to the large porch set on the back of the house. There was a table as well as chairs and on many warm evenings, they dined there rather than inside. There were also a couple of cane back chairs and a comfortable wicker settee on which he would very much like to sit with Gabrielle in the evenings.

"Your home is far more than I ever expected, Tomás. It is quite grand," she said when she stopped to take in the gardens of flowers and vegetables as well as the expanse of the porch, the stone tiles on the floor and the iron lanterns hanging from the wooden rafters.

"I am very pleased you like it. I had hoped you would," he said with pride.

"Papa...come on!"

Felicity was standing in the open space of the large grassy area between beds of flowers. She was waving her arms and bouncing about as well as she could with the limitations of her leg.

"Coming, Felicity...you must learn patience," Tomás called to her and laughed. "She is a handful but I would miss her so much if she was not here. I could not love her more if she was my own flesh."

~*~

Gabrielle saw the love in his eyes and knew he meant what he said about Felicity. There was goodness in this man which made it difficult to believe anyone could think him guilty of any crime worth hanging for, much less murder. She had not asked him about the charge against him and feared knowing the reason. What if he had killed someone? Could a man with such a big heart as to care so much for all these people and a crippled, half-blind little girl be cruel enough to commit murder?

When Tomás suddenly took hold of her hand, she did not flinch away and her lack of reaction surprised her. She allowed him to lead her along a path following Felicity who he had to keep telling to slow down. She enjoyed the warmth and security of his large hand. She had not enjoyed such comfort since the last time she and her father had walked together along the street in New Orleans. It was only the day before the fire took her family and her happy life from her eleven years ago. Had it truly been so long since a man had held her hand as they walked?

She glanced up at Tomás. He was talking, telling her about the beautiful flowers growing along the way. He was so enthusiastic about living and enjoying everything around them, she could not hold back a smile. Suddenly, he halted her, released her hand to her disappointment, and reached out to pluck a bloom from a nearby plant. It was a beautiful red flower which she had never seen before. He turned and looking down at her, tucked the bloom into the hair behind one ear. He gazed at her as if memorizing her face and when she moved to tuck her chin, he caught it with his fingers.

"You are so beautiful, Gabrielle, I believe the flowers are jealous," he said in a low smoky voice.

The way he was looking at her, the tone in his voice, and the touch of his fingertips on her chin made her start to believe what he saw in her was true. Could this handsome, charming, and alarmingly desirable man truly think her beautiful?

Everything around them from the sound of the birds, the breeze rustling in the trees and brush, even the sound of her heart in her ears seemed to go silent as she gazed into his wonderful dark eyes. When his head lowered toward hers, she inhaled in excited anticipation of his kiss. Just as his lips hovered over hers, the sound of Felicity's voice shattered the moment.

"The waterfall, Papa," she squealed drawing their attention.

She was standing several feet away and clapping her hands. Tomás looked to her then back to Gabrielle and she knew he was as disappointed as she was to have missed an opportunity to kiss. The thought pleased her.

"The waterfall, Tomás," she said smiling up at him.

He grinned and took hold of her hand once more and pulled her along to join Felicity. She laughed as she worked not to trip on her skirt. Being so much shorter than Mikaela, it was far too long and she had done her best to hike it up but the sash was not holding it very well. She pulled it up with her free hand and hoped she would not land on her face.

Suddenly, they were in a clearing and before them was a beauty she had never beheld before. She had never seen a waterfall before. It was not anything like the huge tall waterfalls she had heard tales of from her brother, but it was exciting and exhilarating all at the same time. The sound of the water rushing over the top where it seemed to emerge from nowhere amidst the thick foliage and vines was loud. There was a cooling mist flowing through the air from the water striking the large pool below. She looked around wondering where the water went after it flowed downhill. She saw where it settled and slowly meandered off into the jungle presumably back to the sea. Birds were chattering and twittering and occasionally flew from one side of the water hole to the other, sometimes passing close to the falls. If she had not already had a bath, she would be tempted to climb beneath it as well.

Tomás led her down some rocks which seemed to work well as steps. Felicity was already at the bottom kicking off her sandals and tugging at her dress.

"Does she swim?"

"Like a fish but even though she does, she knows never to come here unescorted," Tomás remarked. "I worry less about her drowning than encountering something or someone dangerous."

The thought of this being a dangerous place with all its beauty and serenity had not crossed her mind but she supposed there were still dangers. It was his use of the word *someone*, which sent a shiver down her spine.

"Oh my! Does she always strip naked to swim?" Gabrielle asked when she noticed Felicity was standing alongside the water without a stitch of clothing on her body.

"Tis the way of the islands and tis all she knows," he said with a laugh probably noting the flush she knew must be highlighting her cheeks when he began stripping off his clothes. "Besides, you get cleaner and have dry clothes to put back on when you are done."

Gabrielle looked away when he reached for the front of his britches. She heard him chuckle.

"Perhaps someday you will indulge along with me. I believe you would enjoy the freedom it brings to the soul," she heard him say then heard Felicity squeal with delight before a splash filled the air.

She took a seat on the bank. When she peeked toward the water, she saw Felicity paddling around but Tomás was nowhere to be seen. Suddenly, he emerged from the water directly in front of Felicity making the little girl squeal and laugh before wrapping her arms around his neck. His hair was loose and spread out around his shoulders like an ink spot in the water. He laughed and pressed a kiss to Felicity's cheek before lifting her from the water and tossing her a short distance. She dove elegantly as if she were a dolphin rather than a little girl. Tomás quickly swam to her and pulled her up out of the water again to make sure she was all right. He was such a caring and attentive man.

Even with the normal heat of the day, the sunshine felt wonderful on Gabrielle's skin. She knew she should have worn a hat but with the cooling spray of the falls, and the sunlight caressing her skin so delightfully, she closed her eyes and leaned her head back. She smiled listening to the laughter and giggles emanating from the direction of the water as father and daughter played. Occasionally, Felicity would emit a squeal but she was confident it was from delight rather than alarm.

Suddenly, she felt droplets of water hit her and opened her eyes. Felicity was standing nearby shaking her hair so water sprayed in all directions. *So much for having done the girl's hair.*

Gabrielle laughed and told the child to bring her clothes so she might assist her dressing. She glanced toward the water just as Tomás emerged. A gasp escaped her lips before she could stop it.

The man was naked and beautiful.

His skin was tawny and only slightly lighter where his britches normally covered. He was lean yet muscular with a flat belly and the muscles of his abdomen seemed to have been carved like a sculpture. His legs were long, his thighs muscular but elegant. His cock surrounded by hair as black as that on his head with a line leading upwards to his belly button drew her attention as if framed in ink. He was quite impressive even in a relaxed state. His long black hair clung to his back and shoulders. Her fingers itched to thread through those long silky strands and journey along the expanse of skin covering a broad chest and wide shoulders. His chest was smooth and void of hair. She was used to men who had some hair on their chests so she thought it interesting Tomás had none. However, she liked it. She had seen her brother and his friend, Michel, in the nude when they would swim in the small lake near their home, but never had she seen a man such as Tomás naked. A man so desirable he made her blood heat so it might burst from her pores in steam and who sent quivers through her insides as if a flutter of butterflies filled her belly.

Realizing she was staring, she directed her attention to Felicity and turned so she could no longer see Tomás as he reached for his clothes. The little girl's skin was damp so dressing her was no easy task, but soon she was ready.

"Time for supper," Tomás said from behind her.

Gabrielle was still feeling the flush of heat in her cheeks, although whether from the sun or her desire for him, she was not sure but had no want for him to see it. She did not turn to look at him but hoped he was fully dressed.

"Come on, Papa," Felicity exclaimed and grabbed his hand, pulling him forward.

His clothing properly in place, Gabrielle laughed at her own foolishness and followed along behind the girl and her loving father. When they reached the house, Felicity released her father's hand and hurried into the house. Was it her imagination or was her limp slightly less after her time in the water?

"I think swimming does her leg much good," she remarked as she caught up to where Tomás had halted to wait for her.

"I agree. I have also noticed her limp lessens a bit after a swim," he commented then pulled her close.

He smoothed her now dry hair back from her face. "Did you enjoy the view...of the waterfall?"

Gabrielle knew exactly to what view he had originally been referring and closed her eyes in embarrassment for she could not move her head as he had cupped her face with both hands. She placed her hands on his forearms and attempted to lower his hands, but instead she felt his lips brush hers. Her eyes flew open and he was smiling at her.

"I hope you approve," he said in a low whisper just above her mouth then captured her lips in a deep kiss.

She gave her approval in a soft moan. She approved of everything about this man even if he was a wanted criminal and had taken her from everything she knew. He was handsome both in face and body. He was kind and big-hearted. He was generous and thoughtful. Gabrielle approved of Tomás Alvarez, but did he approve of her?

~*~

Tomás had been wishing to kiss her all day. He had attempted to reach his goal a couple of times before but always an interruption came and he failed, but now she was in his arms. She had not thwarted his advances and had even relaxed her hold on his arms. When his tongue stroked along her lips, she gasped into his mouth and he took the opportunity to taste her completely. He suspected she had never been kissed so thoroughly by the way she tensed, but then she relaxed again and even gave up a small moan. That sound sent a rush of hot blood directly to his cock.

He chuckled against her mouth thinking of the way she had stared when he exited the water. With her eyes on him, hot with desire, it was all he could do to keep his precocious cock from standing at full salute. He had been relieved when she finally looked away for it was already twitching to get more of her attention. Only now it was fully awake and pressing against her belly. If she noticed, she gave no sign. *If she noticed? She must notice.*

"Papa! Gabrielle!"

Felicity's shouts tore them apart and they stood staring at each other, their breaths coming in shuddering pants. He wished he could sweep her up into his arms, carry her back to the waterfall, and make love to her on the soft mossy embankment.

"Papa! Supper is ready," Felicity exclaimed as she hurried toward them. "Did you hear me call?"

"Yes, Felicity, we did hear you call. Your father was...he was telling me about the beautiful flowers," Gabrielle quickly explained then glanced at him.

He laughed and nodded. She must have been aware of his erection and that the blood was no longer in his head but had gone further south to rule his body for she was quick to give his daughter an explanation. Tomás turned slightly so Felicity might not see the obvious bulge in his britches.

~*~

"I am going to gather some for the table. Felicity, please escort our guest to the table and I shall join you all in a moment."

Gabrielle understood his predicament, turned to Felicity and motioned for her to lead the way.

"Come, Gabrielle, we are having supper...outside...on the porch," Felicity explained as they walked along holding hands. "I like it. Tis almost a picnic. Have you ever done a picnic?"

"I did enjoy picnics, when I was a little girl. We would spread out a blanket and my brother and I would stretch out after eating and watch the clouds," Gabrielle told her. "Have you ever looked for animals in the clouds, Felicity?"

"No...it sounds like fun. May we do that after supper?"

"It might be too late but perhaps tomorrow," she answered just as they reached the porch.

183

Mikaela appeared at the doorway carrying a large bowl in a towel to protect her hands from the heat. She nodded her acknowledgment and set the bowl down.

"May I be of assistance, Mikaela?" she asked.

"No, thank you. You and Miss Felicity take your seats," she said then glanced around. "Where is Tomás?"

Gabrielle hid a smile for she certainly wasn't going to tell this woman he was hiding in the brush until his erection died down so she continued the tale she told Felicity. "He wanted to gather some flowers for the table."

"But we already have some," Mikaela said pointing to the vase containing large beautiful blooms.

Gabrielle shrugged. "I guess he wanted more."

The woman stared at her as if she had suddenly sprouted another head then mumbled something in what sounded very much like the Creole Mama La Rue used to swear in whenever she was upset with them. Mikaela shook her head and disappeared back into the kitchen.

Gabrielle looked to Felicity who was rearranging her plate and utensils in front of her then rearranging them again. She smiled thinking how wonderful it must be to be so innocent. She had been so until the fire catapulted her into the realm of reality. She thought about how if it had been any other man pressing his hard cock against her as Tomás had, she would have been horrified. But feeling his eager body against hers, she only wanted more.

"Papa!"

Gabrielle turned to look out over the lawn to see Tomás walking toward them. She smiled at the sight of him. He was carrying a beautiful bouquet. He was a man of his word even when it started as a white lie to save face.

Chapter Nine

Supper was a delight, although somewhat dominated by the musings and constant chatter of a five-year-old and Tomás was sure Gabrielle had enjoyed it. Once the meal was over Mikaela stood and began clearing away plates. Gabrielle stood and without a word began helping. He suspected her actions surprised Mikaela as well for when she returned and passed Gabrielle carrying plates and bowls, she stopped to watch her enter the kitchen then shrugged and returned to her work. Once the table was cleared, Mikaela returned with a tray holding a bottle of Spanish port which she knew he favored after a meal. In addition to the bottle, there were two glasses instead of the usual one. After setting it on the table, she returned to the kitchen and a few minutes later, Gabrielle appeared at the door and he could hear Mikaela telling her to *shoo*.

Tomás laughed aloud at the bewildered expression Gabrielle wore. She straightened her scarf and blouse then returned to the table.

"I offered to assist her with cleaning up the kitchen but she threatened me with a knife if I did not leave *her kitchen*, as she stated it," she exclaimed as she took her seat. "In my employ, I was responsible for kitchen duties as they pertained to the girls. I always ate my meals with them and it was only recently Siobhan had begun allowing them to dine with the adults, but only on very special occasions. By the way, Tomás, as adorable as Felicity is—" She looked to where Felicity was twirling on the lawn like a dancer with her arms held out to her sides and her head tilted back then lowered her voice. "Children normally do not attend their meals with adults."

He leaned in and lowered his voice as she had. "In my family, they do."

Gabrielle gasped as if he had chastised her for the suggestion but when he covered her hand with his, she nodded. "My mistake."

"If we were in a proper society, I would agree with you. But tis a family meal and all of my family is who I wish to have in attendance," he said relaxing back in his chair and reaching for the bottle of wine. "Port?"

"Excuse me?"

"Would you join me in a little port?"

"Yes, please, but only a tiny portion. I am very tired and I fear even a few drops might make me quite inebriated," she remarked. "I-I did not wish to imply there was anything wrong with Felicity—"

"No apology needed. We are merely family," his said interrupting her then laughed as he poured a small amount of wine into a glass. "And I am quite sure you will not become drunk off this small amount." He handed her the glass.

Mikaela reappeared at the doorway and called to Felicity to come inside and prepare for bed.

"I smell a storm coming, Tomás," she said before retreating inside again.

"She can smell a storm coming?"

He laughed as he stood and looked to the sky.

"I do not question Mikaela's talents. She has never been wrong," he remarked. "Felicity, you heard Mikaela...time for bed."

Felicity hurried back to the porch and he reached for as she started up the steps. Pulling her up into his arms, he reveled in her wrapping her slim arms around his neck and nuzzling against his neck. He loved this little girl so much. She pulled back and cupped his face in a manner, which always endeared her even further into his heart.

"Gabrielle is not going away, is she?"

He looked to Gabrielle whose eyes had widened at the question.

"I shall be here for a while, Felicity. Do you mind?" she asked.

Felicity grinned and pushed to get down. She nearly leaped into Gabrielle's lap to hug her tight.

"I hope you shall stay forever," Felicity exclaimed and kissed Gabrielle then turned back to him and put out her arms to once more be lifted into his.

He obliged her and kissed her on each cheek, and then on her puckered mouth.

"I must check on things before the rain comes. I shall look in on you when I return, but you must go to sleep first. Mikaela and Gabrielle are both here to keep you safe." He noted her frown and knew how storms scared her so he tweaked her nose. "All right?"

She tucked her arms in close between them, an action which told him she was not feeling confident about his being away from her during a storm but she nodded. He kissed again and set her down.

"Felicity," Mikaela called to her from inside the kitchen.

"Coming!" Felicity blew a kiss to Gabrielle and then to him before slowly walking into the house.

He watched her go and although always amazed at how she had adapted to seeing only from one eye and fighting the limp which plagued her, he worried for her future. Turning to Gabrielle, he decided now was a good time to present her with his idea.

"You taught your charges how to be proper ladies in society, is this true?" he asked taking his seat.

"I gave the girls lessons and taught them proper etiquette if this is what you mean?" she answered. "'Tis up to every young lady to implement what she is taught to match her personality and trust me, not every young lady always does exactly what she should when in society."

"How would you feel about teaching Felicity proper etiquette? I certainly have no idea the right and wrongs of how she need act and I fear Mikaela has not those skills either," Tomás admitted.

Gabrielle's face brightened at the suggestion which he had hoped it would.

"I would love to do so. She is a bright and energetic child but she is rather wild. Also, good manners and a calmer demeanor might assist her in the future, especially since I know what kind of...well, what kind of cruelties she might be facing," Gabrielle said, a frown pulling her brows together. "She is not going to have an easy life, Tomás. Her disabilities will be a hindrance to her having a fine life or possibly even finding a husband."

"I know. I worry always about her. I know I may not always be here to fight her battles and protect her. I have even considered staying here on this quiet island might not be the best thing for her either," he said running his finger around the lip of his glass. "However, hearing your story about how people have treated you does not give me much encouragement to leave here."

"I am sorry. She is such a lovely sweet child and life has been cruel to her at far too young an age. Although, having only known this condition might be a benefit to her whereas I was fourteen and had so many compliments about my looks that when this happened to me, I was devastated." Gabrielle traced her hand over the fabric covering her arm.

A low grumble of thunder came across the air and they both looked to the sky.

"I need to check on things around the village before the storm comes," Tomás said pushing out of his chair.

He drained his glass and placed it on the tray. He started to pick it up but she stopped him, her warm hand on his.

"I shall take care of this," she said her gaze capturing his.

"Thank you," he said, taking her hand in his and tugging her up from her chair.

Pulling her into his arms, he brushed the hair away from her face and took in her beauty. Scars be damned, the woman was beautiful and had the face of an angel.

"Thank you, for a wonderful evening. The waterfall, the lovely meal, the—"

He stopped her words with his mouth. She relaxed into him, accepting his kiss and this time, her lips parted without his urging. She tasted of port and a sweetness which was hers alone. He wished he did not need to leave as he would have liked to sit with her on the settee while the sun set and the stars filled the sky. But then, they probably would not see the sunset or the stars this night because the wind was already picking up and the light was dimming as storm clouds approached the small island. Not wishing to think of the danger, he allowed his thoughts to go only to the soft woman leaning into him.

She broke the kiss with a gasp and stared up at him with wide eyes which had gone enticingly dark blue. Suddenly, she tucked her chin pulling her gaze from his.

"Do not hide your desire from me, my sweet," he said lifting her face. "It carries a beauty which far exceeds anything else on earth."

She smiled at him and he noted the flush on her cheeks grew deeper.

"I am attracted to you, Tomás," she said in a low whisper as if fearing he would hear it. "My

191

behavior is certainly far from proper. Perhaps I am not as qualified to teach Felicity as you think."

Tomás laughed then hugged her to him.

"Gabrielle, you are far more qualified than anyone. Knowing you desire me has made my heart soar and if Felicity learns nothing more from you than to be open and honest with what life brings, she shall have all she needs," he said then kissed her again.

Releasing her was the hardest thing Tomás had ever had to do but there was plenty of time and she was here. He would see to the safety of the village and supplies and return as soon as possible. Perhaps they might discuss this attraction she had for him at length later.

"Mikaela knows how to prepare the house," Tomás said still holding her. "I shall return soon."

~*~

Gabrielle knew she needed to step away but could not bring herself to move. Staring into his dark eyes which seemed to deepen in color and depth, she felt as though she was falling. The world faded away around them and for a moment, she thought the storm was moving away rather coming closer. All she could hear was their breathing and her blood rushing in her ears. Her breath caught as Tomás brought his mouth closer even as he whispered words in Spanish she did not understand. She only hoped they were words of love because she most certainly was feeling the sentiment.

Suddenly, a crackle of lightning lit the sky and thunderous boom made them both flinch and she gave a small squeal.

"Dios mío, that was right on top of us," Tomás exclaimed in a breathless growl. "I must go now, Gabrielle. You go inside and stay there. Perhaps help with the shutters and tell Felicity, I shall return as soon as I am able. The storms, they frighten her."

"I understand. Go and hurry back. Please be careful," she said with her heart pounding but whether from the clap of thunder or fear over his being out in the storm, she was not sure. "Mikaela and I shall watch over Felicity. Go."

Tomás hesitated then gave her a quick kiss and hurried along the porch as it curved around the house then disappeared. She looked to the sky. It had grown dark and angry as if in a moment. The sun was shining and the air, blissfully calm, just a short while ago but now the sky was filled with dark clouds and the wind was whipping her hair about her face and threatened to pull her scarf from her neck.

She grabbed the tray, nearly losing a glass onto the table but quickly set it right. She caught hold of the lovely cloth napkins they had used at supper before they could blow off the table. She wondered if she could handle the lace-trimmed table cloth as well but before she could try, Mikaela was there.

Mikaela pulled the cloth from the table, doused the lanterns then guided her toward the door so she would not drop the tray. Once inside, Mikaela closed wooden shutters then closed the glass-paned doors and locked them to hold back the wind. When she turned, she laughed.

"Do you plan to hold that all night?" she asked pointing to the tray containing the bottle of port and glasses.

"No-no, I-I just was watching you do the shutters. I thought I might help with the others." Gabrielle quickly set the tray down, catching one of the glasses as it attempted to fall once more.

"Thank you, your help will make it happen faster. Yes, please, come," Mikaela said motioning her toward the front rooms. "You will have to open the window to grab the shutters then pull them closed and lock them. Then close the window."

"I can do that," Gabrielle said hurrying to the one in the dining room while Mikaela went to the one in the sitting room.

She pulled open the windows as they opened into the room and a rush of wind and a bit of rain hit her. She leaned out and unlatched the shutters on each side. The wind was blowing so hard she had trouble getting one of the shutters away from the wall of the house. When she finally did, she pulled them closed, locked them together then quickly shut the inside paned windows. Stepping back, she panted from the exertion. She turned toward the foyer to find Mikaela standing there.

"Not as easy as you thought, yes?"

Gabrielle laughed. "No, tis not," she answered as she shook the dampness from her.

It was then she noticed her scarf was no longer around her neck. She glanced around her to find it had blown under the table. Before she could retrieve it, Mikaela picked it up.

"You wear this to cover scars, no?"

Gabrielle took the scarf from the woman and began to replace it around her neck when Mikaela stopped her. She grabbed Gabrielle's hand and pulled it away so she could look at her scars. Gabrielle snatched her hand away and started to turn, but Mikaela stopped her again.

"Please, I do not like people to see my scars," Gabrielle said fighting back tears.

"You are so pretty. Shame you hide behind scarves and long sleeves," Mikaela remarked. "I can help you. I can make you a salve to soften and lessen your scars. It might not make them go away but will make them feel better. They are tight and pain you, no?"

Gabrielle turned to look at Mikaela. She nodded.

"Yes, sometimes so much it feels like they are burning again," she told her. "You can truly help?"

"Yes, this salve...it will help."

Heavy raindrops began pelting the house.

"Oh, we must get the other windows. I already did the one in Felicity's room," Mikaela exclaimed as she hurried from the room.

Gabrielle hurried after her moving toward her room while Mikaela disappeared into the room where Tomás slept. There were a couple more windows to secure but soon all were done. She and Mikaela stood in the kitchen, each a bit breathless from their efforts and a bit damp. When she used her scarf to dab at the dampness on her face, Mikaela lifted her eyebrows at her action.

"Well, it comes in handy for more things than hiding my scars," she said laughing and holding her scarf up.

"Come, let me see your neck in a better light," Mikaela said drawing a lantern down closer from the ceiling.

"The ones on my neck are ugly but not as bad as the ones on my arm and side," Gabrielle told her as the woman tilted her head so she might examine her neck better.

"You have more?"

Gabrielle slowly lifted the sleeve on her right arm exposing the flesh she never allowed anyone to see.

"Oh my, those are bad ones," Mikaela said blowing out a breath. "And you say you have more on your body?"

"Yes." Gabrielle slid her hand down her side from her ribs to about the middle of her thigh. "My clothing caught on fire making it worse."

"Yes, you are most fortunate it did not reach your beautiful hair or face."

"I suppose. Not that it matters to those who see them because most are frightened I am contagious or something," Gabrielle said on a groan. "You do not though. You and Tomás do not shy away. I suppose others here probably would not either."

"Yes, we are all flawed in some way. I carry scars on my back just as Tomás does," Mikaela said moving to peek through the shutters on the windows in the kitchen. "I hope he is in someone's home until the worst of this is over."

"I hope so too," Gabrielle said noting how the woman had changed the subject. "You have scars? You are so beautiful, your skin so smooth."

Mikaela turned to face her.

"I was born a slave. My master was a cruel man. I was not much older than Felicity when he decided he did not like my *attitude*," she said, her mouth turning down as she recalled the incident. "He took a whip to my back."

Gabrielle gasped and her stomach roiled.

"You were only a child."

"Mattered not to him," she said. "I was his to do with as he pleased."

Gabrielle shook her head feeling sick. This was why her father had despised slavery and refused to own them.

"Soon after, he fell ill and my mother used the opportunity to take us away. We come to Jamaica then," Mikaela said dipping the glasses she and Tomás had drunk the port from in a pot of water then into a bowl then using a cloth, she dried it to sparkling clean. "Of course, I always suspected my mother had something to do with his sickness."

Gabrielle looked at her in surprise and when Mikaela winked at her, she laughed.

"You do not think your mother poisoned him?"

"Oh, most certainly or at least cast a spell on him," Mikaela said with a smile of pure glee. "Many fear my mother and call her *witch* but she just knows her way around herbs, and can cure anyone of most anything. Of course, if you wrong her, she might turn it around on you just as fast."

"Oh, my! Well, whatever she did to him, he deserved it," Gabrielle said picking up the polished glasses and placing them in the lovely cabinet where she noticed others were stored.

A scream made her nearly drop one of the glasses so she quickly set it on the shelf and closed the cabinet silently promising to never touch them again during a storm. Meanwhile, Mikaela had dropped her cloth and left the room. Gabrielle followed and stood at Felicity's door as she watched as the woman cradled and rocked the child. She began humming a tune and was soon quietly singing words in *patois*. The song sounded familiar, something very reminiscent of what Mama La Rue used to sing to her when she was frightened by storms.

She stood there watching and thinking how similar everyone was and how affection was the best cure. After a short while, she quietly stepped away and went to her room. It was best to allow Mikaela to comfort the child for she had been there doing so for many years and surely Gabrielle would just be in the way.

A yawn grabbed her as she took a seat on the comfortable bed she was to sleep in and she realized just how tired she was. She kicked off her shoes and lay back on the bed. Lying there, she listened to the storm as the wind whipped the rain against the house. The lightning seemed to come less frequent and it took longer for the thunderclaps to follow so she thought the storm might be moving away from the island. She hoped so anyway since Tomás was still out in it.

Her thoughts returned to what he said about wanting her to desire him. It was true she was attracted to him. It was true she enjoyed his kiss and it was true she had felt something exhilarating when she saw him naked today but it was all so unexpected, so sudden. Or was it?

It had been weeks since she first met him that day in the marketplace and she had learned much about him since then, including that he was a man with a big heart. Of course, he was also a wanted criminal. Obviously, there was a side to him she had not become acquainted with yet, and she was not sure she wished to.

She was a grown woman, and even as inexperienced as she was in matters of sex, so if she chose to be with him out of pure lust who was there to chastise her? She was alone in this world and Tomás was offering her a place where she might feel welcome and be part of this small community. Did she have feelings for him? Part of her thought she did, but another part felt like that frightened fourteen-year-old girl thrust into the world without anyone to care for her or about her.

Surrendering to Tomás was a frightening proposition. What if when he saw her scars he rejected her? She would never survive seeing a look of horror and rejection on his handsome face. No, she needed to keep her distance for now. She needed to be sure he did not wish to simply bed her and then be done with her. She needed to know he would not reject her once he knew the extent of her scarring. She needed to know the man she was coming to know was the man he truly was.

She yawned and curled onto her side to watch the shadows cast upon the wall by the lightning flashes. Exhaustion was defeating her. Perhaps the salve Mikaela mentioned might help. Mikaela seemed to think it would. She decided she would ask her about it in the morning.

Gabrielle woke with a start. She must have fallen asleep but for how long, she wondered as she looked around the room. The rain had stopped and the wind was no longer whipping the foliage outside her window around making dancing shadows on the wall.

She rolled to her back and grimaced when the skin on her side pulled tight.

She told herself she needed to undress but she was so tired, she simply rolled over again and pulled one of the blankets up over her. Suddenly, the door creaked open. She closed her eyes because if it was Tomás, she did not wish to speak with him right now. She was still so unsure of her feelings and her attraction for him.

"Gabrielle?" She heard him whisper.

It was him and he was in her room. Thankful now she was still wearing her clothing, she felt a bit more secure but feigned sleep rather than allow him to know she was awake.

He whispered something in Spanish then his lips caressed her forehead.

She had no idea what he said but anything from his lips seemed to sound like an endearment so when he spoke in his native tongue, she nearly swooned. She almost opened her eyes so he would know she was awake, but then she heard the door click shut. It was for the best that he went away to his room. She was not ready to be anything more to him than a companion right now. She was not even sure she could be more. Her confidence was never very high before the fire and since then, she had none at all.

Sighing, Gabrielle rolled to her back and stared at the ceiling in the dark room. She wondered what time it was but feared if she got up to find out, she might meet Tomás along the way. Her eyelids slowly betrayed her, keeping her from even trying for they were still heavy with sleep and soon she could no longer keep them open.

~*~

After checking on Gabrielle and finding her sleeping soundly, Tomás walked to the kitchen. Mikaela had been awake when he returned to the house and she was heating some water for him so he might clean up some before trying to sleep.

The storm had been a fierce one and a few of the homes had taken damage. He was not eager for the sunrise to come for he feared what further damage he might discover. He was not even able to ensure his own home went unscathed although Mikaela said nothing unusual had happened. She had spent most of the night with Felicity so, in case she woke again, she would not be alone. She told him

Felicity had awakened not long after the storm began as she had expected.

With the amount of damage he had already seen, he knew he would have to scout some of the other islands for wood supplies to make repairs or return to Kingston to purchase what he needed. He feared he might have to do so anyway but he would face that decision if and when it arrived. He said nothing to Mikaela about it now. He would address it in the morning when he had both women in the same room. He knew there was a chance if he told Gabrielle he was returning to Jamaica she might wish to go as well. He hoped not. He wanted her to stay here—with him.

Once the water was heated, he carried a bucket to his room. There he stripped out of his wet, dirty clothes and after wetting a cloth, he worked some soap into it then scrubbed the mud, sweat, and rain from his body. Exhausted from the day and then the storm, he yanked back the covers on his bed and fell onto it. Pulling the covers over his lower body, he lay back and closed his eyes allowing his skin to air dry which cooled him until he began to feel chilled. Tomás pulled his covers higher and turned on his side. It was time to sleep. Tomorrow would be there when he woke.

Chapter Ten

Morning broke with a brilliant sunrise, fresh clean air, the sounds of the jungle alive and active, and the voices of people out and about proving the storm had not discouraged the living.

Gabrielle dressed but when she looked in the mirror, she knew she could not continue to wear the same clothing each day. She would ask Mikaela about finding other clothes. She only wished she had more than the few dollars which she had tucked into an inside pocket of her skirt. Yes, Tomás was wealthy enough to purchase her what she needed but she had not depended on anyone for her keep since waking orphaned in the hospital.

She brushed out her hair with the lovely brush Tomás had gifted her while aboard La Bella Dama. He had made sure it was brought to the house along with his things. It was something needed and gratefully accepted but if possible, perhaps Mikaela had some extra fabric she could have to make a dress or two. The humid air made her hair curl more than usual so she decided to leave it loose other than a few pins to draw it back from her face. With her hair loose and pooling around her neck, she might be able to forego her usual scarf. The air seemed warmer here than on the island of Jamaica so the scarf was quite uncomfortable.

Thinking she did not look too forlorn, she opened the door to see what the day would bring. Mikaela was in the kitchen softly singing a tune when she reached the center of the house.

"Good mornin', Miss Gabrielle," she said over her shoulder without actually looking at her.

She was busy frying up something in a skillet which smelled heavenly.

"Good morning, Mikaela and please, just call me Gabrielle," she said stepping forward. "I do hope we can be friends."

Mikaela seemed to freeze her action, turned to look at her then nodded.

"Perhaps," she said then returned to her work.

Gabrielle frowned not quite knowing what to say to such a cryptic response. She could only presume the woman truly did not like her.

"May I be of assistance?" she asked changing the subject.

Mikaela shook her head.

"Got everything going fine," she said. "Oh, I did make you up a batch of salve though—" She reached to the table and picked up a small clay pot then handed it to Gabrielle. "You smooth some of that on your scars every morning and every night and your skin will soon feel so much better and look better too."

Gabrielle accepted the jar, pulled out the cork stopper and held it to her nose. It smelled wonderful and so she wondered what was in it. She smelled coconut.

"What is it made from?"

"Only good stuff," Mikaela said as she began ladling batter into another skillet to make what Gabrielle could only presume would be hotcakes. "Oil from the coconut, juice from the aloe plants—all available right here in the brush—a little rosemary for good scent and soothing feel, some juice of the oranges too bitter to eat but they do well for bleaching out whites so help lighten the skin too, and some other herbs to soothe the skin and help smooth it out. It all feels good on the skin."

She looked at Gabrielle.

"All good stuff, cher, it will help."

"It does smell heavenly," Gabrielle said then dipped her finger in and slid some of the oily, somewhat grayish cream across her hand.

It felt cool yet tingled a bit. It did feel good. She pushed her sleeve up a bit and exposed some of the scars on her arm. Sliding some of the concoction over it, her skin seemed to drink it in. It did feel so very nice.

"What say you go back to your room and put some of that on," Mikaela said as she turned the cakes. "You got time before all this be done. Might as well start healing that skin..."

She glanced up at the suggestion and Mikaela looked at her.

"No sense wastin' time," she said with a lifted brow.

Gabrielle smiled at her. Perhaps Mikaela did not dislike her so much as preferred she was not here.

"No time like the present, right? Thank you, Mikaela, thank you very much," she said and hurried back to her room to apply the salve.

When she returned to the kitchen a while later, her skin honestly felt better, less tight and a bit energized. She hoped it would help because there were times when she wanted to rip the rough thick skin from her body. The kitchen was empty but when she looked to the porch, she saw Mikaela and Felicity sitting at the table. She joined them there.

"Good morning, little one, how are you today?" she asked Felicity.

Since the little girl had a mouthful of food, Gabrielle waited as Felicity chewed then swallowed rather dramatically.

"Hungry," Felicity stated with a grin making both women chuckle.

"I can see that," Gabrielle said with a glance at Mikaela who was spooning up food onto a plate.

After she added some fried ham and plantains, Mikaela handed her the plate.

"Oh my, this looks and smells delicious. Thank you, Mikaela," she said accepting the plate and taking a seat at the table. There was mango juice in a tall pitcher so she filled a glass. "Thank you also for the salve. My skin already feels more comfortable," she remarked while slicing into the delicious smelling food.

"You are most welcome."

"I was wondering if you or some of the other women might have some extra fabric I could have to make another dress or two. I have a few dollars so I could pay for it," Gabrielle said around bites of sweet mango slices.

"No. No. No. I have many skirts and blouses. We can fix them so they fit you perfectly," Mikaela said with a wave of her hand. "We can add sleeves to the blouses if you wish. No problem."

"Thank you. Perhaps just one or two maybe, I do not wish to take advantage," Gabrielle said.

"No problem. We take care of each other. Is this not so, Felicity?"

"Uh huh," Felicity grunted as she stuffed more hotcakes into her little mouth.

"Slow down, honey, or you shall choke," Gabrielle told her. "A lady chews small amounts at a time."

The little girl's brows lifted and her eyes went wide. She chewed what was in her mouth then took a long drink of juice before she swallowed.

"Then a lady wipes her mouth gently with her napkin which she usually has on her lap," Gabrielle instructed, handing the child the napkin still folded alongside her plate.

Felicity took the napkin and wiped her mouth then she watched as Gabrielle demonstrated how to spread the napkin and drape it across her lap. Felicity did exactly as Gabrielle then looked up at her. Mikaela and Gabrielle gave applause for her job well done.

"Is Tomás not joining us for this delicious breakfast?" Gabrielle asked.

"No, he ate earlier and went to help with some repairs around the village. This house faired very well except for a palm down in the back." Mikaela pointed across the lawn and when Gabrielle looked, she saw a small palm tree lying on the ground. "He said he would cut it up later. Many others were not so lucky. The house, our dear friend Maria lives in with her little boy had a tree hit on the roof."

"Oh my heavens, are they all right?"

"Yes, no one was hurt but it makes a mess and if another storm comes before the men can fix the roof, they might have to move in somewhere else," she remarked as she placed a few more mango slices on Felicity's plate. "I told Tomás we have plenty of room if they need it."

She had no doubt Tomás would have already thought of that but had allowed Mikaela the pleasure of suggesting it.

"Of course, and I am sure Felicity would enjoy the company. Is that not so, little one?" Gabrielle asked her.

Felicity nodded as she stuffed a slice of mango into her mouth then licked some juice from her hand where it had dripped down her fingers. Gabrielle chuckled knowing it was going to take more than one lesson to teach this little girl the proper use of a napkin.

"They are welcome if they need to come here but we must wait to see what repairs are needed before we promise anything," Mikaela said in a stern tone.

Gabrielle supposed she had overstepped by suggesting to Felicity her friend might come to stay with them. "I apologize. I did not mean to presume they would."

Mikaela topped off Felicity's glass with more mango juice. She looked to Gabrielle and nodded. Gabrielle could only take that to mean she accepted her apology. She had thought they were becoming friends but obviously, she had touched a nerve and undone it all.

Later that afternoon, Gabrielle was sitting on the back porch watching Felicity pick flowers for the evening meal when Mikaela surprised her with a couple of lovely skirts, matching blouses, as well as several folds of lovely fabric.

"I think we can trim these to fit and if you would like this fabric for a dress, I can help you," Mikaela said setting them on her lap when she sat beside Gabrielle on the settee.

"They are lovely. Thank you, Mikaela, thank you very much," she replied.

"I am sorry I was harsh earlier, tis not my place," Mikaela said.

"No. No. You were correct. It was too much for me to assume anyone was coming to stay and not my place to say they are welcome. After all, I am only a guest here."

"All guests are welcome here," Mikaela said her gaze landing on Felicity.

"May I ask something...well, tis rather personal? If you prefer not to answer, I shall understand," Gabrielle inquired.

Mikaela looked at her and nodded.

"Are you—" Gabrielle suddenly was not sure she even wished to know the answer. She swallowed hard then took a deep breath, closed her eyes, and forced the question which had plagued her since she came to this house. "Are you in love with Tomás?"

Mikaela smiled, exhaled, and leaned back against the settee.

"I imagined myself in love with him—" She looked at Gabrielle. "Once upon a time but no, I am not in love with him. I care very much for him as well as Felicity. They are my family." Then before Gabrielle could say anything in response, Mikaela continued. "It would matter not for I have never seen him look at any woman the way he looks at you. He is in love with you, cher."

Gabrielle gasped and stared at the woman wide-eyed. Was it possible? Could Tomás be in love with her? She shook her head. It was not possible.

"No...no, I think he is simply being kind to me...tis all," she said, unable to believe such a man could love her. "You still do not wish me here though."

Mikaela laughed.

"I admit I wish you had not come but you are here, and he wants you here."

"So you do not like me?"

Mikaela looked at her then looked out to where Felicity seemed to be trying to decide if she had enough flowers.

"Tis not that...no, for I wish Tomás much happiness and if he finds it with you, I shall champion you to anyone."

"I do not understand," Gabrielle said trying to understand this mysterious woman.

"Felicity...she likes you very much," Mikaela said her tone soft and somewhat sad.

"Oh my, you are worried Felicity shall prefer me to you," she said with a chuckle. "Mikaela, she adores you. She loves you as the mother she lost."

"But she will not need me if she has you," Mikaela said, wiping a tear from her eye.

"But of course, she will. One thing I know about children...and I do not know a lot...they have huge hearts. Hearts so big they can love many people at the same time. She will always love you and need you," Gabrielle told her taking her hand in hers and squeezing it. "She might grow to love me someday but she has known only your gentle hand and touch since being a little one who just lost her mother. You are the one she cries out for when she is scared and I suspect she always will."

Mikaela looked at Felicity then back to Gabrielle. "Do you really think so?"

"Yes, and I believe her to be the luckiest of little girls for that very reason."

"Thank you. Tis true, I have been cold to you because I was jealous and I am sorry," Mikaela said with a smile. "I wish to be friends."

"Then friends we are." Gabrielle pulled the woman into her arms and the two embraced.

"Is someone leaving?" Felicity asked from next to them.

Neither had noticed the little girl climb the steps to the porch. She was standing beside them clutching a handful of lovely flowers.

"No one is leaving, petite, Gabrielle was thanking me for the pretty skirts I am giving her," Mikaela told her.

"Ooh, very pretty," Felicity exclaimed fingering the skirts with her free hand. "I picked these." She shoved the bouquet into Gabrielle's face.

"And they are very pretty," she told Felicity with a chuckle while pulling back so as not to be scratched by the stems.

Mikaela stood and took the flowers from the little girl.

"Help me put them in a vase and we shall set the table for supper," she suggested to Felicity who clapped her hands and hobbled off into the kitchen.

"Thank you for clearing the air between us, Mikaela," Gabrielle said and received a smile in return.

Feeling truly welcomed here, she gathered the clothing and fabric and took it back to her room. Upon returning to the kitchen, she did not ask what she might do to help but simply started gathering things to set the table.

"Come, Felicity, you are going to learn how to set a proper table," she told the little girl and smiled at Mikaela who smiled her approval.

Felicity clapped her hands and hurried ahead of Gabrielle. Once outside, she told the girl to settle down and pay attention. So busy with her lesson on the proper setting of the table, she had not noticed Tomás had arrived home until she glanced up and saw him standing in the doorway. He was leaning against the frame with his arms folded in front of him and he was smiling.

"Hello," she said which drew Felicity's attention.

"Papa!"

The little girl hurried toward him before leaping into his arms. Tomás scooped her up into his arms and showered her face and neck with kisses making Felicity laugh and squirm. Gabrielle loved watching him interact with the little girl. He might not be related by blood, but he was a wonderful father to Felicity and the two loved each other very much. A more positive observation could never be had by anyone who saw them together.

Her gaze slid to Mikaela who had stepped up behind them. She was smiling at the interaction and now Gabrielle saw the truth. The love she saw in Mikaela's eyes was for Felicity and not Tomás. Oh, there was affection and caring for him easily readable in the woman's eyes but the adoring love she showed was for the little girl.

"Papa, I am learning how to sit a proper table," Felicity said as she cupped her father's face in her small hands.

"I think you mean *set* a proper table," Tomás said with a grin.

"Yes. Sit. Set. You know what I mean," Felicity said with a huff.

"Yes, I do. Let us see what you have learned," he replied and gently set her down.

She was no sooner on her feet but scurrying to get around the table and beat Gabrielle in setting the forks at the next two place settings. Once the utensils were situated properly, Felicity stood back and held her hands wide then curtsied. Everyone clapped and the little girl smiled so big, Gabrielle thought her face would split.

"Perfect, Felicity," she told her and received a hug in response.

"You did this very well, little one, brava," Tomás told her and she shot into his arms. "Have you been a good girl today?"

"Yes, Papa, Mikaela gave Gabrielle some skirts and things," Felicity announced.

Tomás looked to Gabrielle and lifted a brow. She tipped her head in response.

"She was quite generous. I believe we are going to be friends after all," she said with a smile.

"This is good to hear. I am pleased," he said then set Felicity on her feet. "I have something I must discuss with you and Mikaela."

His sudden change in tone sounded serious and a shiver of anxiety swept over Gabrielle. Had the soldiers caught up with them? Mikaela appeared at the door wiping her hands on a cloth. Tomás motioned her to take a seat on the settee then directed Gabrielle to have a seat next to her. Felicity climbed into the space between them. He took a seat in the chair across from them.

"I must leave for a while," he said.

"No," Felicity exclaimed hopping out of her seat to go to him and climb into his lap. "Papa, you just came home." Then the little girl hugged him around the neck.

"I know, honey, but we need supplies to repair damage from the storm. We did the best we could, but need more things. You wish everyone to have a nice home, do you not?"

Felicity looked at him and nodded even as her expression betrayed her sadness. Gabrielle could see the tears streaming down her flushed cheeks and her own eyes were a bit blurry at the moment.

"I hope I shall not be gone long but we might have to search several islands to find what we need and if it comes to it, we may have to return to Kingston," he said looking at her.

"No," she exclaimed and gripped Mikaela's hand without thinking.

The woman patted her hand and Gabrielle looked to her.

"Tomás knows his way around well. He will not let the soldiers see him. He will be fine," Mikaela said with a confident squeeze to her hand.

"Are you sure?"

"Yes, he goes in and out many times and they have been seeking him for years since that ugly woman blamed him for her husband's death."

Gabrielle had not been told the story behind the murder charge and did not wish to have it told in front of Felicity so she decided she would ask about it another time.

"You will be very careful, especially if you go anywhere near Kingston," she said to Tomás.

"Yes, I shall be extra careful," he said with a confident grin.

Then he bounced his daughter on his knee and kissed her cheek.

"What do you wish me to bring you this time?" he asked the little girl.

"Sugar sticks."

"So I shall." Then he looked at Gabrielle and Mikaela. "And my dears, what do you two wish?"

"Well...if you come across some lavender for me to dry, it would be nice. What I have is not keeping the bugs out much anymore," Mikaela said then looked at Gabrielle. "The bugs, they don't like it so stay outside."

Gabrielle knew well about lavender keeping away bugs. She remembered Mama LaRue putting small boxes of dried lavender in the corners of the rooms and the windowsills.

"So I have heard," she said with a smile, realizing only then that they were still holding hands.

I have a new friend.

"And you, my beautiful Gabrielle, perhaps some cloth?"

"Only if you can do so without any trouble...I do not wish you going to Kingston and risking getting caught for cloth. Understood?"

"Understood," he said with a grin which told her he would probably try anyway.

"I am serious, Tomás," she said with real concern.

"Yes, yes, only if I can," he said.

"When will you leave?" Mikaela asked.

"On the morning tide," he remarked then hugged Felicity to him. "I hope to return in a week or so. You will be all right here?"

His question was directed to Gabrielle.

"We shall be fine," Gabrielle answered squeezing Mikaela's hand then looking to his daughter. "Is that not so, Felicity?"

The little girl nodded but then buried her head in her father's neck. Gabrielle knew how she felt for she was suddenly very sad Tomás was leaving. It was not only worrying about his safety, but she wished him never to leave her side again. If only he felt the same way as she, her life would be one of pure contentment here with her new friend and Felicity.

Later, after supper was over and Felicity was finally asleep, Mikaela announced she was going to visit a friend who was pregnant. It seemed Mikaela was also the local midwife and medicine woman. Tomás explained she was very knowledgeable of herbs as well as assisting in childbirth. They had not lost a single mother or child since she came to the island to work her magic.

Now Gabrielle sat on the settee on the porch. She inhaled the perfumed air as the flowers gave off their heaviest scent at night. It made her think of the jasmine which grew in the vicinity of La Coeur de la Terre. The air would be heavy with the lovely scent and she loved going to sleep with it surrounding her.

The sky was clear, the moon full, and slowly the stars grew brighter and brighter until the entire expanse was filled with them. She sighed. This was such a lovely place and she knew she could very easily become accustomed to living here.

Tomás stepped out from the kitchen and she turned to look at him. His hair was tied back and his handsome face looked even more so in the soft light of the lanterns. He had such strong fine features, he looked carved from stone.

"Some port, my sweet?"

"Yes, just a little," she said and a shiver ran over her as he took the seat beside her and set two glasses and a bottle of wine on the side table.

They were alone out here. Felicity was sleeping and Mikaela was gone. She had never been this alone with a man. Well, she supposed that wasn't true since she and Tomás had slept in the same cabin, but there were others nearby and she had not felt so nervous then. Now her insides were shaking, her breathing erratic, and she felt cold even in the warm, humid air. She folded her arms across her chest and tried to calm the nervous energy racing through her.

Tomás poured a small amount of wine into a glass and handed it to her.

"Are you all right, Gabrielle," he asked when she did not take it.

"Yes, I-I," she stammered trying to think of how to explain what she was feeling.

"Take a sip then sit back and enjoy the night sky," he said with a smile.

She accepted the glass and with her eyes meeting his over the top of it, she took a sip, and then another. The port warmed her so her shivering subsided a bit but still did not go away. Suddenly, Tomás took the glass from her hands and set it aside. He slid his hand along the curve of her cheek. Her heart leaped and fluttered in her chest then the shivering came rushing back.

When he leaned in and touched her lips with his, she inhaled on a gasp and closed her eyes. His lips were gentle but she wanted more. Sliding her hands around his middle, she leaned in and parted her lips. When he had kissed her in the past, he had touched his tongue to her lips so she did the same this time. When her tongue ventured forth and tentatively explored his lips, he pulled her close and his tongue touched hers.

At first, she pulled back, her tongue retreating but then she became more adventurous and gave him what he wanted. She tasted him and he tasted her. It was both scary and exhilarating, and rather intoxicating. Her body tingled, and her mind raced. But when his hand slid down to her shoulder and pushed the cloth of the oversized blouse aside so he might allow his lips to trail along the curve of her jaw to her neck, she broke away from him with a small cry. She tugged the blouse up around her neck and turned away.

"Gabrielle, please, I am sorry," Tomás said trying to turn her back to face him. "I meant you no disrespect. I care for you, I desire you, and I hope you feel the same."

Tears had welled in her eyes but his words soothed her—but only a little.

"My scars—"

"I care not what your skin looks like, I see all of you, my beautiful Gabrielle, and your scars shall not diminish the beauty I see before me," he said in a low voice meant only for her ears.

"I cannot...I-I am frightened," she said on a sob.

"No, no, please, I have no wish to frighten you," he said pulling her into his arms. "I only wish to kiss you."

She looked up at him through hot tears.

"Yes, I would very much enjoy making love to you but I know you are not experienced in such things...is this not true?"

She nodded.

"I-I have never been with a man," she admitted and felt heat flush her cheeks.

"Good, this pleases me much," he said with a grin. "I wish you to know only me—but only when you are ready."

"You will wait?"

"Yes, I shall wait forever if need be," he said lifting her hand and pressing a kiss into her palm. "Well, perhaps not forever." He laughed. "You already have my heart, and you shall choose when to have my body."

"You are like no other man I have ever met, Tomás. Sometimes, I believe I have imagined you."

He laughed and poured himself a drink, tipped back the glass then grinned.

"Gabrielle, you honor me in thinking so but trust me, I have not always been so patient," he said.

"Oh...was it impatience which got you a murder charge on your head?" she asked figuring now was as good as any to learn the facts behind the charge and gain a better insight into this man.

He laughed again.

"Not impatience, no...simply refusing a woman and being in the wrong place at the wrong time," he said filling her glass with more port.

"Tell me," she pleaded.

Tomás sat back with a sigh. She knew he was hesitating and worried it was so horrible he did not wish her to know. Or worse, that he was guilty of the crime and did not wish her to know it.

"I was in Kingston. We had stopped there for supplies and to allow some of the men to blow off steam after a long stint at sea. Most of the men had gone to the taverns and were taking in drink and whatever other amusements they encountered."

She knew he meant taking time with the women who survived by selling their bodies. Her time around the tavern in New Orleans had opened her eyes to the seedier side of life even as she fought off the advancements of drunken men.

"I had gone to visit with an old friend, Mikaela's mother," he looked at her. "She is a medicine woman also. She taught Mikaela all she knows. After I left her, I returned to the tavern to check on my men. We did not need them getting into any trouble."

He leaned forward and poured more wine into his glass. He downed it all in one swallow then offered to top off her glass. She covered the top of her glass with her hand so he shrugged and set down the bottle.

"I was leaving to head back to the ship. Liam was in the tavern and I knew he would keep the men in check. As I left the tavern, a woman approached me. She was pretty enough—a bit older than most of the whores who frequented the docks but she was friendly and began talking to me. Perhaps I was feeling lonelier than I thought for when she asked if I would like to come to her home, I accepted. My gut told me to say no, but I accompanied her anyway. She lived in a room at the local inn, not far from the docks. I noted there were men's things scattered about the place. My gut screamed at me to leave. She clung to me, trying to kiss me, and remove my clothing. I pushed her away and told her I must leave. She started yelling at me, cursing, and hitting me. Just then the door flew open and a man entered. He began cursing her and attempted to hit me. I pushed him to the floor and left as quickly as possible. I was only a short distance from the inn when I heard a gunshot. The sound halted me and I considered returning to see what I could do to help when the woman came out onto the street and started screaming. Others came out of their homes and the nearby taverns. She screamed that I had shot her husband and pointed at me. It was her word against mine and I knew the authorities would believe her so I ran. I hid on the docks until Liam appeared. He gathered the men and we left as soon as possible with me hiding in the hold until it was clear. It was not long after that I received word from my friend that there was a bounty on my head. I have been evading the authorities ever since."

"But you are innocent. Obviously, *she* shot her husband. It was probably her plan from the start. To lure some unsuspecting man to her home knowing her husband would come home and find them. Perhaps if you had not left, she might have shot you as well then claimed her husband and you fought."

"Liam had suggested the same thing," he said with a nod. "People will do whatever they must to divert attention from them when they are the guilty ones."

Gabrielle took his hand in hers.

"I am so sorry you must live this way. I wish there was something I could do to change this for you," she said with tears stinging her eyes.

She knew this man was good at heart. He would never kill someone in cold blood.

"Somehow I knew you could not kill someone in cold blood. You are not such a man. All the more reason then you must promise me you will not return to Kingston. If you cannot get the supplies you need, we will figure out how to make the repairs some other way. I wish you were not going at all," she said, lifting his hand to her chest.

Tomás pulled her into his arms.

"I do not wish to leave you either," he said, cradling her head against his shoulder. "I shall return as fast as I can and I will be cautious, I promise. I have much to lose if I am caught."

She looked up at him. He smiled and when he kissed her, Gabrielle wished she could give her body to him as well as her heart. The fear of him not returning was great and she wanted him for her own, but the fear of him seeing her as she truly was and rejecting her was greater.

Chapter Eleven

Guilt settled over Tomás as he and Liam came ashore just outside of the town of Kingston. Gabrielle had believed him when he told her he would not go anywhere near Kingston but even as they had discussed it that evening he had already decided he must return. Not only because they needed supplies they might only obtain there but he needed to satisfy his curiosity about this man, Cuddy.

Her words were haunting him, however. She had said she knew he was not the kind of man to kill someone in cold blood. If Cuddy was the man he sought all these years, could he bring himself to take his revenge on him, knowing how his death would hurt her? If he did so and she found out, he knew he would lose any chance of her loving him the way he did her.

"This is crazy, Tomás," Liam said as they hurried along the edge of town.

They did not dare procure horses so they were walking the distance to the house where Gabrielle had lived with the family of this man he must see with his own eyes.

"I must know for certain, Liam," Tomás said, keeping his hat pulled down close over his eyes.

His long hair was tied up under his hat and he had worn his most worn britches and blouse.

He had borrowed a nearly worn out hat from one of the men. The less conspicuous he was, the more he might move freely around the town without notice.

"I plan to marry the girl, Liam," he said, causing his friend to halt his steps and grab his arm.

"Are ye serious?"

"Yes, very serious. I love her but if this man is the bastard who scarred me, I must know," he growled.

"And if he is?"

Tomás shook his head.

"I am not sure what I shall do," he said and began walking again.

"Well, you are taking a huge chance this fellow does not kill you first," Liam said with a scowl darkening his face. "Of course, I have no doubt he will call the authorities on you and we probably will never get off this island again."

"We shall be fine, Liam. Have faith."

"Ha! I have faith...faith you are going to get our necks stretched yet," Liam said with a shake of his head.

Soon the house where they knew Gabrielle had lived came into view. The two men left the road and moved toward the house using the brush as cover.

"How do you even know he is here? He might be at sea?" Liam asked in a low whisper.

"I had one of the men ask around town. He was told the man was at home," Tomás said. "I want you to remain back here, out of sight. If something goes bad, I want you safe so you might return home to tell Gabrielle and the others what has happened. I do not wish her or Felicity to always wonder."

"They will never have to wonder if you do not do this, my friend. Please, tis not worth it," Liam pleaded.

Tomás embraced his friend then held his finger to his lips before slipping away into the brush. He knew Liam would worry and he hoped his friend would not attempt to follow him so he might have his back. He needed to do this alone and if things went bad, he wanted his friend safe.

When he reached the side of the house, he waited and watched to ensure it was clear before running across the lawn. The shadows were long on this side of the house so the drabness of his clothes and hat helped him blend into the dim light. When he reached the house, he pressed his body against the wall then dipped to move along the façade until he reached an open window. He listened to be sure no one was in this particular room before climbing inside.

The room was empty. It was a parlor room with a settee, two comfortable looking reading chairs facing the fireplace, and a small card table with chairs in the corner. There was an open book in one of the chairs so someone must have recently occupied the room and there was a chance the person could return any moment.

Tomás quietly moved to the doorway, he heard feminine voices coming from somewhere nearby and then he heard a man laugh in a boisterous manner. Suddenly, a man appeared near the end of the hallway. He was facing another room and speaking to someone then laughed again. When the man turned toward the room where he was, Tomás ducked inside before he had a chance to see the man's face. He was certainly a similar size to the man who had tied him to a post and nearly whipped him to death, but he was not sure even yet.

Slipping behind the door, he waited to see where the man would go. He had no need to wait long for the man walked into the room where Tomás was hiding and moved to the chair and picked up the book. As soon as the man took a seat, Tomás closed the door to the room and stepped forward with his hand on the hilt of his sword.

"What the hell?" the man exclaimed as he came to his feet.

As soon as Tomás saw the man's face, he knew it was not the man he sought and he felt a strange relief fill his chest. He would not have to choose whether or not to kill Gabrielle's friend— yet. What the man did next might force him to decide.

"What do you want? I have not much money but if tis what you came for, take it and go but do not harm my family."

"You are the man Gabrielle calls Cuddy?"

"Gabrielle—who are you?"

"My name is Tomás Alvarez and I wish to speak to you," he said in answer.

"Bloody hell, where is Gabrielle? If you have hurt even a hair on her head, I will kill you myself," Cuddy growled, his hands fisting in anger.

"You need not worry, I would never harm my love, nor allow anyone to harm her," Tomás said, lifting his hands to show he meant no harm. "She is my one and only and I plan to marry her."

"Marry—she is safe then?"

"Yes...very safe and I believe content," he said with pride. "I seek a man with a scar such as yours. I needed to find out if you were that man."

"And if I had been?"

"I am not sure. Before I met her, had you been the man, I would have killed you," Tomás admitted. "But now...I am not sure. Gabrielle has much faith in me to do the right thing and I am not sure I could have harmed her friend."

Cuddy laughed and even Tomás could not keep a smile from teasing at his lips.

"You are a ballsy bastard, I will say that about you, pirate," Cuddy said through chuckles. "You risked coming back here to find out if I was the man you wished to kill but would not because Gabrielle would not have liked it...is this what you are saying?"

Tomás considered the man's words then nodded.

"Yes...Capitán Cuddy, I am not a killer. They call me murderer but I am innocent of this charge."

"I know," Cuddy said and took his seat again.

"You know what?"

"Have a seat, young man. Tis all right, I do not bite," Cuddy said with a grin and motioned to one of the reading chairs.

Tomás slowly maneuvered to the chair without taking his eyes off of the man. The man was large and although he was older, Tomás was sure he was as strong as a bull. He did not wish to have to fight the man.

"You obviously have not heard...the woman who made the claim you shot her husband has died," Cuddy said turning in his chair to face Tomás.

"She is? I am not sorry. I hope she rots in hell," he said upon hearing of the woman's death. "Tis not a Christian thing to wish upon someone but she has made my life a living hell since I rejected her."

"So it seems. I suppose she did not wish to tempt the fates for when she knew she was dying, she sent for the authorities and on her death bed admitted it was she who killed her husband that day. She admitted she had tried to blame you because she wanted her husband dead but did not wish to hang for it."

"No, she wished me to hang instead," Tomás said with a hiss.

She might be dead but he still carried anger toward her for the lies she told.

"Well, she cleared your name. You no longer have a murder charge hanging over you," Cuddy said. "However, your kidnapping of Gabrielle is a whole other thing."

"No...no, sir, I did not kidnap her," Tomás exclaimed. "I wished only to protect her because I believed the authorities were using her to bait me and I certainly did not wish her to face the hangman's noose because of me. I swear by the Holy Mother, she came willingly."

Cuddy chuckled.

"I kind of figured she had and it was a good thing she disappeared with you," he said. "I am not sure I could have kept her from the jailhouse. She is a grown woman and if she wishes to be with you, I cannot make her do otherwise—as long as she is with you of her own free will and she is happy."

Cuddy stared at him and Tomás knew the man meant he would do him harm if she was anything but happy.

"I love Gabrielle, sir. I only wish to make her happy. She has had a very sad life and I only wish her to feel beautiful and loved," Tomás said, holding his hand to his heart.

"I see...you understand about her scars." Cuddy was not asking but making a statement and Tomás knew what he meant.

"Yes...she fears I shall not want her but I do not care if she were a leper...I would still love her. I knew from the first moment in the marketplace she was my one and only...the woman born to own my heart," he said placing both of his hands over his heart. "Since I am a free man again, I can marry her openly so please, I know she shall wish for you and your family to be there...so I hope you will consider coming to the wedding."

"You are damn right I shall...if for no other reason to make sure she is all right and that you make an honest woman of her," Cuddy exclaimed, reaching over to slap Tomás on the back nearly knocking him out of the chair.

"Good, I am sure she shall be very pleased," Tomás said, flexing his shoulder to make sure it still worked. "I should tell you...I have not disrespected her, Capitán Cuddy." Tomás shrugged. "She is quite innocent when it comes to...well, you know...I am sure of this, and I shall never push her. When she is ready...I shall wait until then."

"Might be a long wait, son, you prepared for that?" Cuddy asked with a chuckle.

"I hope it will not be too long, but she is worth the wait," he told the man and meant it.

"So where is this wedding to happen?"

"At my home."

Cuddy leaned back in his chair. He seemed to be pondering the information.

"I do not suppose I could convince you to bring her home here for the wedding?"

"If this would please her...I would consider it perhaps, but our home is where I feel it would be best," Tomás said and was determined to have it so.

"You just let us know when and we shall be there," Cuddy said with a laugh. "I know Siobhan would not wish to miss it. Speaking of my wifc...she would probably have my head if she does not make your acquaintance. We are sitting down to the evening meal soon if you wish to join us."

Tomás decided he liked this man. He made no demands on him and right away, had been open about the charges having been dropped. He appreciated the man's honesty. Cuddy stood and motioned him to follow him. As soon as he was in the hallway, he bellowed for his wife. She appeared with her hands on her hips and an impatient expression on her face. All Tomás could think was how he would not rile a woman with such fiery red hair. He stifled a grin when she chastised Cuddy for *hollerin' for her.*

Cuddy apologized and then introduced Tomás. He told her he had invited him to dine with them and she clucked her tongue when he asked her if they had enough.

"I have to feed your ever hungry belly, do I not? Of course, we have enough," she said with a wink to Tomás. "Lad, you look like you could do with a hearty meal."

"I eat very well at home but sea rations tend to put me off my appetite." He turned to Cuddy. "We left our cook at home because he was too under the weather to sail with us."

"Sorry to hear that. I hope he is well soon," Siobhan said then grabbed Tomás by the arm and dragged him into the kitchen. "You will find soap and water over there—" She pointed to a wash table in what appeared to be a mudroom. "Then you are welcome at my table."

"Señora," Tomás addressed her as she started to walk away but she stopped and smiled at him.

"I like the sound of that...so much prettier than Missus," she said.

"I have a-a friend...he is waiting...out there," he said motioning to the brush growing around the house.

"If he looks as hungry as you, get himself in here—now!"

Tomás did as he was told and stepped outside the porch door and whistled for Liam. When the man poked his head out of the jungle, Tomás waved his arm at him to come to the house. Liam hesitated then slowly walked the distance to the porch.

"What is going on?"

"We have been invited to supper, Liam," Tomás told him and proceeded to introduce him to Cuddy and his wife.

A few minutes later, two young girls entered the kitchen. Cuddy introduced his daughters and they each curtsied as they were named. Tomás knew these were the young charges Gabrielle had been teacher and friend to over the past few years. They were young but very well-mannered and pretty. He knew Cuddy would have no problem securing them good husbands. He decided he had been wise to ask Gabrielle to teach Felicity.

Fine food, good drink, and delightful company made the evening go fast. Soon the women had cleared the table and Cuddy pulled out cigars and brandy. It had been years since Tomás and Liam had indulged in either so neither refused his offering.

"So when can we expect this wedding to happen?" Cuddy asked after filling a glass for each of them.

"Tis a good question, only I must ask her and get a yes answer first," Tomás said lifting his glass as if making a toast.

Liam laughed. "The way she looks at you, my friend, I believe you shall get a yes," he exclaimed.

"I wish my confidence was as great as yours."

"You fear she will refuse you," Cuddy asked.

"I believe she fears I will reject her once I see her scars," Tomás said wishing he could change all which had happened to her.

"Keep the lights out, Tomás," Liam suggested.

Cuddy laughed and Liam joined him. Tomás did not laugh for he did not think it funny or something he wished to do.

"I suppose if I must but I do not wish to do so," he said. "Gabrielle is the most beautiful woman I have ever known...at least to me."

"As it should be, Captain, I am glad to hear you say just this," Cuddy said with a big smile. "She is beautiful but she has always worried so over those scars. Many have spurned her for the way she looks but I think if you can convince her they mean nothing to you, she will be fine. Lights on or lights off."

He lifted his glass. "May you not fear asking her and may she not fear accepting you," Cuddy said in a toast.

"Aye, aye!" Liam lifted his glass.

"Thank you...very good advice, Capitán Cuddy, and I shall keep it in mind," Tomás said lifting his glass.

~*~

Gabrielle walked toward the open sand. The gentle surf caressed the shore and a fresh breeze blew curls across her eyes as she looked out over the open water.

"Hola," a young woman's voice said from behind her.

Gabrielle turned to find the young woman Tomás had called Maria when they had first arrived almost three weeks ago.

"Hello," she said with a smile. "You are Maria, am I right?"

The woman laughed. "Si, I am Maria and you are Gabrielle?"

Gabrielle chuckled. It seemed there were no secrets in this little village.

"Yes, I am. Tis nice to meet you, Maria," she said extending her hand.

Maria shook her hand.

"And you," she said. "Little Felicity talks about you so much."

"She does? In a good way, I hope."

"Oh yes, she adores you."

The thought of the little girl talking to others about her made her heart soar. She had grown quite fond of Felicity and wished she was strong enough to own her feelings for Tomás in the same way. She missed him. He had been gone for over a week now and she was eager for him to return.

"I adore her," she said of Felicity. "And I believe you might adore a certain Scotsman as well."

Maria laughed. "Am I so obvious?"

Gabrielle grinned. "Liam is a good man. I like him very much, and he needs someone to love him."

"I would if he would let me. He says I am too young." Maria frowned with a sigh.

"Do not give up on him, Maria, I think he is fearful, is all," Gabrielle told her. "I think he is afraid to love for fear he will lose it again."

"Lose it?"

Gabrielle looked around them then lowered her voice.

"I am not sure I should say, but he had a wife and lost both her and their child."

The look on Maria's face told her she had no idea.

"I am telling you this so you might understand. Be patient, but do not give up on Liam," Gabrielle said.

Maria smiled. "Tis very sad but it explains much. Thank you, Gabrielle...now, what about you and Tomás?"

"Me and—" Gabrielle swallowed hard and adjusted her scarf closer on her neck. "Tomás...no, he is just a very kind man. He thought he had caused me great trouble and so brought me here to keep me safe."

"Hmm...I see how you look at him, and you must be blind not to see how handsome he is and how he looks at you," Maria said with a laugh.

"Well, I am not blind," Gabrielle said laughing too. "I just wish..."

"Wish what?"

"He is very handsome. He can have any beautiful woman he wants, I am sure."

"You are very beautiful, Gabrielle."

Shaking her head, she fought tears and looked out at the ocean.

"I am not beautiful enough, Maria," she said.

"Have you not ever looked in a mirror?"

Gabrielle looked at the woman.

"Of course, but all I see is the ugliness which makes people turn away in disgust," Gabrielle said and started to walk away but Maria stilled her with a hand on her arm.

"I see no ugliness. Why do you think others do?"

Gabrielle hesitated then slid the scarf open on her neck. Maria looked then looked closer and ran her fingers lightly over the flesh there.

"Tis not bad...I know not how you came by these but I do not believe Tomás thinks you less beautiful because of them," Maria said. "I wish Liam would look at me the way Tomás looks at you."

Gabrielle laughed. "He does, Maria, he does. You just have not noticed."

Maria gasped and looked at her with an expression of surprise.

"Do you truly believe so?"

Gabrielle nodded. "And you are truly not disgusted by these?"

"Of course not, and I do not think Tomás will be either. Have you asked Mikaela if she has a magic cream or potion?"

Gabrielle laughed because she had no doubt many thought Mikaela to be some kind of witch woman.

"I have been using a salve she made for me on my scars. Mikaela said it would help and I do think my skin feels a bit smoother," Gabrielle said running her fingers along her neck.

"Oh, yes, keep using it. I have a burn scar on my leg," she said pulling her colorful skirt up along her leg to show Gabrielle her thigh.

From her knee to about mid-way up on her thigh was a wide swathe of skin, which was lighter in color with uneven edges. Gabrielle recognized it as a bad burn but the skin did look smooth and when she reached out to touch it, she hesitated but then Maria told her it was all right.

"Go ahead, I do not mind," she said.

Gabrielle ran her fingertips along the flesh and was surprised at how smooth it was.

"Mikaela's salve did this?"

"Si...I was cooking over an open fire and my skirt caught fire. I was lucky someone dowsed me with water before it got too bad," Maria told her. "Mikaela helped me through it...I got very sick. But after it healed, it was rough and rigid. And it hurt for a very long time. She gave me a lovely salve to put on it. I still put some on after I bathe or swim."

"I shall keep using it then," Gabrielle said with a pleased smile. "I still do not wish anyone to see my scars, but I believe it is helping."

"You are too pretty to worry about such things," Maria said patting Gabrielle's hand. "Besides, those who care about us do not even see such things."

"Do you really believe that?"

"Oh yes...perhaps even Liam cares more than he is willing to admit—he does not see my scar anymore," Maria said with a smile which seemed to grow with each word. "Could it be?"

Gabrielle laughed and hugged the woman.

"Perhaps you might ask him when they return," she said then frowned. "If they return."

"Oh, Gabrielle, do not worry...they always return. It has not even been a fortnight. We shall see them in the next several days."

"You mean they are always away this long," Gabrielle asked.

"Yes...it takes time to get supplies unless they go to Jamaica, but many of the other islands have what they need," Maria said then added with a laugh. "Just not all in one place. Do not worry. I must get these things to Chloe. My friend is going to make some baby blankets."

"Oh yes, she is the one who is having a baby, correct?"

"Yes...tis her third but she likes to make something special for each one," Maria said.

"Is she doing well? I know Mikaela visits with her almost daily now," Gabrielle asked.

"She is doing very well. Come...join me in visiting with her. My Luis is there playing with his friends."

Gabrielle hesitated a moment not wishing to impose upon the woman in her private condition but then agreed. Perhaps she might be of assistance to her or her children. Besides, she enjoyed making new acquaintances and she had begun to dream about a permanent life here on La Isla with this community—and Tomás. Thoughts of leaving were becoming less and less.

"I would truly enjoy a visit with her. Thank you, Maria," Gabrielle said then with one more glance out to sea to send out a wish for La Bella Dama's safe return, she set off with her new friend.

Chapter Twelve

The sound of a bell broke the quiet repose of the afternoon. Felicity sprang from her seat at the table where Gabrielle was teaching her proper letters.

"Papa!"

"We do not know for sure, Felicity, but we shall go to the beach to see," Gabrielle said closing the leather binding on the pages so they would not blow away in the breeze.

She closed the ink and wiped her fingers. She followed Felicity into the house and reminded her to put on her shoes. When they reached the front door, Felicity opened it with such flourish, it banged the wall. Gabrielle laughed at the little girl's enthusiasm although she was feeling quite excited as well, and hoped Tomás had finally come home.

Mikaela had been gone for two nights and nearly two full days. She was with Chloe since the expectant mother had started with labor pains. Gabrielle had been somewhat nervous during each night being alone with only Felicity in the house and since their rooms were on opposite sides of the house, she allowed the little girl to sleep with her. The nights had passed without incident but she hoped Tomás would be home this night so she would not feel so anxious.

Felicity hurried along the path leading to the beach with as much speed as she could muster considering her leg but she was fast enough Gabrielle had to nearly run to keep up with her. When they came out on the beach, she gasped. There was a ship and from the excitement of those gathering on the beach, it must be La Bella Dama.

"Papa! Tis Papa," Felicity exclaimed grabbing Gabrielle's hand. "I knew it. I just knew it."

Gabrielle smiled and allowed the little girl to pull her through the sand until they reached the water's edge. Felicity stopped and kicked off her shoes.

"Oh no! Not today, little one," Gabrielle said grabbing Felicity's arm. "Let's wait until they get ashore this time."

Felicity's shoulders drooped and her lower lip jutted out in a pout. She sat down in the sand and pulled her shoes back on then folded her arms across her chest.

"Do you wish your papa to see you pouting?"

Felicity looked up at her and shook her head.

"Then what do you say to your standing beside me and acting the proper lady when your papa comes ashore?"

Felicity seemed to think about it for a moment then nodded and got to her feet.

"He will be pleased with me, yes?" she asked.

"Very much so, Felicity, very much so," Gabrielle said encouraging the girl and receiving a big smile in response.

Although Felicity had agreed to act a bit more proper than wading into the water or pouting in a pile on the sand, the little girl was still excited enough she could not seem to stand still. She fidgeted and paced, and walked circles around Gabrielle. Understanding her excitement, Gabrielle wanted to jump up and down and wave to the men as they approached in the dinghy but then what kind of example would she be setting for Felicity. Her heart was racing as they got closer and she could see their faces. Tomás was wearing a big smile. Seeing him, she wanted to kick off her shoes and rush into the water just as Felicity had planned.

She chuckled at the thought and got a strange look from Felicity.

"He is almost here, sweetheart," she told the child.

Felicity clapped her hands and hopped up and down.

"Papa!"

Tomás jumped from the dinghy and waded through the gentle surf. Gabrielle patted Felicity on the shoulder and gave her a nod of permission. The little girl sprinted as fast as her shriveled leg allowed and leaped into her father's arms. Seeing such love made Gabrielle's heart swell with emotion. She wished she could do just the same for having been parted from him for almost three weeks had made her realize just how much he was a part of her life now. She was very much in love with Tomás, yet terrified of it being true.

"Have you been a good girl for Gabrielle and Mikaela?" she heard Tomás ask Felicity as they approached.

"Yes, Papa, I have. Mikaela is helping Chloe's baby come," Felicity said with excitement.

"So we are in time. Good." When he looked at Gabrielle, she thought her heart would melt. "Gabrielle, you are well, I hope."

"Yes, Tomás, I am-we are all well," she said with a smile and taking Felicity's hand as she extended it to her from his arms. "And very happy you are home safe."

"We are," he said not looking anywhere but in her eyes. "It was a good trip. We got all the supplies we needed and I have some news as well."

"News? Good news, I hope."

"Yes...very good news," he said then leaned in and kissed her lips.

"Me too, Papa!"

"You too, little one," he said with a laugh then kissed the little girl's puckered mouth.

"Did you bring me sugars sticks?"

"Felicity, tis rude to ask if someone has brought gifts," Gabrielle said with a shake of her head.

The little girl turned her head into her father's shoulder in a pout. Tomás laughed.

"You listen to Gabrielle. What she says is true. However, I did bring you some sugar sticks. You shall have them later," he told Felicity, squeezing her and pressing kisses to her neck making her laugh delightfully, and squeal.

"I might have brought you something as well," he said leaning in and kissing Gabrielle again.

Gabrielle wanted to clap her hands and jump up and down just as Felicity had for no one had brought her a gift since before the fire. Her father and her brother would usually bring her some lovely trinket or a piece of cloth whenever they returned from a voyage, but many years had passed since those lovely days.

"You need not bring me anything, but thank you. I am sure whatever it is, tis lovely," she said with a giddiness which made her smile so hard, her cheeks ached.

"I need to make sure the supplies get unloaded so I must stay here for a while yet but please, you take Felicity home and I shall be there shortly," Tomás said setting the little girl on her feet.

He surprised Gabrielle by putting his arm around her shoulders as well as taking Felicity by the hand when he led them up the beach. He smiled and greeted others as they moved toward the path leading back to the house but he never relinquished his hold on either of them. When they reached the path, he leaned down and whispered something in Felicity's ear. She grinned and nodded. Then he turned to Gabrielle.

"Felicity has promised to behave for you and if she does, she shall be rewarded with a swim at our favorite watering hole before supper," he told her with a laugh.

Gabrielle glanced at Felicity and smiled.

"I have no doubt such a reward will warrant excellent behavior," she said with a chuckle.

"As for you, my beauty—" Tomás leaned in close to whisper. "Your reward shall come after the little one is in bed for the night."

Gabrielle gasped and did not know what to say or expect from such a statement.

"I am intrigued, Tomás," she said feeling a blush heat her cheeks.

"I hope so...and I hope you shall be pleased," he said then he kissed her. "Go now, and I shall be home as soon as possible."

~*~

Nervous excitement plagued Gabrielle throughout their casual supper with just Felicity since Mikaela was still with Chloe. Even with the excitement over learning what Tomás might have for her, her thoughts had continuously gone to the woman birthing her third child and she could not help but worry. Mikaela had been with her going on the third night and the baby had yet to come. Birthing was hard work and dangerous but the baby should have come by now.

"Perhaps I should attend Chloe and see if I might be of assistance to Mikaela," she suggested as she began clearing the dishes from the table. "I am sure Felicity would love for you to see to her bedtime."

A look of disappointment crossed his handsome face and she knew her suggestion was not a welcome one.

"I would prefer you to stay right here. I shall see Felicity to bed if you wish, but I am sure Mikaela has everything under control. She is a miracle worker when it comes to birthing. No babies have been lost under care since she came to this island," he said with a confidence she wished she felt.

"Tis Chloe's third and with each one, it gets more risky," she remarked. "And she has been in labor for a long while now."

"True, but we all have great faith in Mikaela. I am sure the baby will arrive soon and all will be well," Tomás said taking her into his arms. "Besides, I have been away for a long time and I missed you. There is something I wish to tell you about."

"Please do," she said with a smile.

"Later," he said. "After—" He nodded in the direction of Felicity who was trying to fold her napkin into a perfect square.

Gabrielle looked over to the little girl and smiled. "All right."

Tomás rewarded her response with a kiss to her mouth then he announced it was time for Felicity to prepare for bed. When she looked up from her project, she gave them a pouty expression but it quickly turned into a smile when he asked her what story she wished him to read to her.

While Tomás saw to his daughter's bedtime ritual, Gabrielle set to work cleaning up after the simple meal she had cooked for them. She was not the cook Mikaela was but it had not turned out too terrible. Tomás and Felicity had eaten quite heartily even if she had not. Her nerves had the better of her and her appetite was no longer with her.

She was just folding the linens when Tomás appeared at the doorway leading to the porch. He walked toward her, stopped in front of her and gently took the linens from her hands. He set them on the table, took hold of her hands and led her to the settee.

"Sit with me, Gabrielle," he said sounding so serious, a whole new flutter of butterflies took to flight in her belly.

His serious tone made her anxiety double and suddenly she was not sure she wished to know what he had to tell her or what his surprise was. When she hesitated, he pulled her to sit next to him on the settee. Was he going to tell her he was sending her home? Or somewhere else?

"When I left here, I told you I would not go to Kingston," he said holding her hands and when she started to pull them away, he held tighter. "Forgive me, for I did go."

She frowned at him and tried to pull her hands free again.

"You promised," she said feeling betrayed. "What have you done?"

"As you can see, I returned so I was not so foolish," he said with a grin then it faded as fast as it came when she gave him a look of disapproval. "In truth, I was safe going there for I am now a free man."

Gabrielle ceased her resistance and stared at him. Had she heard him correctly?

"You are—I do not understand."

"I went to see your friend, Cuddy. I thought...I thought perhaps he was the man I seek," he said.

"You thought Cuddy was the man who abused you...the man you wish dead," she said, once more attempting to free her hands but he prevented it. "You went there to kill him if he was..." She gasped. "Am I right? What did you do?"

Tomás stared at their hands entangled and for a moment, she wished she was anywhere but here. Suddenly, she had to know what transpired. To think he might have killed the man who had cared for and protected her all these years turned her insides.

"What happened? Tell me the truth, Tomás."

"Your friend, Cuddy, welcomed me. He was not the man I sought."

Gabrielle released the breath she was holding without realizing it on a loud sigh of relief.

"We sat as civilized men and talked. He asked about you and I told him you were well and had accompanied me freely and willingly." He looked up from their hands and gazed into her eyes. "This is true, yes?"

She nodded. She had no idea where this was going and still feared learning that which he wanted to tell her.

"Your friend then told me the woman who had accused me of killing her husband was dead."

"Oh my!"

"Tis good, Gabrielle. It seems she feared the prospect of going to hell for her crime and so made a deathbed confession. She admitted it was she who shot her husband and not me," Tomás said with a smile.

"And the authorities accepted her confession?" She was suddenly hopeful.

"Yes, I am no longer wanted for murder. Cuddy accompanied me into town so we might purchase supplies but first, we went before the magistrate. I am cleared. I can return to Kingston whenever I wish—as long as I stay out of trouble," he said laughing. "I was given a very harsh warning from the magistrate."

"This is very good news, Tomás," Gabrielle said squeezing his hands.

Suddenly, he released her hands and cupped her face. He kissed her lips and she closed her eyes reveling in the pleasure of it.

"Gabrielle, I told Cuddy I hoped you would choose to stay here with me, but if you wish to return to Kingston...I will not like it, but I shall take you," he said then kissed her again.

This kiss was not a short quick act. This kiss was deep and searing. She felt it over her entire body and his words swirled in her head. *He wishes me to stay here with him.*

But in what capacity? Teacher for Felicity? Lover?

Never a lover. He will put me on the first ship sailing away if he ever sees my scars.

When he broke the kiss, he stayed close, his mouth hovering over hers and she slowly opened her eyes. Her head was spinning and she wanted his mouth on hers once more.

"Marry me—marry me and stay with me forever, my sweet Gabrielle," Tomás said in a whisper, his breath warm on her face.

Had she heard him correctly? Before she had a chance to answer, his mouth covered hers again and stole every thought from her head. All she could comprehend at the moment was the way it felt to be in his arms, the way his mouth stole her breath while sharing his, and the way her body reacted pressing closer to him, wanting and needing him. She was on the brink of giving in to the temptation when his fingers traced across the scars on her neck.

Gabrielle jerked away with a small cry escaping her lips. Shaking her head, she stood so fast she nearly stumbled backward and would have if Tomás had not caught her. He stood and held her, not allowing her to pull away again.

"No! I know not what kind of game you are playing but I am not to be toyed with and for sure, you do not wish me to marry you," she said, tears filling her eyes so she could hardly see.

"You think I am lying? Sweet Gabrielle, please, hear me—" He tried to get her to look at him but her fear and shame kept her eyes shut tight. "I wish more than anything in this world to marry you, my love. You are everything to me. You are my one and only. I have known this from the first moment I looked into your beautiful blue eyes and heard your sweet voice. I wish to make a life with you...have babies with you."

She yanked away from him and opened her eyes. He was so handsome and she wanted to be his but she knew as soon as he saw her scars, he would wish her gone. She shook her head.

"Gabrielle, please...I love you," he said with his hands out to her as if begging her to return to his arms.

She wanted to return to his embrace. She loved him more than she could ever imagine and her heart was shattering with every one of his pronouncements of love. She shook her head again.

"Why not?" he asked in a low dejected tone which tore at her heart.

"If you saw my skin, you would not want me. How can you love such ugliness?" she said on a sob.

Tomás relinquished. His hands dropped to his sides and he sighed loudly as if defeated. But what he said next surprised her.

"Show me then, my love," he said. "Show me and then we will know."

Her eyes widened as she stared at him. Could she? Should she?

"Show you?"

"Yes...show me what you fear I shall reject," he said stepping forward and cupping her face. "Come with me...and show me."

He kissed her. He kissed her mouth, her cheeks, her forehead, and when she did not answer, he brought her hands to his lips and kissed her palms. She trembled but whether from fear of his request or desire, she was not sure.

"Please, Gabrielle, show me, please...I wish to see so I might reassure you..." He kissed her again. "I am not toying with you. I have desired you from the first time I held you. Show me."

Nodding, she blinked back tears. He smiled and took her hand in his. Leading her, she followed as if she had no will over her feet. When they reached his door, she hesitated but he lifted her hand to his lips.

"If you wish to wait, I shall wait but I hope you shall not deny me," he said and she knew she could deny him nothing.

"If you are offended by the sight of me, I shall know, Tomás," she said in a shaky whisper. "'Tis a look I have seen far too many times, so I shall know."

"If I am offended, I shall return you to Jamaica on tomorrow's tide for I shall never be able to face you again," he said.

The thought of leaving him threw her into an even more anxious state. She closed her eyes and prayed he would not reject her. He opened the door and waved her through, but her feet refused to move. He remedied the situation by sweeping her up into his arms making her squeak out a small cry then stepped inside and pushed the door shut with his backside. He kissed her lips and whispered sweet words she did not understand because they were in his native tongue. She had no doubt they were words of love but she was sure they would fade away never to be heard again once he saw her horrid scars.

Tomás carried her toward the large bed which sat in the middle of the space. It was a grand bed with a large headboard and matching footboard made from some beautiful dark wood with intricate carving adorning it. Everything about this man seemed to surprise her.

He set her down and her legs wobbled slightly. He lit a lantern on the chest beside the bed and turned it up to a full flame. He took a seat on the bed. She stepped away just out of his reach for fear he would pull her onto that wonderful and inviting bed. She knew not what to expect even as she knew what men and women did when alone in a bedroom.

"Show me, my love," Tomás whispered.

With shaking fingers, Gabrielle reached for her scarf and slowly untied it. She unwound it from around her neck but left her long hair covering her neck and shoulder. She refused to look at Tomás for she feared the look in his eyes when he saw the rough ugly skin with its spidery edges and ridged texture.

Suddenly, he was standing in front of her, his fingers in her hair and before she could stop him, he swept the long strands away from her neck. She closed her eyes tight against the feared expression of disgust she expected to see on his handsome face. But what he did next made them fly open in surprise. He pressed his lips to her shoulder in a gentle kiss then more kisses as he worked his way along her neck. She tried to pull away but he held her firm. Never had anyone touched her this way and certainly, no one had ever touched her scars in such a manner.

When his mouth reached her jawline, he pulled back and looked deep into her eyes. It was not disgust or rejection she saw there but desire. He still desired her.

"Show me more," he said against her lips before searing her mouth in a hot kiss which sent shivers of delight down her body making her feel things she never knew her body could experience.

Gabrielle pulled away from the kiss reluctantly. She was breathless when she tried to speak.

"Worse...the others...much worse," she said then took a deep breath and exhaled. She looked up into his dark eyes. "You might have accepted the scars on my neck and shoulder but those on my arm and down my side are far worse."

"Show me, Gabrielle," Tomás whispered and before she could react, he tugged her blouse up and over her head leaving her standing in front of him in her shift and skirt.

She gasped and tried to pull away but he grabbed her around the waist and pulled her close to his body. His body felt hot, feverish even, against her bare skin. His left hand grazed her upper arm and slid down along her arm tracing the scars which she had always so carefully hid from him and everyone else.

"Do they cause you discomfort?"

Again, he surprised her. He was not disgusted or offended but only concerned for her. If she were not already in love with this man, she would be now.

She shook her head.

"Mikaela gave me a salve and I have been using it daily. It has softened the skin a bit and so it no longer feels as tight or burns me when I have used my arm too much," she told him even as his touch made her tremble.

This time, she knew it was not from fear but pure desire.

"Marry me, dearest...say you will marry me and be mine forever," Tomás pleaded.

"You have not seen the worst of them."

He chuckled then cupped her face and stared into her eyes with such intensity, she thought he could see into her soul.

"Then show me, Gabrielle. Give me a reason to accept your denial of me," he said then kissed her.

This was a kiss like none of the others. This kiss lit a fire in her so bright she knew she could not deny him if he still wanted her after he saw her side. His kiss made her forget everything, her scars, and her fear, and instead had her leaning into him, her arms lifting to wrap around his broad shoulders while her fingers slid into his silky black hair. So surrendered was she to his kiss and the feel of his hard body pressing against her, she failed to notice his fingers had been busy at work untying the laces which held her skirt in place. A cool breeze from an open window touched the hot skin of her legs when the skirt fell to the floor. She gasped and broke the kiss.

"Show me, my love, and I shall show you what pains me much right now," Tomás said in a hoarse choked voice then led her hand to his crotch.

Under her hand, his cock was hard and pressing against the fabric of his britches. Thrilled at knowing she had inspired this lust even as he accepted her scars gave her the courage to reach for the bottom of her shift.

Tomás took a step back and sat on the edge of the bed. Having him watch her undress was strangely thrilling but she still could not look at him as the cloth came up her body then over her face. Cool air touched her hot skin and then she was naked in front of him.

She had not been naked before anyone since the nurses in the hospital bathed dead skin from her body. In truth, never had a man seen her naked in her entire life. Even when she used to swim in the pond near La Coeur de la Terre, she always left her shift on.

Now she trembled as if cold and feared opening her eyes lest she see the horror in his. The sound of something hitting the floor pulled them open. Tomás was looking at her even as he pulled his second boot off. His eyes never left her even when he stood and pulled off his blouse then quickly undid his britches and shoved them down his legs. When he stood upright again, he kicked them aside.

Gabrielle had watched his every movement mesmerized. She had seen him naked before but now his body glowed in the light of the lantern and his cock stood proud and eager. When she realized she was staring at it, she quickly lifted her eyes to meet his. Again, he surprised her. There was no expression of disgust. Not one of disappointment or offense. He was smiling. His eyes glowed with the love she now believed he had for her and her heart soared.

"Ask me again, my love," she said in a breathless whisper.

He pulled her against him. Their naked bodies came together in a manner, which felt completely natural and strangely comforting.

"You are my one and only, my love—my heart, Gabrielle," Tomás said staring into her eyes and capturing her heart tighter with each word. "Will you marry me?"

"Si, Capitán Alvarez, I will marry you," she said, the words barely escaping her lips before he captured her mouth in a kiss then lifted her into his arms.

A moment later, she was lying on the bed, on her back, and he was kissing her neck, her shoulders, her hands, her breasts, her belly, and he even traced his tongue across the scars on her side and down her thigh. She laughed because she was filled with such joy over his enthusiasm but when he kissed his way back up and stopped where her legs came together, she cried out.

"Tomás!"

He laughed and came forward to lean over her. He kissed her, deep and hard. His tongue danced with hers and sent tingles of excitement over her body which she felt clear down to her toes. The greatest amount of reaction came from that place between her legs.

"My sweet Gabrielle, I wish to know all of you. I wish to love all of you. You are beautiful, and you are equally beautiful in this place," he said as his fingers slid between her legs and drew an inhaled gasp from her. "If I must be patient, I shall be but I promise you, I shall taste every inch of your beautiful body."

Before she could argue his promise, he kissed her again. This time his fingers seemed to match the rhythm of his tongue to their actions between her legs and soon she was clinging to him and crying out against his mouth when a strange and wonderful sensation rushed over her. When he released her mouth, she had trouble catching her breath to speak and so could only whimper when his cock breached her maidenhead.

He had prepared her well so her pain was minimal and once more this man, who had a reputation as a pirate and at one time as a murderer, demonstrated how caring, considerate, and gentle he was. Tomás took his pleasure and although her inexperienced body had responded to his fingers, she was not disappointed it had failed to react in the same way to his body. It would come in time and she knew he would no doubt patiently help her along.

When he collapsed against her, his breathing hard and rough against her neck, she smiled. He moved just enough to relieve her of his weight but stayed close against her. She wrapped her arms around him and when her fingers touched the lines of scarring on his back, she pulled him closer.

"You honor me, Tomás. I have never been happier." She pressed a kiss against his mouth. "I love you...I love you so very much."

He smiled at her and smoothed damp hair from her cheek.

"I am the honored one, Gabrielle. I have always loved you. Perhaps now you shall believe how beautiful you are...and loved," he said closing his eyes and pulling her close so they lay cheek to cheek.

Gabrielle smiled. She seemed to float on a cloud of joy. She believed him. She felt beautiful and she knew she was loved.

Chapter Thirteen

Tomás woke in the morning and smiled when he saw Gabrielle curled up against his side. She had agreed to marry him. She had allowed him to see her scars and had willingly given herself to him. He knew he should have waited until the priest gave them the blessing but when he saw her standing before him so beautiful, so innocent and so open to him, he knew there was no going back.

Besides, he planned for them to be married as soon as possible so it was merely a formality. In the meantime, there was building to complete, repairs to be made, and he would have to send word to Cuddy so he might have time to bring his family here for the wedding. That was a piece of information he planned to withhold from Gabrielle until they arrived. He wished it to be a surprise. He knew it would greatly please her to have her adopted family in attendance for their wedding.

The evening had not gone exactly as he had planned but it ended well as far as he was concerned. He knew she would want a wedding dress and although he had not found the most perfect fabric for her to use in making one, he had bought her the finest fabric he could afford. He had hoped to present it to her after she accepted his proposal but after such a glorious night, today would do.

A quiet tapping came on his door and his thoughts immediately went to Felicity. She would be awake soon if not already. He slipped from the bed and pulled on his britches then quietly made it to the door and opened it. Felicity was standing in the hallway in her nightshirt. He slipped out and closed the door behind him.

"Sweetheart," he said, lifting her into his arms.

"I am hungry," she said, rubbing the sleep from her eyes. "Where is Mikaela?"

"I do not think she is back yet from helping Chloe have her baby?"

"Oh. I could not find Gabrielle either, Papa," she said hugging his neck. "I was scared."

"Aww, my sweet girl, you have no need. We are here," he said kissing her cheek as he carried her to the kitchen. "Gabrielle is sleeping still."

When he reached the kitchen, he set her on the edge of the table which sat in the middle of the room. It was used for chopping, biscuit making, and other such things as well as where Felicity would eat or just sit and watch Mikaela as the woman worked about the kitchen.

He pulled up a stool and sat down near her. He took her little hands in his.

"Felicity, what would you think about Gabrielle being your mother?"

"Mother? Oh, Papa! Yes. Is she to be my mama?"

"Yes, little one, she says she will marry me," he said with a smile and then laughed when Felicity threw herself into his arms and hugged him.

"I am so happy," she said with a squeal.

She pushed away and started to climb down. He stopped her.

"Where are you going?"

"To find Gabrielle—to find Mama," she exclaimed.

"I told you, she still sleeps. Let us wait until she wakes. I thought you were hungry?"

Felicity pushed her lower lip out in a pout and frowned at him. He had disappointed her in telling her she could not bother Gabrielle in her excitement. She had to learn she could not always have her way. The sound of the front door opening drew their attention and pulled the pout and frown from Felicity's face.

"Mikaela!"

This time when she squirmed to get down, he allowed her. He watched her run to Mikaela who held out her arms to the little girl. When she hugged her and buried her face in Felicity's neck, he saw her shoulders shake. Something was wrong.

"Why are you crying, Mikaela?" he heard Felicity ask.

"What has happened?" he asked as he walked toward them.

When he reached them, Mikaela lifted her head and looked at him. Tears were streaming down her cheeks.

"I lost them both," she said on a sob and stood up, her hands covering her face.

Tomás quickly moved to take her in his arms. He held her as she sobbed. He knew she meant she had lost both Chloe and her baby.

"I failed them. They are gone," she cried, and he heard a loud gasp from behind him.

He glanced over his shoulder to see Gabrielle standing in the archway with her hand to her mouth and tears filling her eyes. Felicity must have heard her as well because she broke away and ran to her.

Gabrielle caught her and hugged her tight. When her eyes met his gaze over the top of the little girl's head, she nodded.

"Felicity, how about you help me make breakfast for everyone," she said then steered his daughter toward the kitchen.

He led Mikaela to the settee and sat her down then joined her. She wiped her eyes with the backs of her hands then shook her head.

"It took too long. The baby kept trying to come the wrong way so I had to keep turning it around. When the little one finally came, the cord was tight around its little neck," Mikaela said with a great sob.

He held her as she cried some more. His own heart was breaking over the loss of such a tiny life. "And Chloe?"

Mikaela shook her head.

"It must have been too much for her. She was so tired. I had to pull the baby from her because she was too tired to push anymore. Once I freed the little one and realized he was gone, I checked on her. She was quiet. I thought maybe she just sleeping but no...she was gone also."

"I am so sorry, Mikaela, I am sure you did your best, my friend," he told her hugging her to him and allowing her to cry against his chest.

"Not good enough."

Tomás held her away and made her look at him.

"You are the best, Mikaela. Everyone here trusts you to do the best you can. Sometimes, things happen no one can change," he told her wishing his words would allow her to release the guilt she felt over the loss of Chloe and her baby son. "You are not to blame. If God has called them home, you could not stop them from going."

"Then God does not care, Tomás, because now two little ones have no mother and Rodrigo has no wife," she exclaimed, pushed away from him and stood. "I need to be alone."

Before he could respond, she hurried from the room. He dropped his head to his hands. Her words repeated in his head and he thought of the good men who had died when he had survived. His faith had always led him to believe God had a plan for each person, but he had to wonder what merciful god took babies and mothers.

"Tomás?"

He looked up when he heard Gabrielle say his name. He stood, suddenly feeling very tired. All the happiness he had felt upon waking was now shrouded in sadness. He walked to Gabrielle and pulled her into his arms.

"I know we had hoped to celebrate our engagement but sadly now, we must have a funeral first," he said stroking her hair as he held her against his chest with the thought of ever losing her squeezing his heart until he could hardly breathe.

She leaned away and looked up at him. He saw the grief in her eyes and wished he could spare her and Felicity all of the cruelties this world brought.

"So Chloe and the baby—"

"They did not make it."

Her eyes filled with tears and she pressed her cheek to his chest.

"I had hoped I had misunderstood," he heard her say her voice not much more than a harsh whisper then he felt her body tremble with quiet sobs.

Tomás had never questioned his faith, even when he nearly died, but now he had to wonder how a merciful protector of his children could allow a mother and child to die. Holding Gabrielle tight, he swore he would never lose her in such a cruel way. If it meant he would never touch her again in a manner which would get her with a child, then so be it.

~*~

The next day, the small community came together as a family to bury a young mother and her tiny son, and to celebrate her life and the life the little boy would never know. Tomás led Gabrielle to a clearing in the jungle. There was a small cemetery containing only a few roughly carved crosses bearing the names of those who had already passed from this world. The men had dug a single grave for the mother and child. It seemed only right they stayed together.

Gabrielle had gotten to know the young mother well enough to call her friend and the loss hit her as hard as it did the others. She did not know her husband, Rodrigo as well since he had been away with Tomás. To think he arrived home in time to see his son born, only to lose both, tore at her heart.

She watched Rodrigo as he followed the simple casket toward the place set for their final resting place. His two other children were far too young yet to understand what was happening. They only knew their mother had gone away with their new baby brother. She had asked Tomás what the man would do, and he said everyone in the village would assist him.

Looking around at the group gathered, she knew they would all do what they could to help ease the burden placed on him by the loss of his wife. Already, Tomás had reached out and the two little girls were at the house with Felicity and watched over by Mikaela. When Gabrielle asked Mikaela if she was attending the funeral, she shook her head and said she did not participate in such religious practices. She had not said anything more but simply went on with her work. When Gabrielle asked Tomás what she had meant, he simply said she had come from a different way of life.

Gabrielle had heard stories of the slaves practicing religious arts far different from the Christian traditions of the Catholic Church and had even suspected her own beloved friends, the La Rues, only attended church with the Hawkings family because it was expected of them. She suspected Mikaela would attend her friend's grave and celebrate in a different manner when she was ready. In the meantime, Gabrielle honored her friend by not discussing Chloe's death for she knew how she blamed her inability to save her. It mattered not how many times she or Tomás told her she did all she could, Mikaela did not wish to be absolved of the loss.

The ceremony was brief but poignant. The sky was blue and the air smelled sweet with blooming vines climbing the nearby trees. Several people spoke, including Tomás who told Rodrigo everyone would forever cherish his wife's memory and would always be here in support of him and his children because they were family. When he said this, several people responded with an *Amen*.

When Liam stepped up and sang a mournful tune she had never heard before but touched her heart, she began to cry. Tomás curled his arm around her shoulders and pulled her close while pulling a kerchief from his pocket and handing it to her. It was surprisingly fine and she felt guilty wiping her tears and nose on it.

When Liam was finished, he approached Rodrigo and the two men embraced. Liam then returned to stand with the others. It was then she noticed Maria was standing with him. A small smile teased her lips when she saw Maria slip her hand into Liam's. Had the girl finally taken things into her own hands and told Liam she was interested? She hoped so because Gabrielle suspected the Scot was as stubborn as his hair was red.

When the ceremony was over and the men lowered the box into ground, Rodrigo stepped forward and scooped up a handful of dirt. He whispered something in Spanish then tossed it into the grave. He then accepted a bouquet of flowers from one of the women, held it to his nose, and as he tossed them in, Gabrielle heard him speak the words, *te amo.* Knowing he had told Chloe he loved her, Gabrielle felt it straight to her heart like an arrow. Tomás must have as well, for he squeezed her tight against his side.

After Rodrigo stepped aside, each person took their turn scooping up dirt and tossing it into the hole. When it came time for her to do so, Gabrielle hesitated. She looked to Tomás and he nodded.

"If you do not wish to—"

"No, I-I do...I shall," she said then reached down and gathered a handful of dirt.

As she approached the edge of the hole, she wobbled a bit but Tomás was there. He grabbed her arm and steadied her as she tossed the dirt onto the box below. Then still holding her arm, he reached down and grabbed a handful of dirt and tossed it in.

"Go with God," he said in an almost whisper.

Her heart went out to him for he was as sorrowful as anyone. Perhaps he blamed himself for keeping Rodrigo away so long when he probably wanted to be home with his wife. She slipped her arm from his and wrapped it around his waist instead. She wanted him to know she was here to support him just as he was for her.

He looked down at her and gave her a small smile then he led her to stand and watch the others follow the same ritual. He never let go of her and she prayed he never would.

After everyone had taken their turn, the men who had dug the hole began filling it. It was then, the man everyone knew as Cook aboard La Bella Dama stepped forward and announced that the good ladies had prepared some fine food for all of them. Rodrigo nodded and shook the man's hand then waved everyone along back toward the village. When they arrived back where their homes sat, she discovered the women had indeed done what Cook had stated. Set on tables placed mostly in front of the house where she lived with Tomás, Felicity, and Mikaela was an assortment of foods, which would have made a holiday at La Coeur de la Terre look shabby in comparison.

When she announced she would see how she could help, Tomás stopped her. He turned her to face him and she worried he had changed his mind about marrying her and was about to tell her so. Nervous, she looked away.

"Dearest, I know this has been most upsetting to you," he began then rested a hand against her cheek and made her look at him. "Once all this sadness has passed, we shall give everyone our good news and soon these lovely ladies will prepare such a grand meal for our wedding celebration."

He still wants to marry me!

Gabrielle thought her heart was going to leap from her chest. She did not know what to say and began to stammer but his mouth captured hers and she relaxed. She leaned into him and cared not that they stood in the middle of all the activity, even when she heard a few catcalls from the men. She felt more than heard Tomás chuckle in response.

"I suspect more than a few already know what is happening between us," he said with his mouth less than an inch from hers then he kissed her again.

When he released her, she was breathless and wished they could escape the party which was growing before their eyes and go somewhere to be alone.

"Come, eat, and someone fetch the children," Tomás called out.

Just then the front door of his own house opened and Felicity hobbled toward them. Rodrigo's children ran to their father and Mikaela stood in the doorway. Gabrielle saw the sad expression on her face and went to her.

"Come, Mikaela, join us," she said taking the woman's hand.

"I would rather not," Mikaela said with a sigh. "But may I have a moment with you?"

"Of course." Gabrielle stepped inside into the foyer and Mikaela closed the door.

"Mikaela—" Gabrielle began wishing to comfort her friend, but suddenly Mikaela embraced her.

"Felicity told me the news," she said holding her away from her then embracing Gabrielle yet again. "I wish you to know I am so happy for you and Tomás. You have become a dear friend and I know you will be a good mother to Felicity."

"*We* will be good mothers to Felicity," Gabrielle said. "She loves you, Mikaela. You shall always be as much a mother to her."

"Perhaps, but she will not always need me," she said.

"Someday, she shall need neither of us, my friend," Gabrielle said with a laugh.

~*~

Tomás watched Gabrielle disappear inside with Mikaela and wondered if she might be able to cajole their friend into joining everyone at a time when the comfort of others was most needed.

Felicity hugged his leg and he smiled. He reached down and lifted her into his arms. Pressing a kiss to her cheek while she hugged his neck, he had never felt more grateful to have this precious child in his life. The only thing which might make his life more complete was having a child with Gabrielle. However, after what had happened to Chloe and her babe, he was rethinking the idea completely. Perhaps Felicity was enough for both of them.

The door to his house opened and Gabrielle emerged. She closed the door behind her and he knew without asking Mikaela was going to forego the festivities.

"Is she all right?" he asked her as Gabrielle approached.

"Yes, she simply prefers to be alone right now." When she was close enough, she lowered her voice so only he and Felicity might hear. "She wanted to wish me happiness on our engagement."

271

Felicity reached for her and Gabrielle hugged her.

"I hear your papa has already told you the news," she said to the little girl.

"Uh huh, and I am so happy," Felicity said with a big smile then hugged Gabrielle around the neck. "You are to be my mama."

Tomás chuckled and slipped the child's legs around Gabrielle's middle.

"I shall get us some of that roasted pig before it is picked clean," he said nodding in the direction of the pig on a spit.

"Good idea. We shall wait over here," she said and headed to a nearby section of the long table someone had put together where there were three empty chairs together.

As soon as he knew they were settled, Tomás managed to obtain three full plates of food and delights, including a large chunk of the delicious smelling pig. Liam and Maria joined them near the end of the table. He saw Gabrielle hug Maria, and then she pinched Liam's cheek making the man blush a bit.

As he set the plates on the table, Tomás asked what it was all about and Liam mumbled something. Gabrielle asked him to repeat it. When he did not, Maria announced with her head held high that she and Liam were courting. This announcement resulted in a round of applause from the gathering, a few toasts of congratulations, and some ribald comments from their sailor cohorts.

While Liam blushed and cursed them all, Maria smiled and Gabrielle laughed. Tomás knew he should be feeling sad but if ever there was proof upon the loss of loved ones that life continues, this was it. He felt blessed. His own future was bright with Gabrielle soon to be his wife, and his family coming together with sweet, darling Felicity who would be a daughter to both of them.

When someone mentioned their parties would never be the same without Chloe's delicious Syllabub and her decadent rum-soaked cakes, there was a moment of silence then Rodrigo raised his glass.

"May my beloved never want for anything ever more and may she dine on the finest of treats for she has taken the best with her," he said.

"Hear, hear," everyone said in unison and raised their glasses in a toast.

Tomás nearly choked on his rum when he heard Felicity ask Gabrielle a question, which drew everyone's attention. "When can I start calling you Mama?"

Gabrielle's eyes shot to him and when he glanced at his old friend, Liam, the man was staring at him with a lifted brow.

"Yes, Tomás, when can she start calling Gabrielle...Mama? Is there something we have not heard?" his old friend asked in a curious tone.

Then it came loud and clear from the innocent mouth of Felicity.

"Papa and Gabrielle are getting married, Uncle Liam. She is to be my new mama."

Liam broke into laughter.

"And what is so funny, Liam Campbell?" Gabrielle asked with a scowl while wielding the knife she had been using to cut up Felicity's food.

Liam nearly choked. "Nothing. Tis wonderful news...tis wonderful indeed."

Tomás stared at him.

"Damned right, tis wonderful, my friend," he said annoyed.

"So she said yes. Huzzah! Tis about time. When is the happy occasion?" Liam asked.

Gabrielle looked to Tomás with the same obvious question in her eyes.

"As soon as my beautiful bride to be can have her dress made," he answered with a smile.

"And what exactly am I going to use to make this dress, pray tell—palm fronds?" she asked.

"That was the second part of my surprise, my love," Tomás responded then lowered his voice to a whisper. "If you remember, we did not get that far."

Whether Liam heard it or simply gathered the connotation from his action did not matter for the man's laughter was enough to fill Gabrielle's cheeks with a red flush of heat.

"Liam Campbell, you have a dirty mind," she said and grabbed the rum-filled tankard Tomás was holding and took a long drink before coughing a bit.

When she handed it back, she swiped the back of her hand across her lips then laughed a bit. She shrugged. "I guess it is ridiculous to deny the truth, do you not think?" she asked him.

"Very true, my love," he said then stood. He leaned down and kissed her mouth before lifting his tankard. "May I take this opportunity to announce to all present, I have asked the beautiful, Gabrielle Hawkings to be my wife and she has consented."

A cheer went up and Rodrigo stood.

"My Chloe would be so happy for you, Tomás, for she always said you needed a good woman...and you have one in Gabrielle. May I be the first to offer my congratulations and best wishes," he said with a lift of his glass.

"Hear, hear," everyone cried out in unison and lifted their glass in a toast.

"Thank you, my friends, we are happy to share our good fortune with you and you are all invited to the wedding which shall be as soon as it can be sufficiently planned." He looked down into smiling blue eyes and after taking his seat, Tomás leaned in close and kissed Gabrielle again. There was no happier man than he.

Chapter Fourteen

Gabrielle smoothed the beautiful dark blue velvet fabric Tomás had surprised her with after proposing. His surprise gift for her upon his return from Jamaica was yards of blue velvet so dark, it was nearly black and yards of beautiful gold silk for her wedding dress. He said he did not know what was appropriate but when he saw the blue velvet he thought how beautiful it would look against her fair skin, golden hair, and how it would bring out her gorgeous blue eyes. Although it was not very traditional, she loved it all and was very excited about her dress.

Several of the women in the village were assisting her in creating her ensemble and she hoped to have it ready soon for Tomás had prepared everything for their wedding ceremony and celebration and it would commence in less than a week. She was anxious about her dress and nervous about the ceremony and celebration because it meant being the center of attention. Something she was far from comfortable with doing. She surprised the ladies by asking them to help her design a dress, which would leave her shoulders and arms bare. Mikaela had smiled and hugged her when she heard of the design.

"You are beginning to believe in your beauty, my dear friend," Mikaela had told her.

Gabrielle had smiled in response. Whether truly beautiful or not, she could not say but she knew her skin was looking so much better since using the salve. It was softer, less pink, and certainly smoother. She had Mikaela and her magic salve to thank for that but she had Tomás to thank for making her believe in his words.

They had not made love again since the night he proposed, but he assured her it was only because it was not proper for them to be together until their vows were spoken. She had worried he might have changed his mind and had hesitated in bringing it up but when he said he was going to travel back to Jamaica before the wedding, she worried he was getting cold feet.

"No, no, I am simply giving you the respect you deserve. I do not regret our night together, but I should not have taken advantage of you before we are wed," he explained to her.

She wrapped her arms around his waist and leaned in against him. Looking up at him, she smiled.

"I do not regret our night either and have wished to repeat it but if you prefer to wait until we are properly married, I shall accept your decision," she told him.

He grinned, threw his head back and laughed.

"You are making my decision quite difficult, my love," he said then cupped her face in his hands and kissed her. "I think time away to retrieve a priest to do the honors shall be a good thing for I do not think I can continue to resist you," he said then kissed her again.

Tomás had been gone now for over a week and she missed him terribly. She had made him promise to be safe and return as soon as the winds would allow. He promised he would be back sooner, but still he was not home. She knew not to worry but with the wedding planned and coming up soon, it would not bode well for the groom not to be there.

After spending the last hour with two of the women working on her dress, fitting it, pinning, and adjusting the cloth, and having to stand still she needed some peace and quiet. Gabrielle decided to stroll through the jungle which abutted the property where she lived with Tomás and pick some flowers. As she strolled along, she smiled at the beautiful birds singing their songs and flying about displaying their colorful plumage. Her pick of flowers was extensive and as she perused the lovely blossoms, she mentally decided on which ones she would like for her wedding.

The sound of the waterfall became more noticeable and she suddenly realized how far from the house she was. She had promised Tomás a long time ago, she would never come here alone or even with Felicity. She peeked out at the lovely pool of water and reveled in the freshness of the air around the waterfall.

"Well, what do we have here?" a gruff male voice said from nearby and when she turned toward the sound, she came face to face with a partially toothless grin surrounded by a dirty dark beard with a scar cutting through it similar to the one Cuddy had.

Gabrielle dropped her flowers and turned to run but the man caught her by the waist and lifted her into the air. She screamed and kicked hoping to make him release her but he held firm to her. He spun her around and laughed when she pressed her hands against his shoulders and kicked her feet at his legs.

"Leave me be. You have no right," she screamed at him.

"Oh, I have the right to do whatever I wants to do, and I be wantin' you," the man hissed and proceeded to try to kiss her.

His breath was as rotten as his teeth and she nearly gagged. She pushed and kicked moving her head in all directions to evade his mouth. When he dropped her against his body and grabbed the back of her head, his hands clasping her hair tight in his fingers, she screamed in pain.

"Please stop! Please, leave me be," she screamed at him.

Suddenly, the man's hold on her weakened enough she gave one good shove so she fell backward onto the ground. When she scrambled to her feet it was to discover the man was standing very still with his hands up and away from his body. Standing behind him was Tomás, his sword pointing directly between the man's shoulder blades.

"Tomás!" She wanted to run to him and throw her arms around him but she knew it was not the best time. "This man...he—"

"I know, dearest, I know. Are you all right?" Tomás asked.

Gabrielle nodded and smoothed her skirt. She was wearing a top she had made from some fabric Mikaela had given her and although any other woman would have worn the drawstring neckline with more slack, she wore hers tied so the blouse clung to her shoulders. The tie had come loose and now her blouse hung off of one shoulder. Feeling a blush rush to her cheeks when Tomás noticed and smiled, she did not like this ugly man seeing her this way. She tugged up the blouse and tied it tight.

"Turn around, bastard, we do not appreciate strangers coming to our island and molesting our women," Tomás said to the man and to prove his point, dug the tip of the sword into the man's back enough to make him flinch.

"Son of a bitch, if you did not have that sword, I would throttle you," the man growled and spit.

"Turn around," Tomás ordered him.

The man slowly turned to face Tomás and when he did, Gabrielle heard her fiancé gasp on a loud inhalation. The expression of surprise on his face caught her attention.

"Do you know this man, Tomás?" she asked.

"Gabrielle, I wish you to return to the house. I have a matter—a very private matter to discuss with this man." He glanced at her, his expression dark and for the first time ever, she saw such anger it scared her.

"Is this the man you have sought all these years?" she asked with a rush of fear racing down her spine.

"Gabrielle, please go to the house—now," Tomás said in a voice which told her he was not going to ask again.

"Do you wish another murder charge on your head, Tomás?" she pleaded.

"Who the bloody hell are you?" the man with the scar growled at Tomás.

In reaction, Tomás pushed the tip of his sword against the man's chest.

"Unless you wish another scar like the one on your face across your neck, you shall watch your tongue," he hissed in an angry tone she had never heard from him before.

"Gabrielle, please—leave," he growled at her in a low voice of warning. "Now!"

She flinched when he roared at her but now she was angry with him.

"I will go but if you kill this man, you shall never see me again," Gabrielle said in anger then turned and hurried through the brush.

She needed to find Liam. He might be able to stop Tomás. The thought of him killing the man, no matter what he had done to him in the past, was more than she could imagine. She knew what this man had done, and it was unforgivable but for Tomás to kill him would unforgivable for her.

Out of breath and scared, she finally reached the house. Calling out to Mikaela, she rushed to the back porch. The door opened. She expected to see Mikaela but instead, it was her dearest friend, Cuddy. She threw herself into his arms and cried.

"He will kill him. Someone has to stop him," she exclaimed through sobs.

"Who?"

"Tomás?"

"Someone is going to kill Tomás?" Cuddy asked his expression growing dark.

"What is happening?" The question came from Liam.

"Oh, Liam, that man...the one with the scar—" She pointed to the path leading to the waterfall. "He is here. He...oh, Liam, I think Tomás is going to kill him."

Liam took off running toward the jungle while Cuddy held her by her arms.

"Tis all right, girl, we shall take care of this. I will not allow him to harm himself if it hurts you," he told her. "Stay here."

He gave her a quick kiss on the forehead and ran down the steps and across the lawn.

"So much excitement here...I thought we were just coming for a wedding," a familiar voice said from behind her.

She turned to face the woman who had been so dear to her.

"Siobhan," Gabrielle exclaimed with half joy and half anxiety then found comfort in the woman's arms as well as those of Sara and Fiona.

~*~

If the sound of someone crashing through the brush was meant to distract him, it was not going to work. Tomás finally had his prey before him and he was enjoying seeing the man sweat as he kept him pressed against a tree with his sword tip at his throat.

"Tomás," he heard Liam say in a tone he knew was meant to calm him. "I know you want this man's blood but do you wish to once more be wanted for murder and because of this man, of all people?"

"He is right, Tomás, think of Gabrielle, of your family," Cuddy said breathlessly as he came to a halt alongside Liam.

"Who the bloody hell—" The man began but when the sword tip nicked his skin, he shut his mouth.

"You wish to know who I am—" Tomás began through gritted teeth, his anger making his words catch in his throat. "You probably do not remember whipping a young man nearly to death because he would not answer your questions. The reason being he could not answer because he did not understand your words yet you kept on and on until his back was shredded, bloody, and raw."

Tomás lifted the sword so it pressed harder against the man's neck and both Liam and Cuddy gasped and took a tentative step forward.

"I have sought to find your despicable hide since you left us on an island to heal or die," he told the man. "Tis true, I wish to kill you."

"Wait—" The man lifted his hands slowly. "I was only doing what was ordered of me," he groaned, real fear showing on his ugly face.

Liam started laughing then he nudged Cuddy and pointed to the man's lower body. Cuddy chuckled and then he was also laughing aloud.

"Tomás, this coward is not worth you losing everything. He is so afraid, he has pissed himself," Liam said between guffaws.

Tomás glanced down. His anger suddenly replaced by pure satisfaction. He grinned then chuckled. When his gaze returned to the man's face, he noted how his skin had become even whiter against the filthy beard he wore. The man was a coward. Only a coward would hide behind orders and attack lone women. He relaxed his sword arm but did not lower the blade. He still owed the man for the scars on his back.

"You are right. I am about to marry my beloved, my one and only. I have a family, a good life, and good friends. Killing a piece of scum like you is not worth wearing the hangman's noose," he said and he visibly saw the man relax. "However, it does not mean I do not owe you."

With a quick snap of his sword arm, he flicked the tip of the blade across the man's cheek opposite the one where it bore a scar and split the skin from just alongside his eye down to his mouth. The man screamed in pain and sunk to the ground holding his face.

"We shall call it even now, you gutless coward," Tomás said as he stepped back. "If you ever come near any of our women or homes again, I shall not hesitate to slit your throat next time. Now get out of here."

The man did not hesitate. He stumbled to his feet then hurried toward the waterfall, slipping along the embankment and a few minutes later, they heard a splash and cursing.

The three men laughed and Cuddy and Liam slapped Tomás on the back.

"Good job, son," Cuddy said with a laugh and shook his hand.

Liam embraced Tomás then slapped him alongside his head. "What the hell were you thinking?"

"He attacked Gabrielle and when I saw who it was, I just wished to take my revenge," Tomás admitted.

"He attacked Gabrielle," Cuddy roared. "Give me the damn sword...I shall end his miserable life myself."

Now it was Tomás and Liam's turn to keep the older man from ending up at the end of a hangman's noose. Before long, the three men were laughing again.

"This is a really beautiful place here," Cuddy said peering out at the pool of glistening water and the falls feeding it.

"Yes, tis why I planned our ceremony here," Tomás said with a prideful grin.

"Well done, my boy, well done," Cuddy said slapping him on the back and nearly causing him to lose his footing.

"I suppose my plan to surprise Gabrielle with her family has now gone astray," Tomás said with a frown.

"I would say so," Liam said with a guffaw and gave Tomás a playful shove. "What do you say we go ease the lass's worry, eh?"

"Yes, no better idea, my friend," Tomás exclaimed. "I have not even kissed her hello yet."

The three men laughed and joked about the coward with the scar pissing his britches as they walked back to the house. When they emerged into the open lawn area, Tomás heard Gabrielle call his name. He stopped, handed

Liam his sword, and caught her in his arms when she ran across the open space to him.

"I love you, Tomás. I did not mean it when I said you would never see me again. I could never abandon you," she exclaimed through tears. "But please, tell me you did not kill him."

He kissed her long and hard then smiled at her.

"I did not kill him," he said gazing into her wet blue eyes. "However, he shall forever remember our encounter."

"In more ways than one," Cuddy exclaimed with a loud guffaw.

Gabrielle looked at them all with a puzzled expression.

"I shall tell you all later, right now I only wish to know what you think of my surprise," Tomás asked her.

"I love it," she said with a big smile. "Having my adopted family here is the best gift ever. I love you even more for doing this wonderful thing. Now our wedding shall be perfect."

For the first time in many years, Tomás felt truly free, free of his anger, his hate, the memory of that time, and free to embrace the future with his beloved, Gabrielle, and his family. His wish now was to give his bride a perfect wedding.

~*~

And perfect it was. When the day came, it arrived with beautiful blue skies, a gentle breeze, and more anxiety than Gabrielle ever thought she could feel. As she stood before a looking glass in the room she would be sharing with Tomás from this night forward, she was rethinking her decision to wear a dress, which left her shoulders and arms bare.

"You are so beautiful, my sweet Gabrielle," Siobhan said from behind her.

Gabrielle turned to face her with a grimace.

"I fear everyone seeing my scars. I should have made a dress with long sleeves and a high neck. I shall embarrass Tomás," she said with tears filling her eyes.

"Tomás would never be embarrassed and you do look very beautiful," Mikaela said as she swept into the room carrying a lovely bouquet of flowers she had obviously just gathered from the jungle. "He loves you, my friend. He loves you more than I have known him to love anyone and I assure you, he would strike down anyone who ever criticized you."

"But—"

"But nothing, he shall be so pleased with what you did with the wonderful fabric he brought you," she said setting down the flowers and coming to stand before her.

Mikaela took Gabrielle's hands in hers and smiled.

"You only see the scars, my dear Gabrielle, he only sees you as do I, as does Felicity, and all of our other friends—beautiful," she said squeezing her hands gently. "Look at how much smoother and softer your skin is now."

Mikaela turned her to face the mirror again, and then gently traced her fingers across the scars. Gabrielle had to admit they were not as prominent as before and since she was careful not to allow her skin too much sun, the tissue was nearly the same shade as the rest of her skin.

"Tis true, Mikaela, your magic salve has worked wonders but I still fear—"

"Then you shall wear this about your shoulders," Siobhan said holding up a piece of rich dark burgundy satin edged with delicate lace, which although it did not match her dress with its rich dark blue velvet bodice and skirt covered in ruffles of gold brocaded silk, was beautiful. "I wore this as a veil the day I married Cuddy and so I brought it just in case you wished to wear it too."

"Oh, Siobhan, tis truly beautiful," Gabrielle exclaimed. "I would be honored."

She accepted the cloth, draped it up and over her long blond hair which she wore loose down her back with only the sides pinned up and turned to face the mirror. The beautiful shawl hung down over her arms and covered her neck.

"I believe I shall feel much more at ease like this," she said and smiled.

In the reflection, she noted how Siobhan and Mikaela looked at each other and shrugged.

"I know it would probably be better draped as a shawl but I am not ready to bare my flaws to everyone quite yet," Gabrielle said.

"Honey," Siobhan said stepping forward and hugging her against her side as they gazed into the mirror at each other. "You could be wearing a burlap sack and that man would still see an angel before him. Never have I seen a man more in love."

"She speaks the truth, my friend," Mikaela said with a laugh and picked up the flowers. "If you are ready, your man is probably wondering if you ran away."

Gabrielle turned and accepted the flowers thinking of the many times she thought of running away. "I am so very ready and I will never run away."

With Mikaela and Siobhan at her sides, she walked along the path leading to the lovely swimming hole and waterfall. Excited yet nervous, Gabrielle could only think of Tomás waiting for her there. Today was her wedding day. She was marrying the most handsome and generous of men, a man with a heart as big as the Caribbean and she only hoped she could be the best wife to him.

When they came into the open, her eyes went directly to him. Tomás looked so handsome, so eager, his expression made her heart flutter. He stood at the water's edge dressed in black britches, black boots, a white silk blouse, and a burgundy sash at his waist which looked very similar to the shawl she wore as a veil.

She glanced about at the gathering of people, all familiar to her for they were the members of their village. Liam and Maria stood alongside Tomás with Felicity smiling and bouncing on her heels with excitement. Cuddy stood across from Tomás and stepped forward to take her arm. Siobhan and Mikaela moved to stand alongside the priest who had come from Jamaica to give them the blessing of marriage.

"You look beautiful, Gabrielle," Cuddy said near her ear before pressing a kiss to her cheek. "I am honored to give you in marriage to this man."

"Thank you, Cuddy. Since my father and brother are not here, I can think of no better man than you to do the job." She smiled up at him.

"Then let us get this done," he said with a grin then turned to face the priest and Tomás.

When the priest asked who gave her in marriage, Cuddy told the crowd in a loud booming voice that he did making everyone laugh. He then placed her hand in her groom's and stepped to stand next to Siobhan who he gathered against his side with his arm.

"You look wonderful, my love, so beautiful," Tomás said smiling.

Gabrielle felt heat rush to her cheeks and started to tuck her chin but he caught it with his fingers and lifted. When her gaze met his and she saw the love there, she stood proud and smiled. It was then she made a decision. She took hold of the lovely cloth acting as a veil and dropped it down to rest lazily on her shoulders. She noted how his eyes widened when he saw her bare shoulders and neck but instead of being horrified, Tomás smiled.

She heard gasps from those gathered to watch and started to draw the shawl back up but then she heard the whispers—*so beautiful...she is so lovely...what a beautiful dress...Tomás is a lucky man*—and she relaxed.

"Gabrielle, you are more beautiful than you know. I was right to pick this dark blue for it so compliments your eyes, the water behind us shall be green with envy," Tomás said and she truly believed him.

Smiling, she turned to the priest and the man began the ceremony joining them in the marriage. It seemed to happen so fast the next thing she was truly aware of was hearing the man tell Tomás he may kiss his bride.

Tis me. I am his bride.

She looked up at Tomás and he was beaming. He cupped her face in his hands and lowered his mouth to hers. She completely forgot all of their guests as his kiss carried her away to a place where only the two of them existed. When he finally broke off the kiss, he kissed her again then scooped her into his arms. Gabrielle laughed and totally forgot about her scars or anything else because she was his wife now and Tomás believed her beautiful, and so she was.

"Let the celebration begin," Liam hollered and everyone cheered.

And celebrate they did. There was plenty of food, drink, music, laughter, and she left her shoulders bare and did not tuck her chin once the rest of the day. The expression of love in the eyes of her adopted family, her friends and most of all, in the eyes of her husband told her all she needed to know. None of them cared about her scars for they each carried their share, whether external or internal. They only accepted her for who she was and they loved her.

As the party began to wear down and the sun began to set beyond the trees, she leaned against Tomás and smiled. Felicity was on his lap and the little girl's eyelids were growing heavy. Suddenly, Maria gave out a squeal and threw her arms around Liam's neck. This drew everyone's attention including Felicity's who sat up with a start.

"What is happening, Liam?" Tomás asked then winked at her as if he knew something.

Liam stood, a bit wobbly from a day of drinking rum. He lifted his cup so everyone else did so also. "Today, I watched my best friend marry his one and only—he told me she was just that the first time he met her." He gave a big wink in their direction.

Gabrielle smiled at Tomás then pressed a kiss to his beautiful mouth.

"Well, I figured if it was good enough for him...it was good enough for me," Liam said, swaying slightly. "So I just asked this lovely lady—" He looked down at Maria. "If she would do me the honor of becoming my wife—"

"And I said, yes," Maria exclaimed jumping to her to feet.

While everyone cheered and toasted their good wishes, Liam pulled Maria into his arms and kissed her like there was no tomorrow. When they came up for air, Liam grinned like a man in love, and then promptly passed out hitting the ground like a dead body. Everyone laughed, including Gabrielle and Tomás while Maria attempted to wake him.

Tomás stood, shifted Felicity to her lap and moved around to where his friend lay on the ground.

"Best wishes to you both, Maria," Tomás said giving her a hug. "We shall make sure he gets to bed."

Maria came to her feet and shrugged. "I just hope he remembers his proposal in the morning."

Everyone laughed. Tomás motioned to a couple of the men. They stood, rounded the table, and lifted Liam then carried him to where Maria directed. Still laughing, Tomás returned to stand by his seat.

"I think this little one is ready for sleep," Gabrielle said of Felicity who had fallen asleep against her chest.

Tomás nodded. "I hope you are ready for bed as well...but not for sleep. Tis been a very long wait," he whispered near her ear then lifted his sleeping daughter and cradling her in his arms.

She felt the heat of a blush fill her cheeks. *The wedding night.*

She had been disappointed when Tomás told her he was going to honor her by not visiting her bed until they were properly wed but now the night was here, and suddenly she was as nervous as a virgin should be on her wedding night. Gabrielle wasn't a virgin but it had only been that one time with Tomás and now nervous energy had taken hold of her and she only hoped he did not regret his decision to marry her.

Carrying Felicity, he waited as she stood. Mikaela stood and joined them. Together, as a family, they entered their home to the cheers and good wishes of their friends. Mikaela took Felicity from his arms and wishing them well, she disappeared into their part of the house.

The foyer was nearly dark except for a bit of light coming from a lantern hanging in the center of the kitchen. Gabrielle was not sure what to do. Did she head for his bedroom and disrobe? Did she wait to see what he wished her to do? Suddenly, he was there in front of her, his hands on her bare shoulders which sent shivers of nervous delight over her skin. She could not help the tremble which rushed over her.

"My love," he said drawing her shawl up around her. He pressed a kiss to her lips then lifted her hand to his mouth. "Give me but a moment to make things ready then I shall return."

He kissed her hand and disappeared through the doorway leading into the dark hallway leading to his bedroom.

"Make things ready," she whispered to the darkness and smiled.

Suddenly, her excitement changed from nervous to eager. She wondered what he was doing and what he had planned. She thought back over the day and hugged her arms around her middle, smiling. Her wedding day could not have been more perfect. Well, it could have, and would have, had her brother been there to give her away but Gabrielle appreciated Cuddy doing the honors. Still, she could not help but wish Beau had been here to do the job.

A chill washed over her as if something terrible had just happened and her thoughts went to Beau. Where was he? Was he alive or had he died on one of his many journeys? A tear swelled in her eye and it slid down her cheek before she could stop it.

"Tears, Gabrielle, you do not regret marrying me, do you?" Tomás asked as he returned taking her in his arms.

"Heavens no! I shall never regret marrying you, my love. This was all so perfect but I was...I was thinking of my brother. I only wish—"

"You wish he was here. I know. I left word at the taverns in Kingston with the hope he would come before today."

"What?"

"Yes, I thought it was worth the effort. If he came to Kingston and visited any of the taverns, someone would surely recognize him and tell him where to find you," Tomás said.

"Oh, Tomás, doing so has given me so much hope I may see him again someday. Thank you, tis the best gift you could ever give me," Gabrielle said pulling his head down and kissing him.

Chapter Fifteen

Had Tomás known how much it would please her to know he had left word of her whereabouts for her brother, he would have told her about it when he first returned from Kingston. Of course, whether or not he was even alive was an unknown and he did not wish to burden Gabrielle with such a thought. Instead, he allowed her happiness at the thought of someday seeing her brother again.

"Come, my love," he said, taking her hand in his and leading her through the darkening hallways to stop before his bedroom door.

"You are my angel, Gabrielle, my one and only love. Tonight, we start our life together. I promise to honor all of my vows to you but I also promise to always think of you first, keep you safe, and if a time ever comes I must sacrifice myself for your well-being, I shall do so."

"Oh Tomás, do not speak of such things," she said placing her hand along his cheek. "I wish to believe such things shall never happen and we will always be together."

He placed his hand over hers and turned his head to press a kiss against her palm. He nodded. He knew life was never what anyone expected but he would do his best to keep his promises to her. She was the most important person in his life.

Tomás opened the door and stepped aside so she might enter. When he heard her quiet gasp, he knew she appreciated what he had done. Candles flickered with light from around the room. There was a tray holding a bottle of wine and two glasses on the table beside the bed. Fresh flowers set in vases filled the room with a sweet fragrance and on the bed was a package tied with a ribbon. He watched her walk to the bed, pick it up and turning, he saw her face beaming with a big smile.

"Is this for me?"

"But of course, my love."

"Tomás, you have already given me so very much," she said, her eyes becoming moist so they glittered in the candlelight.

"Ah, but you could say this is for both of us," he said coming to stand alongside her. "Open it, Gabrielle."

Without hesitation, she untied the ribbon and opened the cloth wrapping.

"Oh my," she exclaimed as she pulled the elaborate lace from the package.

When she held it up, he grinned with pride. It was a dressing gown made of pure ivory lace infused with gold thread. When she clutched it to her bosom and looked up, her blue eyes glistened wet with tears.

"Tis too much, Tomás, this must have cost a small fortune," she said. "I have never had anything so beautiful."

"It pales in comparison to your beauty, Gabrielle," he said, cupping her face.

He kissed her then, the lace all but forgotten. She wrapped her arms around his neck and pressed into him. She kissed him in return, the way he had taught her with her tongue exploring his mouth and filling him with a desire greater than any he ever thought possible. His hands slid along her bare shoulders and down her back to quickly unlace the back of her bodice. He wanted to claim what was now his and only his, and as soon as possible.

Gabrielle pushed away and with a breathless whisper, she said, "Wait."

Tomás started to object but she hurried away behind the dressing screen in the corner. Not wishing to waste another moment with clothing, he untied the sash at his waist, pulled his blouse off over his head and tossed it into a nearby chair. He took a seat on the edge of the bed and pulled off his boots. He stood and was about to shuck his britches when she reappeared from around the screen.

His wife was vision standing in the candlelit room wearing nothing but the lace dressing gown. It was sheer so he could see the warmth of her skin through the lace. The gold threads enhanced that blush of pink and her hair, loose now, glowed in a golden halo around her which paled the threads in comparison.

"I imagine this is meant to be worn over a sleeping gown but I suspect this is the part which is your gift," she said in a breathless tone. "Am I right to present it this way?"

Tomás started to speak but his throat did not wish to cooperate. He had to clear his throat for she had taken his breath away. He nodded rounding the bed.

"You are my greatest gift, Gabrielle," he said meeting her halfway. "The gown is simply wrapping. I am honored to be the one to unwrap you."

She smiled up at him.

"I love you, Tomás. You are *my* everything," she said, her voice not much more than a whisper.

He scooped her into his arms and carried her to the bed. Setting her down on her feet, he pulled open the single tie holding the gown closed. Spreading the lace open, he feasted on the sight before him. High firm breasts above a narrowing waist greeted his eyes. Her pink nipples were already eagerly awaiting his mouth and he did not disappoint them. Taking a seat on the bed, he pulled her to him, his mouth capturing an erect pink tip and stroking his tongue around it. When she moaned her delight, he sucked it in and caressed it until she threaded her fingers through his hair and pulled him closer. Not wishing the other one to be jealous, he released the sweet morsel and captured the other which had been waiting with eagerness. Her moans deepened and he felt her fingers pull the leather tie from his long hair. She slid her fingers down the length of his hair grazing his bare skin and sending shivers of delight over him which in turn made his cock more eager, straining harder against his britches.

He wanted her. He wanted her more than he had ever wanted any woman but he remembered how she had been a virgin and completely inexperienced the first time so he wanted to take things slow for her. He wanted this night to be everything positive for it was the beginning of the rest of their life together.

Lifting his head, he gazed into her beautiful face. She smiled down at him.

Her hands came to his face and cupped his cheeks then she leaned in and kissed him. It was a sweet, tentative kiss but full of love and he desired it. He desired her.

Tomás led one of her hands down his chest, her fingers trailing gently along his skin and when her fingertips grazed his abdomen, he sucked in his breath. Her eyes widened as if suddenly struck with the power her touch had over him. He smiled at her.

"My body craves your touch, Gabrielle," he said, his voice sounding hoarse to his ears. "It wants more."

His hand led hers to his crotch. When her hand covered the hard bulge there, her eyes widened even more. She gave a small moan and her gaze dropped to his lap.

"You see how your touch affects me, my beauty," he said. "I am yours to explore."

As if his words gave her permission to do something she had only fantasized about doing, Gabrielle's lips turned up in a sly smile and her hand began to move on him, caressing him through his britches. He groaned in reaction to her touch and closed his eyes trying not to give in to the sensations and embarrass himself. When her other hand traced down his chest to a hard nipple and her fingertip encircled and teased the nub, he nearly lost control. Grabbing both of her hands and bringing them to his lips, he took deep breaths trying to push back his desire for release.

"Did I do something wrong, my love?" she asked with such innocence, he nearly laughed but did not for then she would think she had.

"No. No, your touch is everything right," he said. "My willpower is just not strong enough to resist it, tis all. Come."

Tomás stood. He turned her and slowly slid the lace gown from her shoulders then draped it across the chair where his blouse had landed. When he turned back to face her, she had tucked her chin and wrapped her arms around her mid-section. He knew she was still self-conscious of the scars marring the surface of her beautiful skin along her right side down along her hip and thigh nearly to her knee. He took her into his arms, lifted her, and laid her on the bed among flower petals sprinkled across the covers.

"These petals shall shrivel and hide because they cannot compare their beauty to yours, my love," he said pressing a kiss to her lips.

His words made her smile and that pleased him. He stood back and slowly undid his britches. Her eyes watched him and when he pushed them down his legs, she leaned on one elbow as if eager to see what he uncovered. This pleased him nearly to orgasm. She wanted him.

He kicked away his britches and stood tall. Her eyes widened and he knew she was looking at his proud cock, which was eager to encounter her and please her. Leaning forward, she

301

reached out a hand and caressed his length. He had to grit his teeth to keep from coming in her hand. He gave her a moment then clasped her hand in his, and kneeling on the bed, Tomás leaned over her.

~*~

Gabrielle had stared in awe at the way Tomás looked standing there before her, naked and fully aroused. She had thought him the most beautiful creature she had ever seen when she saw him emerge from the water that day long ago, naked and wet but now, she thought him a rival to the gods of myth. When they had been together before, she had not known his body other than how he felt inside her but seeing him, touching him, it was all so much she was both scared and exhilarated at the same time. Had her body truly accommodated him when he had made love to her before? His cock was both beautiful and terrifying. How had he not ripped her apart when she had been a virgin?

When he leaned over, she rolled to her back expecting it to be as it was the first time—without any pain this time, so she hoped. But he looked down at her, smiled then climbed over her to lie on his side facing her. She rolled until she was facing him.

"Tell me what you are thinking, dearest," he said to her and his words surprised her.

She felt heat engulf her cheeks and so she lowered her eyes but found them looking at his chest, his erect nipples, and a trail of dark hair which led to that which fascinated her. She closed her eyes.

"I suppose I am a bit frightened."

Her eyes flew open and she glared at him when he laughed.

"Gabrielle, you have nothing to fear from me. I shall never cause you harm or injury," he said with a smile.

"Tis just...you...I had no idea you were so...large," she said hesitantly, and her embarrassment was enough for a hot flush to fill her face again and make her look away.

Tomás tucked a long finger beneath her chin and forced her to look at him. He was not laughing but his eyes were gentle and his mouth soft.

"Your body accepted me before, it shall again. You have nothing to fear. In truth, my beautiful wife, I plan to give you more than myself this night."

Her eyes widened and she glanced around.

"There is no one here but us," she said.

He laughed again and pulled her on top of him.

"I do not mean to share you—ever," he said, his chuckle bouncing her as she lay on his chest. "I mean I plan to give you such pleasure you shall never fear my body or think making love with you shall ever cause you any pain."

"Oh," she said feeling foolish for thinking he meant another person was to join them.

She had seen such things when she worked in the tavern back in New Orleans, quite often two women servicing one man and so had thought he had meant something like it for them.

Suddenly, he rolled her onto her back and half leaned on her. He kissed her and when his tongue entered her mouth, she tasted him and tangled her tongue with his. She knew he liked this, and she had grown to appreciate the effect it had on her body as well. When he kissed so, it left her breathless and wanting more. She wasn't quite sure what the more was but she remembered feeling as if she had been pulled from her body then dropped back in it when he caressed her between her thighs the last time they were together. Perhaps he would do the same this time.

She was just about to suggest it when he broke the kiss and slid his lips along her jaw to her neck. While his lips caressed her neck sending delicious shivers down over her skin, making her moan and tangle her hands in his long silky hair, his hands slid over her breast and teased a hard nipple. When he gently pinched it between his thumb and forefinger, she nearly shot up off the bed.

"Did I hurt you?" he asked looking at her with a frown.

Breathless, she shook her head and he smiled.

"Good." He gently pinched it again and she groaned because she liked it.

This time she realized it had not been her body which nearly shot off the bed but her hips pushing upwards as if seeking something. When his lips replaced his fingers and his hand slid down over her belly gently caressing the skin and teasing her by passing over the place at the top of her thighs to trace down her thigh and then slowly, gently, and enticingly move up the inside of her leg, she involuntarily moaned in reaction.

"Tomás, please," she urged, her voice barely a whisper, her legs falling open in invitation, and her fingers pulling gently on his hair.

"Your wish is my command, my love," he whispered then he surprised her by spreading her legs further and tracing his fingers across that sensitive place between her legs.

She moaned, sighed and closed her eyes. He said he was going to give her pleasure. She smiled and hoped she experienced the same thing as last time. When suddenly, she felt his tongue where his fingers had been, she nearly sat up. She grabbed his hair and tugged to remove his head from between her legs.

"Tomás...no...what are you doing?" she exclaimed and tried to close her legs.

He lifted his head. He was smiling and he chuckled.

"Gabrielle, my love, I told you I was going to give you so much more," he said. "Trust me, please. You shall like this very much."

"I-I—"

"Trust me," he said and placed a hand on her belly and gently pushed her back so she lay against the pillows.

Gabrielle did as he wished but she could not relax. When he returned to his administrations, she was wholly conscious of his being between her legs. At first, he did not do much but kiss her inner thighs and tease her with his fingers but then his tongue hit a spot which drew a loud gasp from her and reflexively forced her hips upward to press against his mouth.

Whatever he was doing was brilliant and she wanted more.

This time when she clasped his head and tangled her fingers in his long hair which was now spread across her white thighs as well as his broad back, she wanted to hold his head there rather than remove it. The sensations that coursed over her body were intense, thrilling, breath-stealing, and when her body seemed to feel again as if it was being pulled from her body, she gave in to the feeling and again experienced something she could not put a name to but wished it would go on forever.

As she lay breathless, feeling unable to move as if her body had exploded in a delicious heat, after being engulfed in sensation and an unexplainable pleasure, Tomás crawled up and over her. He looked down at her and all she could do was smile at him. He chuckled and lay down next to her.

"You liked that, did you not?" he asked and all she could do was nod. "Good. Someday, I shall teach you how to pleasure me in the same way."

Gabrielle was not sure what he meant for he was made different from her but if she could give him the kind of pleasure she had just experienced, she was more than happy to learn.

She turned to face him and once more traced her fingers down his chest. When she reached his belly and he sucked in his breath, she felt bolder this time, more confident in knowing what he might like. Without hesitating, her hand slid down and clasped his hard cock in her palm. It was hot, soft yet hard, and when it twitched in her hand, she smiled. It was a powerful feeling to know her inexperienced touch could create such a reaction. It seemed to swell more as she stroked it and when she glanced up at Tomás, his eyes were closed and his lips parted. She was giving him pleasure.

It was then she thought of what he said about teaching her to give him pleasure in the same way he had her. Had he meant with her mouth? She recalled seeing the women in the tavern seeming to suck on men's cocks. She looked down at his cock in her hand. There was a glistening drop of moisture beaded at the tip. She leaned down and licked the drop away. Tomás groaned loudly and jerked in response.

"Gabrielle, please...I am having a hard enough time controlling my body," he exclaimed and pulled her up and away from hips. "Do you wish this to be over before we even get started?"

"I only wished to—" She had not meant to offend him.

"I know. I know...tis all right, my love...I want you to want to do so and more, but not now," he said with a chuckle.

"So tis something you wish me to do?" she asked touching his lips with her fingertips. "I feared I had offended you."

"Offend me? My dearest, you honor me," he said smoothing damp hair back from her face then kissed her.

His mouth still tasted of her body and although strange, she liked it. She kissed him and pushed him to his back. She straddled his hips with her legs. She wished to look at him. Surprising her, he did not object. Instead, he relaxed into the pillows and put his hands behind his head. Smiling at her, he seemed to be enjoying the view she presented him as well. She had not thought of how her body would be exposed to him in this position but she liked that it pleased him.

She ran her hands over his chest, his belly and down to where his cock stood up in front of her. She caressed it. It was an interesting part of the body and seemed to do as it pleased. Suddenly, Tomás clasped her hips and lifted her so she leaned forward on her knees. He moved a hand to his cock and then she felt the tip of it there between her legs. She knew then what he wanted. He wanted her to lower herself on it while straddling him. She knew this was possible for she had witnessed it often in the tavern.

She smiled at him, braced her body, pushed his hand away to take his cock in hers, and guiding him, she lowered herself onto him until he was sheathed completely inside her. The sensation was nothing like before when he breached her. This time it was more. It was incredible. It was arousing, and thrilling.

With his hands on her hips, he showed her how to move her body giving both of them the most pleasure. Once she had the rhythm, he moved one hand to between her legs and rubbed against that magic spot which stole her breath. Now as she moved on his cock, his fingers stroking her, and his other capturing her neck, Tomás kissed her mouth. With his tongue stroking hers and their bodies moving together, what the combination did was amazing. Her body tightened on his cock, and when she soared on waves of pleasure this time, his cock throbbed and stroked her from the inside, while his hand stroked the outside and his mouth claimed hers. She was his, and only his. And she wanted it no other way.

Tomás groaned against her mouth and heat filled her inside even as her body throbbed against his. She tore her mouth from his and threw back her head as once more that unexplained pleasure captured her body, and stole her soul before sending it home again before she collapsed on her husband. With his breathing heavy against her ear pressed to his chest, Gabrielle smiled.

They made love several more times over the night. And in the early morning with the sun just beginning to fill the room with a soft glow, Tomás told her what he wanted and how to do it so she took his hard cock into her mouth. She did as he instructed and when he lost control and she claimed him, Gabrielle knew he was hers forever.

~*~

Emma turned the page but there was nothing more there. She looked at Sam and he was staring at her with expectation.

"And...well...so what happened next? What about the gold? Did Beau ever find her? He must have because Felicity must've gone to live with him and Emily. Read on, Emma girl, read on," he exclaimed.

"The next pages are blank," she said.

"No...can't be," Sam said taking the journal from her. "Well, shit...there has to be more journals then. Tomás Alvarez was a very wealthy man. I'm thinking he had a lot of gold from his pirating English or even French ships but that still wouldn't explain why it was Spanish gold."

She watched him shake his head and ruffle the pages of the journal as if searching it for more information. He was right about Tomás Alvarez being wealthy. So if he gained his riches from English ships meaning his wealth was probably in English coin, where had the Spanish gold they found come from?

"Wait...wait," Sam exclaimed, silently reading the words on a page. "Here's more about Tomás and Gabrielle. Here, you read it. I think your reading the words is what makes us go there."

She laughed. She didn't know what magic took them back into the past to seemingly witness the events but that last trip and feeling like they were spying on Tomás and Gabrielle's wedding night had her feeling like she would rather be doing other things than reading at the moment. However, the eager look on Sam's face told her he wanted to know more.

Emma could wait, she supposed. But when she was finished reading these pages, she was going to make love to her husband, whether he liked it or not.

Chapter Sixteen

A little more than a year later...

Tomás paced the floor in the drawing room. With each groan he heard coming from their bedroom, he cursed himself. When Gabrielle first told him she was with child, he was elated but terrified at the same time. He had sworn he would never put her life at risk and he would never cause her pain. Now she was having his child and every so often, she let out a scream which rent his heart in two.

When Mikaela had told him Gabrielle was nearing her birthing date, he had sent Liam to Jamaica to retrieve Celie James, Mikaela's mother. Most folks who knew her called her Mama Celie. Mikaela had been so worried after losing another mother to childbirth only a few months after Chloe and her baby died she suggested her mother come see to Gabrielle's birthing. She could not bear to lose her dearest friend or the child...or worse, both. Fearful of losing Gabrielle as well, Tomás had agreed.

Now, with her labor having arrived, he was a bundle of anxiety and wished he had never lain with her for childbearing was far too dangerous. Felicity was enough family for both of them. Crossing himself, he said a silent prayer to keep his beloved Gabrielle and their child safe. When another scream of pain echoed from the direction of the bedroom, he cringed. Perhaps he would go to Liam's and check on Felicity. He had sent her to stay with Maria and Liam for he did not wish her to hear her adopted mother in such pain. He hurried to the front door, hesitated then turned back. *What if Gabrielle needs me?* No, he would be right here if she needed him.

Sudden yelling outside drew his attention. He turned back to the door and opened it to find out who was causing such disturbance and put a stop to it. He did not want Gabrielle upset by petty arguments. Before he had a chance to even speak, someone roared and shoved him back into the foyer.

"Where the hell is she, Alvarez? I am told she lives here. Is this true? My sister lives here with *you*? She had better be in your employ and not your whore," the man, Tomás now recognized as Hawke Hawkings bellowed at him as he pushed him against a wall.

"Capitán Hawke," Tomás said in more of a groan than words since the man had him pressed tight against the wall, his broad chest holding him there. "Tis good to see you."

"Bloody hell, Alvarez," Beau Hawkings growled. "Tell me where she is."

A high pitched scream echoed through the house just then startling both men and making Tomás come alive. He pushed Beau off him and hurried toward the back of the house. He had not realized Beau had followed him until the man slammed into the back of him when he reached his bedroom door. Another scream filled the air.

"What the hell is going on?" Beau did not wait for an explanation but threw the door open.

Tomás tried to move past him but Beau caught him by the neck, spun him around and punched him square in the face with his big fist. He stumbled backward and vaguely heard Gabrielle scream his name through the ringing in his ears. Hitting the credenza, which sits across the room from the bed, once he steadied his swirling head, his eyes lit on his sword hanging from a hook in its scabbard. He grabbed it, pulled the blade from its sheath, and brandished it at the man.

"Beau...Beau, please stop," Gabrielle commanded from the bed. "Tomás, put down your sword—he is my brother."

"Gabby?" Beau stood staring at her as if he was not sure it was her.

"Tis me...you came, thank goodness. I have been hoping and praying since Tomás said he left word that if you came seeking me, you should be sent here," she said then her face crumpled into an expression of pain and she fell back against the pillows.

Celie stepped forward.

"Cap'n Beau, you picked a truly bad time to come visiting your sister. She be having a baby. Now get you out of here...and you get out too, Cap'n Tomás. Puts that sword back or I use it on both of you," she said and Tomá knew she would do as she threatened.

Tomás sheathed his sword and hung it on the hook. He stepped as if going to the bed but Celie blocked him. He looked past her to his wife who was breathing through the pain she was experiencing.

"She doing all right, Celie?" he asked in a quiet voice.

"Yes, yes...now let me get back to her. You all get out," she said rubbing her hand along his arm to soothe him.

"I want to know what is going on here," Beau exclaimed.

"Beauregard Hawkings, I shall tell you what is going on here. If you strike my husband again, I shall climb from this bed and use his sword on your backside myself. Now behave," Gabrielle hollered from the bed then cringed as a pain grabbed her before letting out a scream.

"Go," Celie ordered pushing them toward the door.

Tomás stopped in the doorway and looked to Gabrielle. His heart ached to take away all of the pain she was experiencing.

"Take care of her, Celie," he said. "She is my life."

Celie nodded and pushed him through the doorway. Beau Hawkings and his second in command, Michel LaRue stood in the hallway with pale faces as another scream of pain ripped the quiet.

"Celie?" Michel said as the door started to close and he noticed Celie froze for a moment then closed the door.

"You got that witch woman here. Why?" Michel asked.

"Because the son of a whore got my little sister with child and now she is birthing his bastard," Beau said with a growl and clenching his fists.

"Did you not hear Gabrielle tell you I am her husband?" Tomás growled back in response. "She is my wife, so get used to it."

He pushed past the men and headed to the kitchen, grabbed a bottle of rum from the pantry and a glass from the cupboard and went out to the porch. He took a seat in the nearest chair and pulled the cork from the bottle with his teeth and filled the glass. Before he had a chance to drink it, Beau snatched it from his hand and downed the liquor in one swallow.

"Of course, help yourself, Capitán Hawke...or shall I call you Beauregard?" Tomás asked with a chuckle.

Michel laughed behind him then approached with two more glasses. He handed one to Tomás and kept the other for himself.

"I do not even remember his own mama calling him Beauregard," he said snorting as he held the glass out to be filled.

Tomás chuckled and filled the man's glass. When Beau leaned forward from the chair he had taken a seat in, Tomás ignored him, filled his own glass then set the bottle down on a side table. He would make the man get his own drink.

"Beau will suffice," Beau said with a growl as he stood to retrieve the bottle. "I want proof you are married to my sister."

Tomás groaned, downed his drink, stood and stalked to his desk in the drawing room where he opened a drawer and removed a paper scrolled with a ribbon around it. He stormed back through the kitchen, stopping briefly to retrieve another bottle of rum since he had two huge men drinking the one he had thought to comfort him through what promised to be a very long night. When he returned to the porch, he noted the men had filled their glasses again but had filled his as well.

He shoved the paper in Beau's face and waited until he took it then returned to his seat and downed his drink. He set the new bottle alongside the nearly empty one on the side table then watched as his brother-in-law rolled open the document. It was a signed testament of them having been married by a priest in the Holy Sacrament of Marriage whether Beau Hawkings liked it or not.

Beau sat back and exhaled a long breath.

"Well, I—'tis true then," he said then looked up at Tomás. "I just assumed you...she...I apologize. She was so young when I saw her last."

Then as if the situation happening in the bedroom had finally sunk in, Beau stood looking alarmed.

"Is she all right? Having a baby is serious business," he said with a groan and looking pale.

"You should know, Beau," Michel said with a chuckle then held his glass out to Tomás for a refill. "You left your wife home expectin' one too."

"What? You are married and there is to be a babe?" Tomás exclaimed and laughed when Beau nodded. "Gabrielle shall be so happy.

Come, we are brothers now...let us drink to our good fortunes."

He stood, filled each glass then lifted his own into the air.

"To the women we love, God Bless them for putting up with us," Tomás said.

"Hear, hear," Beau and Michel said in unison and joining him in his toast.

"Señor Michel, you know our Mama Celie?" Tomás asked as he filled their glasses again.

Beau laughed and Michel scowled.

"I know her. She is a witch, that one," he said knocking back his rum in one swallow.

"She is a miracle worker, that one. I sent for her to assist with the birthing because her daughter felt she needed her to make sure Gabrielle and the babe are truly safe," Tomás told them before downing the rum in his glass.

He hoped Celie James could work her magic and keep his one and only safe. As if she had heard his thoughts, a scream filled the air. He silently swore he would never touch her again if she comes through this all right. He never wished to put her through this again.

"It all be part of birthin', you know, the pain," Michel said. "My maman said you put a knife under the bed to cut the pain. Maybe you need to put that big ass sword you got under the bed."

"Maybe he needs to stay away from that bed," Beau grumbled.

"Your wife, she has brothers?" Tomás asked him.

Michel laughed. "She got two of them and one of them damn near took his head off just like he done you."

"Ah-ha, so he was not too pleased with you being with his sister but you did it anyway, right? Because you love this girl?"

Beau nodded. "She is my everything."

"Si...and your sister is mine. If I could trade places with her right now, I would, as I am sure you will wish to do when your time comes," Tomás said, knowing it was the truth.

Beau nodded. Tomás leaned forward and when he held out the bottle, Beau lifted his glass to be filled.

"I guess I overreacted. I almost did not recognize her. She is so grown up," he said leaning back. "How did she come to be here?"

Tomás explained by telling them what Gabrielle had told him leaving out the part of her being burned. He decided she would not want her brother to learn of all her pain at once. When he finished, he looked to Beau.

"How is it you did not know she is married? Did not Capitán Cuddy tell you?"

"Ha! I suppose he would have had Beau not hightailed it out of there as soon as the man told him where Gabrielle was," Michel said with a snort and holding his glass out for a refill.

Tomás wondered how much rum these two men could hold.

"I suppose I was simply eager to find her," Beau said with a shrug. "I had not seen her in a very long time. More than a dozen years, I suppose."

"She has missed you, I know this. Tis why I left word if you ever came seeking her to direct you to Capitán Cuddy. He is a good friend to us, and family to Gabrielle."

"Family?" Beau rubbed his hand along his jaw. "I suppose he is since she thought she had no one else. Damn, I should have gone home a long time ago."

"What is done is done and you are here now. You are in time to celebrate the coming of a new child into this world and I hope you shall stay a while to visit with your sister," Tomás said with a grin.

"Oh no...as soon as she and the baby are well enough, I am taking them back to New Orleans with me," Beau said.

Tomás came to his feet and slammed his glass down on the table.

"You shall do no such thing," he growled. "She is my wife and she stays with me."

Beau came to his feet and glared at him. Suddenly, Michel was between them.

"I am thinkin' this is somethin' for Gabrielle to decide," he said in a low voice.

The two men stared at each other past Michel's shoulder. Tomás refused to back down. This was his home, after all. If his new brother-in-law did not wish to act as good company, he could leave and sleep in the street for all he cared.

Suddenly, Mikaela appeared at the back door.

"Tomás," she said with a tone of urgency.

He turned to face her, pushed past Michel who was staring at her and followed her inside.

He watched her fill a bowl with hot water which had been simmering over a low flame for most of the day since Gabrielle first began her labor. She went into the pantry and retrieved a bottle of rum.

"Rum?" he asked.

"It will help her with the pain. Tis close now, Tomás, and her pain will increase. I want to warn you, all is well so far but she will scream and we shall let her," Mikaela explained resting her hand on his arm.

"I shall never allow her to do this again. She shall have a room of her own and I shall not seek out her bed from now on," he said feeling a bit sick over the thought of her pain becoming worse than it had already been.

Mikaela chuckled. "You men...you all say the same thing. Tis what bringing life into this world is like for us women. Many a woman has said she wishes never to it again but women keep giving birth. You shall love her again and most likely, she shall give you more children. In truth, she is worried about you even though she has cursed you to hell a few times." She laughed when he frowned and rested a hand on his arm. "She wanted to know if her brother had killed you yet."

"No, not yet but I might kill him. He thinks he is going to take her away from us," Tomás growled.

"I would not worry over it, my friend, for your wife would have much to say about that," she said hugging him. "I must get back. As soon as the babe is here, I shall tell you."

Mikaela picked up the bottle of rum and tucked it under her arm then picked up the bowl of hot water. As she turned to leave, she stopped. Tomás turned to see what had halted her movement and found Michel standing there.

"Ah yes, Mikaela, this is Michel La Rue. He is with Gabrielle's brother," Tomas said with a nod. "Señor, this is my good friend, Mikaela."

"Nice to meet you, sir, I must go now," Mikaela said with a smile then hurried from the kitchen in the direction of the bedroom where another scream filled the air.

"She lives around here?" Michel asked still looking in the direction where Mikaela had turned the corner and disappeared.

"She lives here with us—with Gabrielle, Felicity, and me," Tomás said opening the pantry to retrieve another bottle of rum. "She and Gabrielle are good friends and she helps take care of our adopted daughter, Felicity."

"I see."

"If you know Celie, I am surprised you do not know Mikaela," Tomás said as he moved past the big man to return to the porch. "She is Celie's daughter."

Moving to take his seat and refill his glass, he turned to offer Michel a refill but the man was not there. He turned to look back at the doorway and found the big man standing exactly where he was when he last spoke to him.

"Is there something amiss, Michel?"

"What is wrong, my friend?" Beau asked looking concerned.

Michel turned then slowly walked to his seat and sat. He shook his head and mumbled something under his breath then looked at Tomás.

"She is Celie's daughter?"

"Yes...I have known her for many years and when I built this place, she offered to come live on this island so we had a medicine woman. She was a grown woman and could make her own decisions," Tomás said while filling their glasses.

"Who is her father?"

Beau cursed under his breath when Michel asked the question. Tomás halted his movements to look at both men.

"I do not know. I do not know if Mikaela knows. Do you have a problem with Celie and Mikaela? They are good friends to me and Gabrielle," Tomás said glaring at the man as he took his seat.

"Do you know where she was born?" Michel asked.

"You do not think she could be—" Beau was unable to finish his words before Michel interrupted in an angry tone.

"Mine. Did you bloody well see her, Beau? She looks just like my maman," Michel exclaimed.

"Good Lord, you think she is your daughter?" Tomás asked with surprise then glancing toward the open door, he lowered his voice. "Is it possible?"

Michel looked to Beau and Beau sighed. Michel shrugged.

"Celie was—is my wife, so anything is possible," Michel said with a groan.

"Heaven bless you, my friend," Tomás said with a chuckle. "Here, I think you need many of these."

He reached out with a fresh bottle of rum to fill Michel's glass. Michel obliged and Beau stuck his own out as well. Once he filled their glasses, Tomás held his high.

"My friends, may God protect us from the women we love," he said with a grin.

"Hear, hear," Michel and Beau said before tossing back their drinks and then Beau began to laugh.

Michel scowled at him but then began to chuckle. Soon all three were laughing, filling glasses, and drinking far too much rum.

~*~

Several hours must have passed for when Tomás squinted open his eyes the sun was shining on them from the east. His head ached, although his back pained him even more from sleeping in a porch chair. When he sat up straighter, the action only drew a groan from him and made him grimace. He looked to his drinking companions. Beau was asleep with his head back, his mouth open, and the occasional snore competing with the songs being sung by the morning birds. Michel had been smarter than either him or Beau for he had stretched out on the settee, although he did not fit well and his long legs were hanging over one armrest.

Tomás stood with a loud groan, obviously disturbing Beau for the man snorted and his head came upright causing him to grimace and screw up his face in pain. He imagined the famed Capitán Hawke had as wicked a headache as he had.

Tomás half-stumbled and half-waddled down the steps and into the nearby brush to relieve his aching bladder and when he returned to the porch, the other two men were trying to rouse themselves to probably do the same thing. He took a seat and rubbed his temples with his fingers.

"Too much rum...far too much rum," he said.

Michel groaned, closed his eyes, and lay back against the back of the settee.

"Do not mention the demon liquor. I do not think I shall ever drink it again," he said making Beau chuckle.

"You say that every time, old man...every time."

"I can make something to cure your heads," Mikaela said from the doorway.

Michel surprised them all by coming to his feet almost immediately even if he turned a bit green under his dark skin.

Tomás stood as well, turning to face her.

"Gabrielle...how is she?"

Mikaela smiled. "She is well, Tomás. Would you like to see her—and your new daughter?"

"Daughter? I have a daughter?" he asked wondering for a moment if he was still asleep and dreaming.

"Yes, you have a beautiful black-haired daughter. Come, see her for yourself," she said waving him forward.

"May we—" Beau began.

"Come, you are family," Tomás exclaimed then suddenly feeling as fit as on any other day, he hurried past Mikaela, through the kitchen, turning the corner into the hallway toward his bedroom so fast he nearly stumbled.

However, when he reached the door, he hesitated.

"She is waiting for you, Tomás." Mikaela had followed him.

"You are sure she is all right?" he asked.

"She is good. She is a strong one, our little Gabrielle," Mikaela said with a smile then hugged him. "Go on, she has been worried about you."

He put his hand on the doorknob just as Beau and Michel came around the corner and walked slowly toward him. He leaned over to Mikaela.

"Perhaps you might brew up one of your magic potions for my friends, yes?"

She laughed and nodded. "I shall have some for you too. Now go."

She shoved him through the door with a snort.

Once inside, he looked to his beautiful wife. She was sitting up with many pillows behind her. She wore a clean nightshirt and fresh linens covered her from the waist down. Her golden blonde hair still damp around her face looked like a halo around her head and shoulders and her cheeks wore a bright flush of pink. In her arms was a small bundle—his daughter.

"Tomás," Gabrielle spoke his name snapping him out of his apparent trance. "Come see your daughter."

He looked to her face and she was smiling with such happiness and pride, he found it hard to believe only hours ago he had heard her screaming in agonizing pain. Without hesitation, he hurried to the side of the bed. Celie stood on the other side and when his gaze met hers, she smiled.

"Thank you, Celie...thank you for taking care of my wife and child," he said.

"Of course, tis what I do," she said then stepped back from the bed.

He leaned in and pressed a kiss to Gabrielle's lips.

"My love...you are well?"

"Yes, Tomás, I am tired but I am quite well," she said then kissed him again. "Say hello to your little one."

He looked down and if it was possible to fall in love instantly with two women upon meeting them, he had—first, Gabrielle and now, his baby daughter. She was sleeping, her sweet little mouth puckered as if waiting for a kiss, her cheeks were still red from the exertion of struggling to enter his world, and abundance of damp thick dark hair covered her tiny head.

Gabrielle was glowing but he saw the exhaustion in her eyes even as she never looked more beautiful. She smiled at him and then looked to her daughter. She slid a finger into the little girl's tiny hand and his daughter squeezed it. She was a strong one and he could not be more pleased. He reached out, tentatively, and Gabrielle chuckled.

"You can touch her, my love, she will not break," she said.

He gently caressed his daughter's head and when she squirmed a bit and grimaced, he pulled his hand back. Trying again, he traced a fingertip along her little cheek and she seemed to smile. She completely captured his heart at that moment. He tucked his finger into her free hand and she clasped it in a tight grip.

"She is quite strong for being so tiny," he said with a laugh.

"*She* needs a name," Gabrielle said looking up at him.

"My mother's name was Carolina," he suggested.

Gabrielle seemed to think on it for a few minutes. If she preferred another name, he cared not for all he could see was his beautiful daughter. She was now the dearest thing to his heart only after Gabrielle. Felicity had a new sister and he could not wait to introduce them to each other as soon as mother and daughter had rested.

"How about Caroline? I think it is close enough to be a tribute to your mother," Gabrielle said.

Tomás looked at her. "Yes. I like it. May I?" he asked holding his hands out toward the baby.

"Of course, you are her papa," Gabrielle said with a big smile while shifting the baby in her arms then settled her properly in his arms.

Tomás stood, his daughter cradled in the crook of his arm. He had never held an infant before and was amazed at how tiny she was.

"My darling Caroline, welcome...I am your papa but you are as beautiful as your mama," he said in a soft quiet tone.

She opened her eyes and looked at him.

"She has your blue eyes," he said with a smile.

"All babies have blue eyes, Tomás. We shall have to wait to see if they grow dark like yours. She certainly has your hair."

"That she does. She is so beautiful, Gabrielle. Thank you for such a wonderful gift," he said feeling an immense sensation of pride as he looked at his sweet daughter.

"May I see my niece?" Beau asked from behind him at the doorway.

"Beau," Gabrielle exclaimed with a big smile. "Come here, big brother."

Beau moved around to the opposite side of the bed, greeted Celie then leaned down to hug and kiss his sister.

"This was not how I expected to find you, Gabby, but I am so happy you are safe," Beau said and Tomás swore he saw tears in the man's eyes.

"I sent message after message to La Coeur de la Terre in the hope someone would know I survived the fire," Gabrielle said with tears streaming down her cheeks. "I did not know where you were or even if you were still alive."

"As you can see, I am very much alive, beloved, as are you. I feared the worst when I returned to New Orleans too late and discovered our home nothing but ashes." Beau continued to hold her hand as if he feared the loss of her again. "I believed you had perished along with our parents and could not bear to return to La Coeur de la Terre nor stay in New Orleans so we set out to sea again. By the time we returned, much time had passed. When I was told you might still be alive, I began searching with earnest. I found your letters among the unread correspondence at our home and it gave me great hope. When a friend returned from Jamaica and told me there was a notice for me posted telling me you were living in the islands, we came as soon as possible. Now, here you are."

When he rubbed her hand and his hand traveled too far up her right arm, Tomás saw her flinch.

"Are you hurt, Gabby?" Beau did not wait for an answer but lifted the sleeve of the nightgown. "What? Oh, my sweet girl, what happened?"

"I survived the fire but did not do so unscathed," Gabrielle said and Tomás saw the panic in her eyes and knew she feared her brother giving her a negative reaction.

He started toward the bed but when Beau cupped the side of his sister's face, he halted his progression.

"I am so sorry, Gabby. I should have been there for you. I have failed you," Beau said lifting her hand to his lips. "Do your injuries still pain you?"

Gabrielle shook her head and traced her hand alongside her brother's face. Tomás noted she appeared to wipe away a tear.

"You did not fail me. Never could you fail me. I am fine, Beau. The scars are many but with help from Mikaela and the love of a good man—" When her gaze met his, Tomás smiled at her. "I rarely think of them anymore."

"Good. I am glad, Gabby, for you are too beautiful to worry about a few scars." Beau hugged her again and kissed her forehead. "By the by, you have a new sister. You will adore Emily, and she, you...and soon your little one will have a new cousin."

"Oh Beau, that is wonderful. Is she with you?" Gabrielle asked with eagerness.

"No, she is still in Virginia. I thought it best she stay there for her confinement. She is with family and safe. You shall meet her soon enough." Then he looked to Tomás. "May I see my niece?"

"But of course, come," Tomás said with a proud grin.

Beau walked around the bed and peered down at the bundle he cradled as if she was worth a hundred times her weight in gold. Beau put out a finger and his daughter clasped her uncle's finger as she had done his.

"She is beautiful and strong," Beau said with a chuckle.

"How 'bout me?"

Tomás and Beau turned their heads to see Michel standing in the doorway.

"Michel," Gabrielle exclaimed holding out her arms toward him. "So very good to see you, my old friend. Come, please."

Michel entered, stopped to peer at the baby a moment and grinned at Tomás then moved around him to lean down close to Gabrielle. He hugged her and pressed a kiss to her forehead. Tomás watched as his wife placed a small hand against the dark man's face and smile. A tear slid down her cheek.

"I should have known as long as you were with my brother, all would be well," she said with a sigh then pressed a kiss to the man's scruffy cheek. "Thank you."

"You have more to worry about with this one than me, little sister," Beau said coming around to slap Michel on the back. "We nearly lost him on the journey home from England. If it had not been for Celie, we would have for sure."

Everyone looked at Celie, except Michel.

"When was this? You were in Jamaica?" Gabrielle asked with a frown pulling her brows together. "We were so close but you had no idea of me being there."

"I suspect you were already here rather than in Jamaica when we stopped but had I known, I would have found you then, my sweet," Beau said reaching out to caress her cheek.

"Aye, and even after we learned you lived, he had other prey to chase," Michel said with a laugh. "But we found you now."

He pressed a kiss to Gabrielle's cheek then stood tall. Michel looked at Celie who had been watching him throughout the encounter.

"How is your arm doin'?" she asked him.

"It is well healed now, thank you," Michel responded then he opened his mouth as if to say something else but hesitated when Mikaela came sweeping into the room with a large basket and blankets over her arm.

Tomás watched the big man as his eyes followed Mikaela. When she stopped, put down the basket and stood next to her mother, Michel's expression turned to a scowl when he looked at Celie

331

"Is she—" Michel started then swallowed hard. "Is she mine, Celie?"

Mikaela seemed startled by the question whereas Celie did not. Mikaela looked at her mother who seemed to be looking everywhere but at any of them.

"Oh, my," Gabrielle exclaimed with a sudden clap of her hands. "I always thought Mikaela reminded me of someone I knew. You look so very much like Mama LaRue as I imagined she must have looked as a young woman."

"Is it true?" Beau asked with an expression of someone displeased with another.

Celie James turned to face her daughter who wore a puzzled expression.

"I never told you who your father was because we parted on such bad terms and I did not think you would ever know him," she said taking her daughter's hands in hers. "I was-I am married to this man."

Mikaela looked at Michel and then to her mother. She started to pull her hands away but Celie held them fast as she continued.

"It was an arranged marriage. One neither of us chose." She looked at Michel then down at Mikaela's hands. "I-I was so willing to love him and be a good wife but he loved another. I could not face that truth anymore, so I ran away. I got abducted on the road by two white men. They sold me to Master Jenkins."

"Jenkins? That black bastard was one of the worst owners in all the parishes. Why did you not send word? Master Hawkings would have come to get you," Michel said taking a step forward but when Beau put his hand on his arm, he halted.

"I tried to tell him I was a free woman but he did not care. He forced me to stay put by lockin' me up each night. When I discovered I was carrying your babe, I tried to convince him it was his by offering my body to him. He took what he wanted but still locked me up at night. After Mikaela as born, he became wicked mean. I believe the bastard could count after all and figured out she was not his. I did my best to protect her while waiting for a chance to escape."

She looked up at Mikaela and when his friend wrapped an arm around her mother's shoulders, Tomás knew what she was going to reveal.

"One summer, Mikaela spoke up to Jenkins when he slapped me for not moving fast enough and he took a lash to her backside."

Beau cursed under his breath and Tomás saw Michel's gaze go to his daughter. His eyes glistened with the tears of pain he felt for her even as his hands fisted.

"I gave him a brew to make him sick, too sick to mind us. It was our chance to escape. I took Mikaela and what little money I had and we sailed on the first ship going wherever. That ship brought us to Jamaica," Celie said.

"I remember when Jenkins died. Some blamed yellow fever," Beau said then laughed. "Celie fever was more like it. Good for you, my old friend. He deserved a worse death than that, but good for you."

"All the times we came to Jamaica over the years and you never spoke one damn word, not one. You just make me believe you hate me," Michel growled at her. "I remember seeing a little girl playing nearby and all the time, she was my daughter. You truly are a witch, Celie."

Angry, he said not another word but stormed from the room.

"Mama, how could keep this from me or him? I remember him coming with Cap'n Beau. Every time he came. I used to wonder why he looked at you as if he hated you. Why? Why did you not tell me?" Mikaela asked with tears in her eyes. "Why did you not tell him? He might have saved us from so much. You had no right."

She turned with a sob and rushed from the room. Tomás understood his friend's pain. Celie looked to each of them and when her eyes settled on Beau, she shook her head.

"You know how he hates me," she said. "I was not the one he wanted."

"I never believed he hated you, Celie. He was so hurt when you left him without a word," Beau said.

"He did not care. He never loved me," she said with tears in her eyes. I was not *her*."

"Did he not? If he did not love you then why is it he never took another woman after you left? *You* are his wife still," Beau said coming around the bed and taking the woman in his arms.

Celie rested her head on his shoulder a moment then looked up at him with tears on her cheeks. "Never?"

"Never," Beau said. "I believe it was more than vows keeping him loyal to you."

Celie gasped.

"But he never said...he loved...I thought he only loved—" Celie started to step away but Beau held on to her.

"He has carried a lifetime of anger and resentment toward you, Celie, because when we found you in Jamaica you showed no desire to be with him. I know he wished to bring you home and he would have been so pleased to know about Mikaela. Now, I think his anger has just grown twofold so be careful how you approach him," Beau said then pressed a kiss to her cheek and hugged her. "You have much to amend for—with both of them."

Celie nodded. She looked to Tomás, and then to Gabrielle who nodded as if giving her permission to go deal with her family. Celie gave her a weak smile.

"She needs to rest, Tomás. I will send Mikaela to make a bed for the little one," she said to him then looked to Beau. "I need to talk to Michel...but he might not be willing to listen, will you—"

"Come, he can be stubborn but his heart is as big as he is," Beau said taking her arm and began leading her from the room. He stopped at the doorway. "You rest, little sister, we shall catch up later."

Gabrielle smiled at him then he and Celie left the room. Tomás watched them go then turned to look at his wife.

"Imagine that...all this time...Michel had a family he did not know about," she said with a sigh.

"I understand how he must feel. If you had left me before I knew you carried my child and I missed knowing about this beautiful creature...well, I believe it would kill me when I found out," he said then leaned forward to place his daughter in his wife's arms.

"Trust me, my love, you shall never be rid of us so easy," she said with a quiet laugh.

Tomás knew how blessed he was. He kissed her again, a little longer this time since they were alone then knelt alongside the bed and leaned his chin on his forearms and watched his little daughter sleep in the arms of his beloved, his beautiful one and only love.

Chapter Seventeen

Emma relaxed against the pillows on the bed and sighed. "Can you imagine? All that time, Michel had a wife yet," she said. "And a daughter—Mikaela."

"And it was the witch woman, Celie," Sam said with a laugh. "These folks certainly didn't lead a dull life."

"Very true."

"So what happened next?" Sam asked with eagerness.

She laughed for it surprised her how caught up in the lives of people long dead Sam had become. She turned the pages looking for the next entry of their lives but only found a single page. On it wasn't an entry, per se, but more an explanation and notes as if Emily was filling in the blanks which Emma had pretty much thought she had been doing all along.

"Emily writes that Tomás and Gabrielle's story was gleaned from a time she spent with them when they visited La Coeur de la Terre about a year and a half after Caroline was born. They all came as a family to visit. By that time, Emily and Beau's twin daughters had been born and their time together was joyful."

"That's it," Sam said sitting up and looking disappointed. "What about the gold? What happened with Michel and Celie? And Mikaela?"

Emma turned the page.

"Wait...it says here that Tomás decided they would settle in Louisiana but he had to return to La Isla to attend to the community. Gabrielle decided to go with him so they could stop in Jamaica to say goodbye to the McGillicuddy family. They decided to leave Felicity, Caroline, and *Mikaela*—"

"Ah ha! So I wonder if Michel stayed with Celie or if Celie returned to Louisiana with Michel," Sam said. "Or maybe they just stayed apart. Nothing about them?"

"Nothing other than that," she said with a shrug. "Maybe we can find out more about them."

"Did Tomás bring all his riches with him? Or does he return to La Isla and then bring it back?" Sam was still eager to discover how the gold got to the United States.

"Just a minute..." Emma continued reading through the notes. "Okay, it seems Tomás and Gabrielle never returned."

She lowered the journal to her lap.

"How sad...it says they never knew what happened to them but when Beau went searching about a year later, he found their little village burned to the ground and several unmarked graves."

"Disease, perhaps...measles or yellow fever," Sam suggested but she could tell he was sad to learn of their deaths.

"I guess that's how Emily and Beau ended up raising the two girls as their own. They never changed their surnames though."

"How do you know that?"

"Because their marriages are listed here," Emma said.

"Really? Where?" he asked leaning in.

"Here—" She pointed to a list near the back of the journal then read aloud. "Felicity Alvarez married Daniel Baxter of Virginia."

"Virginia? How did she meet a man from Virginia if they were living in Louisiana," Sam asked.

Emma thought about it a moment and then shrugged.

"Who knows...maybe they all visited Emily's family in Virginia at some point and she met a man while they were there or maybe it was just chance and he was in Louisiana," she suggested before looking at the page again.

"Oh...well now, this is interesting though...she and Daniel Baxter had a daughter named Sarah who was born in Virginia so they must have been living there," she said pointing to the names in the list.

"Sarah, huh? Do we know Sarah Chambers' maiden name?" Sam asked leaning in and trying to read the list.

"No," Emma replied. "Can that just be a coincidence? If we were back in Virginia, we could check the archives."

"Maybe Walt could check into it for us. Do you think he might?" Sam asked.

"I don't see why not. I know he's as fascinated by all of this as we are," she said. "I'll give him a call tomorrow."

"You know, if it's the same Sarah, it could explain a lot about how Jeremiah got a hold of the gold he had. If Gabrielle and Tomás brought gold to Louisiana and left it with Beau and Emily while they returned to La Isla, I would imagine Beau to be the type to keep it as the girls' dowry. And Tomás said he kept a share which was to be Felicity's dowry. So if Felicity went to live in Virginia, it would only make sense that if her daughter needed her share, Beau or perhaps Emily would make sure it was delivered to her. If it wasn't already there."

What Sam suggested made so much sense. It also would mean that Emma was directly related to Felicity Alvarez which was quite fascinating. Now she was eager to know for sure.

"What about Caroline?" Sam asked peeking over her shoulder at the pages.

"She's here too. She married a man named Jonathan Devereux of New Orleans. They had three sons. Oh, my...listen to this...one of the sons was named Samuel." Emma looked to Sam whose eyes had grown large.

"I wish I knew more about my ancestry because the names are ringing all kinds of bells," he said. "I seem to recall a cousin or someone saying one of the grandmothers' names was Gabrielle. Naw, I think it's just a coincidence. Besides, I was born in Baton Rouge."

"I thought you grew up in New Orleans."

"I did, but I was just a kid. I was born in Baton Rouge," he said with a shrug. "My parents were from Baton Rouge...well, my mother's family had lived in Baton Rouge for a few generations, I think. My father came to Baton Rouge to work for the governor. He was actually from Houston."

"Really? Well, here it has Samuel Devereux marrying Marie Dupont of Baton Rouge and they had two sons," she exclaimed with wide eyes.

"What? Really?" Sam looked at the page. "Hmm...I wonder if they lived in Baton Rouge. It's all certainly interesting. What do you suppose the odds are that we are both related to these folks?"

"I don't know but it's looking like a mystery still needs solving. It looks like we need to do a little digging into the family tree of Caroline Alvarez Devereux," Emma said with a grin.

She closed the journal and sighed.

"What?" Sam asked when he realized she was staring at him.

"You were a kid when you came to New Orleans? Was that when you came to live with your uncle?"

"Emma, it's late and I really don't want to get into that," Sam said rolling to the edge of the bed.

"Sam...your uncle might have some of the pieces of the puzzle if he knows anything about your family tree," she said putting the journals aside.

She crawled across the bed and wrapped her arms around Sam's shoulders from behind.

When he pushed her arms away and stood, she grew angry.

"Samuel Martinelli, you've got to stop locking me out," she nearly yelled at him.

He turned to face her. He wore an expression of sorrow, which surprised her.

"What is it with you and your uncle? The man raised you when you had no one else," she said sitting back on her heels.

"He may have but he's not part of my life now and never will be," Sam growled then walked into the bathroom and slammed the door.

Emma sat staring at the closed door for what seemed liked hours then climbed off the bed. She walked to the door and gently tapped.

"Martinelli, I'm sorry. I know he's a sore subject for you but I really wish you'd just tell me why and be done with it," she said through the door.

The door suddenly opened and Sam pushed passed her. He had stripped down to his boxer briefs and brushed his teeth for she could smell the toothpaste. He walked to the bed, pulled back the covers and climbed in. He took off his watch and laid it on the side table.

"Oh...okay...so you're just going to go to sleep, is that it?" Emma asked coming to stand alongside the bed with her hands on her hips. "That's your answer for everything, isn't it? Ignore it and it will go away."

"I'm not in the mood, Emma."

"Well, I'm not in the mood either, Sam. Anything you don't want to discuss, you just shut down, ignore it, and hope I won't bring it up again. Was that your thinking when you decided to not tell me about your relationship with Tina?"

"Damnit, Emma," Sam growled and sat up in bed. "I told you it was only the one time and it was before I ever met you."

"I know, Sam, I know...but it still hurts, you know. Knowing you and Tina had that between you all those years and kept it from me hurt. It hurt a lot."

Tears were sliding down her cheeks. She didn't know if it was the pain of learning her best friend and the man she loved had had a sexual relationship once upon a time or just her hormones wreaking havoc on her emotions, but she couldn't stop crying. Sam pulled back the covers and climbed from the bed. He wrapped his arms around her and cradled her against him.

"I'm sorry. I forget how all of that affected you. It just never occurred to me to tell you about it. By the time it mattered at all, you and she had become such good friends and I didn't want to be the one to throw a wrench into your friendship. It never dawned on me that she was still interested at all," he said near her ear in a calming voice.

His deep melodic voice could always take the sting out of her when she was mad. She leaned back and looked up at him then wiped her tears away with the back of her hand.

"Sometimes it's the things unsaid that hurt the most. Perhaps it's time for you and your uncle—"

"Hell no!"

Sam spun away and climbed back into bed.

"Martinelli, here me out," she said moving to stand next to him.

When he rolled over so he was facing the other way, she climbed over him so he had to look at her. He closed his eyes and pulled the pillow over his head. She pulled the pillow away and pushed it behind her. He groaned and started to roll back to the other side, but she quickly straddled him and held him to his back.

"Emma, please let it go and get off of me. I want to go to sleep," he growled and grabbed her hips to lift her off. "I don't want to hurt you."

"No...you don't...so listen," she said grabbing his hands and pushing them back on the bed.

"Damn, girl," he said with wide eyes.

"You said he was always into researching your family's history. He might know what we can't find out. Don't you want to know if Caroline Alvarez...for that matter, Gabrielle Hawkings Alvarez...was your great, great, whatever great grandmother?"

Sam stared up at her as if thinking over what she was suggesting then shook his head, pulled his hands free, and rolled her off of him.

"All right, Martinelli, then I guess I'll track him down myself."

He turned to glare at her.

"You don't think I will? Well, whether or not he has information that might help us, I think I'd like to tell him that he's going to be a great uncle," she said pushing her nose into the air and folding her arms across her chest.

"Emma, don't you dare—" Then his expression changed as if a lightbulb had gone off over his head. "Tell him he's going to be a—are you?"

She nodded but kept her nose in the air.

"When? How?" He laughed when she glared at him. "I don't mean how did you get pregnant, I mean...oh hell, I'm not sure what I mean. Are you—really? Not a trick to distract me?"

"I can think of many other ways to do that, Martinelli. Yes, I'm pregnant," she said looking at him with one eyebrow cocked.

"How long? How far along are you?" Sam ran his hand down her flat belly.

She laughed then. "Not as flat as it used to be. I'm not showing yet but will be soon enough. I'm already four months along," she said covering his hand with hers.

"Four months?" he exclaimed in loud anger so that Emma put her hand over his mouth. He shook his head until his mouth was clear of her hand. "When exactly did you plan to tell me? After you dropped it on the ground...maybe at an excavation site or out in the fields during harvest?"

"Ha, ha, ha," she said shoving his hand away from her belly. "I was going to tell you but then you decided to take bring us here and I thought if you knew, you wouldn't let me come with you."

"Oh baby, I would never have left you behind. This was more a honeymoon than anything else so if we're going to have a kid with us, I guess this is the best way," he said rubbing her belly. "Wow, my kid is really in there?"

Now he was grinning from ear to ear and she knew he was pleased.

"Our kid is really in there...yes."

Sam looked up at her and his brown eyes were glistening. Did he have tears in his eyes? She cupped his face and kissed his lips.

"You're going to be a daddy, Sam," she said in a near whisper.

"Shit," he whispered and she frowned but then he grinned. "And you're going to be a mommy, my beautiful Emma," he said rolling her beneath him. "I just hope I don't lose you."

"You'll never lose me or your child," she said laying her hand alongside his cheek. "I'm not that easy to get rid of and I suspect any kid of ours is going to be tough as nails."

"That's not what I mean," he said leaning his forehead against hers. "It always seems as if when I think I've got everything I've ever wanted, something happens or someone interferes and it all goes away. I lost you for five years, Emma, five long years when a day didn't pass that I didn't think about you and regret my foolish actions."

"And when we learned the truth, I forgave you, and now we are married and having a baby, Sam." She kissed his mouth. "Nothing or no one is going to make me go away, break us apart, or ruin things. I promise."

Sam stared down at her as if he feared she would disappear right now then he sighed. "Do you realize you're wearing entirely too much clothing for what's about to happen?" he asked with a sly smile.

She laughed. "I do feel a subject change is in our future."

She rocked her hips against him making him groan and his cock grew harder than it had already after rolling her beneath him.

"Oh shit...can we? I mean, it won't hurt the baby or anything?"

Laughing hard at the bewildered expression Sam was now wearing, she kissed his mouth. "Martinelli, how can anyone with as much education as you have, not know sex has never harmed a child in the womb?"

"Ha, ha! Okay, so I just had a total brain fart. I've never been a father to be before so I never thought about it," he said with a scowl. "So if it's okay and you're all right, I'd like to make love to my wife."

"Well, all you had to do was say so."

She pushed him aside, climbed from the bed, and began a slow striptease as she removed her clothing. Sam watched every moment grinning and when she finished, he pulled her close to the side of the bed and kissed her belly.

"Come to bed, little mama, big daddy has a treat for you," he said with a waggle of his dark brows.

She slid her fingers into his thick dark hair and laughed.

"I suspect the treat I give you will be even better, she said as she pushed him to his back, hooked her fingers into his briefs and yanked them down his legs.

Before he could react or trap her in his arms, she climbed up his legs and began making love to him with her hands and mouth. She made him moan, felt him tangle his hands in her hair, and soon had him begging her to straddle him like before. She loved this man with all of her being and whether he liked it or not, she would have her way with him tonight and tomorrow, Emma would have her way when she insisted they call his uncle. The truth was close and the key to the past was right here in New Orleans.

—Coming Soon—

Join Emma and Sam as they uncover more
about the mystery gold in
Where Loves Lives Forever

While honeymooning in New Orleans, the
Seekers of the Past, Emma Wells and Sam
Martinelli hope to find more answers now that
they know the origin of the gold found on the
family farm.

Emma suggests asking Sam's uncle who lives in
New Orleans for more information on their
family tree, but Sam balks at the idea. When
she surprises Sam by announcing he will be a
father and he might want his uncle to know his
reaction is not what she expected.

When things take a dangerous turn causing
increased tension to build between the
honeymooners, Sam tries to protect the woman
he loves but Emma quickly makes it clear she
will do things her way. Sam now realizes if he
doesn't reconcile with his past, he might not
have any future with her at all.

Join Emma and Sam as they discover their
connections to the past, to each other, and that
love is the real treasure they seek and worth
holding onto forever.

More Books from the Author

Journey to Where the Past Meets the Present
and Love Lives Forever
in the Seekers of the Past series...

***Each book in this series can be read as a standalone historical romance with the first and sixth books set in the present.

Seekers of the Past – book one

After inheriting the family farm, archaeologist Emma Wells returns to a place she loves even as the memories of the past haunt it. While doing much needed cleaning, she discovers letters and a journal from the time of the Civil War. She begins to think the family tale of lost treasure might be true only she needs help to find it. Assistance comes but it is the last man on earth she ever wants to see again.

Still in love with her, historian Sam Martinelli will use any reason to get close to the woman he foolishly betrayed five years earlier. Now that he is here with her, he hopes to regain Emma's trust and love...if she will ever forgive him.

The search for treasure becomes real but not without dangers and when things take a deadly turn, the truth becomes the real enemy. Emma begins to question if she can trust anyone...especially the man who still holds a claim on her heart.

For the Sake of Honor – book two

The Seekers of the Past begin a search for the origin of the gold only to find it begins in post-revolutionary Virginia in 1799...

Brought up as a man of honor, his heart will only ever belong to the girl he left behind, but Joshua Embry knows the bride chosen for him by his parents must be his future.

When the only man she ever loved returns from England with a future bride, Anna Pelt questions her place in his world. Even as fate brings her the potential for an independent life, she feels betrayed and discarded.

Joshua claims to love her even as honor forces him to marry another woman, but Anna questions his intentions. Not wishing to make the same mistake in life her mother had, she now faces a decision which will change her life forever—keep her self-respect or surrender it to be with the man she loves.

In the Arms of Her Angel – book three

Still seeking the origins of the gold, the magic of the journal sends the Seekers of the Past to the busy Port of Charleston in 1802...

A man who enjoys adventure, Captain Daniel Embry begins to yearn for a life more settled. When a thief enters his room in the middle of the night, he discovers the culprit to be a beautiful woman instead of a filthy wharf rat of a boy. She needs help and he is more than willing to assist her. But he also suspects she carries many secrets and soon his life becomes more unsettled than he ever imagined.

Haunted by her past and desperate to do whatever it takes to rescue her father from a dangerous man, Ginny Blackwood turns to the handsome and caring captain who caught her thieving. With only a strange riddle to guide them, she partners with Daniel to solve it but fears trusting him with the terrible secrets it will uncover—as well as her heart.

To Love and Be Loved By Him – book four

As the Seekers of the Past continue their search for the origins of the gold, they are taken on an adventurous journey by sea in 1805...

Not one to abide by rules, independent thinking Emily Embry wants only to escape marrying the aristocrat awaiting her in England. When tragedy strikes her ship, the handsome and irritatingly arrogant captain who rescues them begins to plague her thoughts and awaken her innocent desires. Knowing such a man makes her arranged marriage even less palatable.

A man of the sea, Captain Beau Hawkings enjoys his freedom with no need for a wife or inherited title. When he rescues the woman his grandfather contracted him to marry, he desires to make her his but his desire for freedom remains greater.

When each sets a plan in motion to escape the other, fate intervenes to make the scheming go awry and then throws them together with nowhere to go.

When It Doesn't Stay In Vegas

Things that happen in Vegas need to stay in Vegas...

Abby Matheson trusts in her skills as a smart, savvy corporate lawyer but knows she is not very smart when it comes to relationships. Now too much champagne and a passion-filled one night stand in Las Vegas with a very sexy and unforgettable man might destroy her career.

With the sale of his company in the works but still not sure he wants to sell, tech genius Mitch Braxton cannot think about business when the memory of a passionate night with a mysterious and beautiful woman keeps distracting him. He decides to leave the decision-making until after his sister's wedding, but business follows him and lands him in the same bridal party as the woman closing the deal. The same woman he spent that amazing night with in Vegas who left behind her crystal heart, and just might have stolen his.

What to do? *When it doesn't stay in Vegas...*

A Convenient Engagement

Sometimes fate has other ideas...

Karma just added one more thing to Eden Murphy's life she did not need. Of all the people to move in across the hall...did it have to be Will Trask? The only guy in high school she ever had a crush on—and also humiliated her.

Still so good looking...still the guy women flock to...but he doesn't remember her. Thank heavens for small miracles. When they discover being single seems to be holding both of them back in their careers, Will comes up with a temporary solution. Pretend to be engaged.

At first, Eden rejects the idea but then she sees an added benefit to his scheme—get what she wants at work and maybe exact a bit of revenge on Will.

But sometimes the best-laid plans go awry.

A new paranormal series based in the mythology of the world's gods coming soon

The Elysian Realm series

Elysian Hearts Never Forget
Elysian Evolution
Elysian Rising
Elysian Resisting
Elysian Reunited
Elysian Retribution

About the Author

In addition to being an author, Amy Valentini is a free-lance editor at Romancing Editorially and romance reviewer at Unwrapping Romance as well as an Avon Addict—a super reader group for Avon/HarperCollins. She has always loved reading, working with words, and creating stories that make readers think, laugh, cry, and escape the realities of everyday life. Writing romance keeps her belief in true love alive.

A graduate of Mary Washington College in Virginia, now the University of Mary Washington with a Bachelor of Arts in English, she has always had the dream of being a published author. Finally achieving that goal with her debut romance, SEEKERS OF THE PAST, she hopes readers will take a chance on her stories because love and romance come in many forms entwined with adventure, mystery, magic, and fun. She enjoys mixing things up for her characters as well as for the reader and if she can introduce a reader to new and different storylines all the better.

Amy lives in Virginia where, in her spare time, she reads and reviews romance.

If you can do me a great favor, please leave a review of this book at your favorite vendor or review site. Thank you, and Happy Reading!

Follow me on Facebook, Twitter, Bookbub, and Instagram.